Also by Isla Gordon

A Season in the Snow
The Wedding Pact

As Lisa Dickenson

The Twelve Dates of Christmas
You Had Me at Merlot
Mistletoe on 34th Street
Catch Me if You Cannes
My Sisters and Me

Isla Gordon lives on the Jurassic Coast of England with her T. rex-sized Bernese Mountain Dog. Isla has worked as a dance teacher, a manager, and an editorial assistant but has been writing professionally since 2013 (and unprofessionally since she can remember). She also has five romantic comedies published under the name Lisa Dickenson.

Isla can't go a day without finding dog hair in her mouth.

A Winter in Wonderland

ISLA GORDON

SPHERE

SPHERE

First published in Great Britain in 2021 by Sphere

1 3 5 7 9 10 8 6 4 2

A CIP catalogue record for this book is available from the British Library.

ISBN 978-0-7515-8511-7

Typeset in Caslon by M Rules
Printed and bound in Great Britain by Clays Ltd, Elcograf S.p.A.

Papers used by Sphere are from well-managed forests
and other responsible sources.

Sphere
An imprint of
Little, Brown Book Group
Carmelite House
50 Victoria Embankment
London
EC4Y 0DZ

An Hachette UK Company
www.hachette.co.uk

www.littlebrown.co.uk

To my family at Christmastime

Prologue

Summer

~ *Then* ~

Perhaps it was the hot weather, the sizzling heat and bright sunshine that made my hay fever a billion times worse and the far-off thunderstorms creep closer. Perhaps it was because I felt a little on edge, a little guilty, for walking out of yet another job in the middle of the day. That's the whole reason I was even in the card shop, to buy a 'sorry' card for my agent at the temp office.

It's not like it was unusual to see small hints of Christmas appear in shops when it was still summertime, but this time, *this year*, the tall display of red and green and snow-white cards really bothered me. I hadn't been expecting this today, this feeling of foreboding, not while I was still wearing shorts; not while I was sipping on the last Frappuccino I would be able to afford for a while, so had got extra pumps of raspberry sauce and whipped cream. Not while it was still *August*.

It made me want to do something very bad, very badly.

My fingers twitched as I imagined pulling down the cards from the display and throwing them in the air; in my mind I watched them flutter to the ground, raining down around me like cherry blossom. Like a slow-motion scene in a movie, sales assistants would be racing over, other customers protecting themselves from the downpour while I just stand there with my arms wide in blissful rejoice. It would be beautiful.

Hold on. Stop. Let me just clarify something.

I'm not a horrible person. I don't *hate* Christmastime. I don't self-righteously mock people that celebrate Christmas. It's just that, for me, all the worst things that have happened in my life have occurred at this time of year, so I like to avoid it – at all costs.

The other reason I like to keep away from all the festivities as much as I can is to protect my friends and family, because I am, I know, a buzz-kill. Christmas just brings up bad memories for me, so I have simply closed the door on it. No, thank you; not today, Santa.

A breeze – polleny and warm, like the gust of a hairdryer – wafted in from the open door of the card shop and tickled the dark waves of my hair and made me sneeze.

Get a grip, Myla. I really mustn't pull down the display; that would be a very unlike-me move. I should just leave.

Jingle! Jingle! Jingle! Jingle! Jingle!

Over the shop radio came a jingle-themed jingle, like the sounds of ten tiny reindeer prancing over my dead corpse.

'Here in Big Bag of Cards, it's never too early to start thinking

2

about Christmas,' came a chirpy, pre-recorded voice. '*Check out our fantastic stock of Christmas cards today, for all your loved ones, or even the Scrooges in your life! Stock up now, and make this year your best Christmas ever, and a Christmas to remember. CHRISTMAS!*'

I fanned myself from the heat prickling my body. The weather was turning, some blobby, dark clouds rolling in to release a hot, summer rain shower. But it didn't seem like it was just the outside temperature causing me to feel like this. My mouth was dry, the Frappuccino shaking in my damp hand. My breathing turned shallow. I had to get out of there.

People may call me Scrooge, or Grinch, or even the 'least festive girl in England' according to a mug my sister gave me a few years ago, which she'd wrapped in birthday paper lest I burn my fingers on candy cane printed foil wrap. But each year I know what I need to do. And what I need to do is to avoid Christmas until it's over, because that way, I can survive it.

To the tune of *jingle jingle jingle!* I ran from the shop. I ran all the way home. And in silent protest, I ran right into my garden to sunbathe in the hot, smattering August rain.

Chapter 1

Autumn

~ *Now* ~

Clickity clackety, clickity clackety. Here I was, super high-powered office exec, typing out reports and living the metropolitan life again. I liked this office, it was one of the swishest I'd worked in this year, with its big, tall windows and faux-leather spinning chairs. There were free drinks and snacks in the kitchen, a chill-out lounge for when work became too stressful, and everybody called me 'Mylo' instead of Myla for some reason, but I didn't mind because it felt like I had a secret, corporate identity.

I'd been here for a little over two weeks now, and I'd just got off the phone to Sophia, my agent at the temping agency, where I'd told her I might just stick this one out.

'Might?' she asked me, and I could almost hear her eyes rolling. 'Myla, it's a three-month placement. You're supposed to be there until January . . . '

'I *will* stick it out,' I confirmed. 'Of course, I will.' Besides, this seemed the perfect place to have a job over Christmas. Everybody kept to themselves, it was very serious and joyless, and I could stay as little anonymous 'Mylo', under the radar for the whole thing.

'Good,' said Sophia. 'Well, they seem to like you. I had a check-in with your manager earlier today and she was telling me they've got a big project they want your help on now you've settled in.'

'Juicy,' I commented, sipping on one of the four free kombuchas I'd lined up on my desk. 'What is it?'

'She didn't say, only that it would probably take up quite a bit of your time and that it was the perfect job for a temp.'

'Bet you ten quid it's digitising old paperwork.' I didn't mind doing that, and it usually meant I got to be on my feet a bit more which I liked, more so than being in front of a computer. Even though the spinning chairs were super comfy.

After we'd hung up the phone, I went back to writing my reports, and that's when an email came through.

'Hello, project,' I whispered, spotting my manager's name at the top. Most emails that I get at work are company-wide newsletters, or HR asking me again to complete the workstation assessment, or HR thanking me for suggesting they provide bean-bag chairs, which I made during said workstation assessment.

They said they would need to come back to me at a later date about it.

I opened the email, and I liked already that my manager, Evangeline, had jazzed up the request with a meme at the bottom, until I noticed what the picture was.

6

My heart dropped.

Will Ferrell's face was beaming out at me from my computer. He was dressed as Buddy the Elf. I'd seen the movie; my friend Willow had me watch it three years ago after telling me it was a 'heartbreaking drama about a man trying to win the attention of his estranged father'. Sneaky.

I read the body of the email, my mind already mentally calculating how many of those free drinks and snacks I could fit into my shoulder bag when I left today.

Hi Myla,

Hope the reports are going well. I have a nice surprise for you. One of the things I'm really keen to have you work on, since you'll be with us over the whole festive period, is our annual office Christmas party! In fact, I'd like you to organise the whole thing, from the venue to the music right down to the mince pies and mistletoe! I'll need to approve anything before you book, of course, but otherwise I'd love to leave it all up to you. I'm sure it'll be a fun job that you'll have a lot of fun with.

It's a bit late in the day so let's get you started ASAP.

Could you begin by finding a date that the directors agree on, and go from there?

Thanks, and Merry Christmas!!!

Evangeline

'How does that sound?' came a voice behind me, and I turned to see Evangeline smiling down at my perspiring forehead, her hands on her hips.

'Um,' I croaked.

'Fun, right? Not a bad job. God, I wish I could spend the next couple of months diving into all things Christmas. By the time the party comes around you'll be the most festive woman in London.'

'We can swap if you like?' I asked. I'm sure I could do her job. What was her job again?

Evangeline just chuckled, and plonked a folder on my desk, not so subtly pushing aside the stack of swiped Nakd bars I'd been stockpiling from the kitchen. 'Here's some info you might find useful from the last few years' parties. You need somewhere that can hold a couple of hundred people, and the main requirement is that it's just as magical as you can make it. We should have got onto the planning of this much sooner so it's not going to be easy. Just do whatever you have to do to get it proper Christmassy. OK?'

She walked back to her office before I could say another word, so I opened the folder, finding a glossy brochure with a post-it note stuck to the front that read 'CONFIRMED – Xmas'. The brochure displayed a magical winter wonderland created inside a ballroom, where silver and white decorations, including – wait, were those *real* trees lining the walls? It was very Narnia. I flicked further into the folder and saw a masquerade ball, a Mariah and Wham! log cabin theme, a shooting stars set-up which seemed to be based around the aurora borealis.

They weren't messing around; these were proper Christmas parties. They would take work.

A lot of work.

All-consuming work.

Work that I would just absolutely flop at. And someone else out there could, and would, shine at, and love it, and they deserved to be here being paid to do this, not me. Not me.

I guessed I'd better call Sophia back.

Chapter 2

I stayed until the end of the week. Nearly. Until the report writing was done anyway, though when my peppy replacement arrived on Thursday morning already wearing a subtle pair of gold reindeer earrings, Evangeline let me go early.

I sat in the Try To Find A Better Temp waiting area, watching Sophia's closed door. Why did she want me to come in? Did I need to do another typing test, or maybe she had some ideas for my résumé? Normally by now she just calls with a new job opportunity, gives me a stern but kind pep talk, and then emails me the information.

Perhaps I could ask her this time to just put me forward for positions where I work on my own. Like . . . a lorry driver. Or a work from home role, telemarketing, selling something summery, like paddling pools.

I'm telling you, it's this time of year. It doesn't agree with me one bit. If I could, I would hibernate throughout it, but I live in London and rent is steep and so I have to work, which

I understand sounds rich right now coming from someone who just walked out of her fifteenth temp position this year. Sixteenth? Who's counting.

Actually, now that I think about it, it was my twenty-first job this year. Yeesh.

'Myla.' Sophia appeared at her door and rode my name atop of a sigh. 'Come on in.'

'Hellooooo,' I said, bashfully, moving through the sleek waiting area filled with other temps, picking my way over neat shoes and past complicated-looking water coolers and into Sophia's office. I took a seat and avoided her eyes by nudging aside a snow globe and fiddling with the dangly leaves of a spider plant on her otherwise-minimalist desk.

'It happened again, didn't it?' she said, sitting opposite me. I felt like I was in the principal's office. Only trendier.

'It did, yes, but next time I was thinking—'

'I'm going to stop you there,' Sophia said, prising the delicate leaves from my clutches and moving the plant out of reach. 'Myla, I don't think I can help you any more.'

'Well, actually, I was wondering—'

But she was shaking her head. 'It's not really working, though, is it?'

'What do you mean?'

'I mean, we – as an agency – have to maintain a relationship with the companies that use our services. So we need staff to commit to the placements we put them on, and not keep walking out. We have talked about this before. Remember when you walked out of the retail job I put you in during the spring?'

'In my defence, I don't think you were quite clear on that one. You said it was a decoration shop. I thought you were sending me to Oliver Bonas, not a year-round Christmas store.' Which I took one look at and walked straight back to your office, I added internally.

'And before that? The fashion assistant role was an absolute diamond of a job and yet, you quit.'

'Ah, yeah.' I smiled for a moment, remembering. 'That *was* good. Fast-paced. A whole new ball game, as they say.'

'Right?' Sophia said, the twitch of her fingers giving the game away that she wanted to reach across her desk and slash at my cheek like an angry cat. 'It was exactly what you asked for.'

'But don't you remember? The designer then screamed at me in front of the whole office just because I didn't know what "Nordic Fair Isle" was.'

'Yes, yes, I remember. It's the knitted Christmas jumper-type pattern, isn't it? I do think in situations like that you could just ask rather than heading out of the studio for the whole day to collect samples and coming back with ... what was it?'

'One cream cushion I'd bought at a Norwegian furniture shop in West London. It was a nice cushion. It just, apparently, wasn't going to help with inspo for the next autumn-winter collection.'

See? Christmas causing trouble again, even in February.

'I got better though,' I argued. 'I stayed at lots of things over the summer.'

'That's because I was mainly putting you in short-term

jobs, a few days here, a week there. What about the PR firm I sent you to in Chelsea? You barely lasted two days.'

'I stayed *three* days!' I shot back with triumph. 'But anyway, I didn't gel with the boss, so that wasn't really my fault.'

It totally was my fault, and both of us knew it.

Sophia raised her HD brows at me. 'What was so wrong with the boss?'

'Don't you remember him? Big white beard? Booming laugh? Personality just a bit *much*?'

'I do remember him. Nick's my father-in-law, actually.'

A sinkhole opened under her desk and in I slipped, never to be seen again. Gulp. 'He's a lovely guy. Maybe that was more to do with me than him.' His name was *Nick Klaus*, and it just gave me a bad feeling.

'I thought you wanted to make an effort and that's why I agreed to try you again with longer placements.'

'I did, I do,' I protested. 'But I just couldn't bring myself to do this project, that's all.'

'There's always an excuse though, Myla. Either it's not close enough to your dream job, or it's too far to travel, or it doesn't excite you, or it's too exciting, or they want you to plan the Christmas party, God forbid.'

I chewed on the peely bits of my bottom lip, my heart thumping. 'What are you saying?'

'I'm saying we need to stop representing you.' She squinched up her face like she was dreading my reaction, but I'm pretty sure all I did was continue to stare at her. I was getting fired from my temp agency? 'It feels a bit like a break-up, doesn't it, although in this case it really isn't *me*, it's *you*.' Sophia laughed, then coughed. 'Sorry, that was a bad joke, a bit inappropriate really.'

What had become of me? Less than a year ago I was working in that elusive, wonderous 'dream career', and I was happy. And then Christmas had hit, and I was let go. And now, ten months later, I couldn't hold down a job. I couldn't even stick out a short-term temp job.

'I'm sorry, Sophia, could I have another chance? I'll work really hard at the next one, no matter what it is.'

'I'm sorry, it's too late.' She stood. No – not the *please leave my office* stand-up?

'It's not too late. I can change.'

'I think you've said that a few times before.' She walked to her door and opened it. 'It's out of my hands now, and I've been asked to let you go.'

I stepped out of my chair and collected up my bag, the last of my stolen Nakd bars falling to the floor. I picked it up, took a breath, then picked myself up.

'No hard feelings?' Sophia said, with a sympathetic face and a one-armed hug, the other hand not leaving the door in case she needed to slam and bolt it with haste.

'Of course not,' I answered. 'I do understand. Maybe if anything comes up you could still consider me? Even just a one-day thing?' By this point I was talking to the closed door, and I turned, leaving the agency, and stepping into the blustery October air.

Around me, brown leaves scratched along the pavement in twos and threes, pushed by the breeze. The ground was as grey as the skies, the buildings and the power suits that passed me by without a second look. Wind slipped inside my coat and I pulled it tighter around myself.

I considered jumping on the nearest Tube and going home, but I knew I should save my money. So I walked, the long walk back from Tottenham Court Road to Earl's Court. And though I tried not to think about Christmas, it was sneaking into my subconscious from all around me. Shop window displays, some men fixing Christmas lights atop a lamp-post, shopping bags with their seasonal makeovers swinging from hands.

To distract myself, I called my older sister. She'd know what to do.

'Hi, Shay,' I said, in a super-casual manner. 'Just wondered how you were?'

'Uh-oh,' she answered. 'It's mid-morning on a Friday and you're calling to say hi, this is not good.'

'No, it's fine, everything's fine, *so* fine,' I lied. 'You still work in recruitment though, right?'

I heard a sigh, followed by the grunt of a pregnant woman (my sister) lifting herself off the sofa. 'Hold on, I need a drink for this.'

'Wait, Shay—'

'I mean a cup of tea. I'm going to put you on speaker-phone a mo.'

'All right. Is Tess there?'

'No, Tess is at work, and I was also working,' she replied pointedly. She works at home on Fridays. 'Now why are you asking about my job?'

Reaching Marble Arch, I turned off the road and entered Hyde Park, following the path of autumn leaves. 'I'm just in the market for a new recruitment agency, that's all, so I thought of my sister.'

'You know I recruit for international seasonal work, right? Are you planning to run off and live abroad? Besides, I thought you got on with ... Sophia, was it? She certainly seemed patient with you.'

'Sophia and I have decided to part ways. A conscious uncoupling, as it were.'

'Why?'

'They say absence can make the—'

'Myla. Why?'

Hmm. I thought I'd better come clean. 'I walked out of another job?'

'*Another one?*' I heard a teaspoon being furiously thrown into a sink. 'Why? What happened this time?'

'They wanted me to plan a party for them. It's not my expertise.'

'A party? That was it? You do know probably ninety-nine per cent of people have to do some things they don't like as part of their job, right?'

'Yes, I know, but this was different. It was a very large party and it was going to be my main big task for like, at least two months.'

Shay sighed and then was silent for a moment, except for the sounds of angry clattering around her kitchen. 'Wait ... what kind of a party was this?'

'A Christmas party.'

'The Christmas thing again? Myla, come on.'

'I didn't ask it to come around every year,' I protested.

'Maybe it's time to let it go,' Shay said, her voice softening just a little.

'Maybe it's time I move somewhere that doesn't celebrate Christmas and then I won't have to deal with this.' I heard her sigh down the phone. 'It's fine, I'll find a new dream job again soon and then everything will be fine.'

'Oh, the "dream job",' Shay replied, clearly adding quotation marks around the phrase. 'And how's it been going – any luck finding that new dream job yet?'

'No … but you know it took me a long time to get that role before, so …' When I'd landed the position of Junior Artworker in the art department of a big advertising firm in the City, it felt like the stars had aligned. Having studied Art at university, and worked my way through various jobs to gain experience in office work and design, I'd finally been offered one that I could do well and that I was happy in.

Then, I wasn't in it any more. And all that hard work fell flat, and, I don't know, I became a little disillusioned by the whole thing. Leaving that job was heartbreaking, and since then I've slipped in and out of roles like they meant nothing.

Shay and I were getting a little scratchy with each other, so I bid her adieu and went back to my stroll through the park.

I know everybody finds my Christmas thing bothersome, but I can't help it. Every time the winter rolls around, I feel my guard going up, because I don't want to have to relive these memories, or add any more to my collection.

OK, I'd better explain. I don't want to get really into it, but first, there was ...

CHRISTMAS 1999 ~ AGED EIGHT
This was the start of it all, really. My sister, Shay, and I, got into a huge brawl in the middle of watching Home Alone 2 *about whether or not Santa Claus was real. Long story short, I ended up spending that Christmas in hospital with a scratched cornea and accompanying head bump. But you should have seen the other guy! Just kidding. My sister was fine, other than a sore bit on her crown from where I'd pulled a fistful of hair out. But it hurt, and it was scary, and it wasn't like any Christmas I'd had before.*

Then there was ...

CHRISTMAS 2004 ~ AGED THIRTEEN
It was the first day of the Christmas holidays, and Mum came downstairs with two suitcases. Shay and I didn't know what was going on at first, I think I shouted something about, 'Are we spending Christmas in DISNEYLAND?' before I saw my parents' red-rimmed eyes. After months of bickering, Mum was leaving. The house, Dad, us. She walked out with days to go before the big day, and though my dad tried to make everything normal and happy for us, there wasn't quite enough merriment in the house to go around.

Mum lives in Malta now. With a whole new family.

Anyway, then followed the always-horrendous few years of growing up as a teenager, which wasn't helped by ...

CHRISTMAS 2007 ~ AGED SIXTEEN

I'd been ready, more than ready, for my first kiss. And at the school Christmas dance I was finally going to tell Rick, my friend who I'd been in love with since for ever, how I felt. But as 'Bleeding Love' played out of the speakers, my heart was doing just that. There on the dance floor was Rick, wrapped instead in the arms of my other friend, Ashley, looking like they were just beginning their own happy ever after. And I stood, alone, under the mistletoe.

I know that unrequited high school love might not seem like much now, but at sixteen, it was everything.

It was around about here I think I started to distrust Christmas in general. The (many) happy memories began to sink to the bottom of my mind while the rising tally of bad memories stayed buoyant. Like how you can receive a hundred compliments but the one insult is the one you sew onto your shoulder and carry with you.

But it was another four years before the next bad Christmas happened, and this was a big one. One that scared me then, and scares me to this day ...

CHRISTMAS 2011 ~ AGED TWENTY

I'd been looking forward to coming home to the Isle of Wight for Christmas, after a particularly stressful term at university. My sister would be coming home too, and it would be nice for us to all spend some time together again; I hadn't seen her in months. Only, when I arrived home, Shay wasn't there, the house was quiet, the lights around the door hadn't been switched on. Inside I found Dad on the phone, and we found out from her friend

19

that Shay had been silently suffering with alcohol addiction, and had been rushed to hospital. That Christmas she wouldn't come home at all, instead moving into a rehab clinic. I never even knew anything was wrong; I should have been paying more attention.

Shay's been sober since that day. But that Christmas was hard, not being able to see her, hold her, not being able to comfort Dad who thought he'd failed his eldest daughter. Going home to Dad's for Christmas never felt the same after that. Excited anticipation had moved aside for nervous anticipation, that was only relieved when I rounded the corner and I saw the lights on around the door.

   After that, along came . . .

CHRISTMAS 2016 ~ AGED TWENTY-FIVE
It was meant to be a joke at my own expense. My friend Callie was having a Christmas party to celebrate her engagement. Trying to combat my nervous energy, I started performing what, at the time, I thought was a funny, self-deprecating monologue about how I hate Christmas (which was so silly, since, as mentioned, I don't actually hate Christmas). It escalated to me mocking Callie's decorations, and accidentally pulling over the beautifully perfect tree. It ruined her big night. I ruined a friendship.

I still feel awful looking back. My stomach twists in knots, not letting the mistake lie. Callie said she forgave me, but I couldn't forgive myself, and I let us drift apart. I really wasn't good company at this time of year, so now I just don't tend to get involved if my friends are doing something festive. It's safer for everyone that way.

And most recently . . .

LAST CHRISTMAS ~ AGED TWENTY-SEVEN
This was last year, right before our office Christmas party at my dream job. I was even beginning to feel a little bit festive, like I might actually let myself enjoy it all this year. And then I was given the news that because of company cuts, I was being let go. All that work, all that hope, gone. At Christmastime. Again.

I know, these aren't the worst things that have ever happened in anyone's life, but they're the worst things that have happened in my life. So that's me. The life of the Christmas party, hey?

As I neared home, I found myself pondering Shay's words. So much so, that I almost stopped noticing the tell-tale signs of Christmas around me, like the display of Quality Street tubs stacked in the window of Tesco. Almost.

Was my sister right, was it time I stopped reading so much into this time of year? Stopped acting like a cursed being and, well, got over it? It *would* be nice to not have twenty-one different jobs next year. It *would* be nice to be able to stand beside a Christmas tree without wanting to knock it over. It *would* be nice to want to spend the holidays with my family again, and have them want to spend it with me. If I let my guard down, though, would some sneaky little elf run up and bite me on the arse?

21

Wait . . . I'm mixing up elves and imps, I think.

Perhaps, just for the rest of the day, I would see how it would feel to not assume the worst was about to happen and focus on finding myself a shiny new job. Yes. Today was going to be a positive step forward. One for Myla, Nil for Christmas Curses.

I arrived on my doorstep and walked straight out of my shoes and into the kitchen to pour myself a tea, because tea can still solve everything, right?

'Hey,' said Jamilia, my flatmate – *and friend?* – of two years, walking into our kitchen holding a box.

'Oh hey, why aren't you at work?' I asked her.

She raised her eyebrows at me. Jamilia works long hours as a banker in the City, so it was unusual for her to be home in the middle of the day. Yes, unlike me, it was not unusual for me to be home in the middle of the day, I didn't need her manicured eyebrows to tell me that.

'Didn't you see the email?' She started pulling cookbooks off the shelf and dumping them in the box.

'What email?' I got my phone out, and there, among a sea of unread notifications, was a message from our landlord.

'He wants to flip this place over Christmas, so needs us to move out. He's giving us our month's notice, but my friend Louise has a room going so I might just head over sooner.'

As Jamilia's belongings were piled into the box, I guessed there wasn't any 'might' about it.

Wait, what? 'Wait, what? We have to move out?'

'Yep.'

'But . . . we live here. Can we not just stay while he decorates and then he can rent it to us again?'

Jamilia shrugged.

But this was my home, this was where I laid my head at night, falling asleep to the sound of the trains and waking up to, well, the trains. I liked that noise, it was soothing. I liked this house, with its white pillars and black railings. I liked my room, with its sink in the corner. I liked Jamilia. Well, she was OK.

'Jam, this is so sad,' I wailed.

'Yeah, no, I know,' she said, inspecting a chipped mug before lobbing it in the bin.

I followed her from the kitchen and to her room. 'Where does Louise live?'

'Quite close to my work, actually; her place is really cool, not far from Carnaby Street.'

'That sounds nice. Do you think she'd like a two-for-the-price-of-one?'

'A what?' Jamilia stopped at her door and frowned at me.

I smiled. 'Maybe I could move in too? Temporarily. And then we could find a new place, together.'

Jamilia pushed her door open with her bum and slid into her room. 'Yeah, no, sorry, I don't think there's enough space for you. You'll find something great, though. Mkay?' And with that, for the second time that day, I was left staring at a closed door.

Losing my job and my flat on the same day. I think that might be Two–Nil to Christmas Curses after all.

Chapter 3

By the weekend, I was living alone in my flat. Jamilia had gone, leaving me with a broken clothes horse, two bags of her stuff to go to a charity shop, and both our shares of the cleaning. She said she was coming back to sort it all out before the end of the month, but when she was leaving she also said, 'Bye, babe, I'll miss you. Text me if you're ever around.'

'We'll see each other in a couple of weeks though, right? You're coming back over?'

'Yeah, no, sure.'

I knew I wasn't going to be seeing that sultry goddess again.

I wandered about my flat for most of the weekend, in and out of spaces left empty without Jamilia, and felt a heavying weight of doom pressing down on me. Where was I going to live? Where was I going to work? How, in the space of a day, had I become such a mess?

I called my friends, even my acquaintances, to see if they knew of any rooms, or jobs, going, and they all said they'd let me know. Also, none of them were free to hang out at the weekend, so in the end I bought myself two pizzas and spent Saturday night from five p.m. onwards binge-watching *Riverdale* and chain-eating pizza slices.

By Monday, I was facing down my sister.

Behind her desk, Shay shifted her pregnant belly and handed me a bag of jelly babies together with a disapproving sigh. In her office she was surrounded by snazzy posters of exotic destinations covered in words like 'Best summer of your life!' and 'Why wait?' and 'Say no to boring this season'. I think I was making the right decision.

'To what do we owe the pleasure, dear sister?' she asked me.

'I want you to send me somewhere to work for the season,' I answered, my back straight and my chin lifted like a totally confident person who has their shit together.

'This season?' Shay clarified, and looked at the date on her phone. 'Even though it's already late October?'

'Yes. I've thought about it a lot, well, since Friday, and if I don't have the burden of a job and a home then I can be free to go somewhere else for a change. Somewhere sunny. Somewhere they don't celebrate Christmas, please.' This was actually the perfect plan; I knew there was a silver lining to everything cocking up. I wanted to escape over the festive season, and had planned to just try and avoid Christmas by keeping blinkers on and staying home as much as possible. But what if I could avoid it altogether, without needing to turn into a hermit? I could be free in the sunshine and enjoy December as if it were just another month on the calendar.

'Sunny, no Christmas, last-minute,' she made a note.

'That pays nicely and provides accommodation,' I added.

'It's lucky you don't have a massive wish list.'

I leant forward eagerly, trying to turn her monitor towards me. 'So what have you got?'

'Very little, Myla.' She swung her computer back to face her. 'Companies recruited for their winter season staff back in the summer, the spring even. Right now, I'm sorting out placements for people next summer.'

Oh. 'But you must have something. A spare place on a turtle sanctuary in the Caymans, perhaps? What about fruit picking in Australia? I'd even ...' I paused. 'I suppose I'd even consider working in a chalet in the Alps.'

Shay rolled her eyes. 'How thoughtful of you.'

'It's just that my preference would be to avoid the snow and all that "white Christmas" mumbo-jumbo.'

'Are you sure you don't want to come and spend Christmas with me, Tess and Dad? We won't make you eat any turkey or have any fun whatsoever.'

'Thanks, but I think I really want to get away.'

Tapping away on her computer, Shay wasn't giving much away, so I let my eyes roam about her office again. On her desk was a framed photo of her and Tess on their wedding day. I wondered if she'd replace it in three months with one of the two of them and their new baby. They were going to make a cute family.

Shay started laughing, a slow, quiet laugh that reminded

me of a Bond villain, which she then turned into a cough and sat up straight again.

'Actually, I do have one thing.'

'OK.' I sat forward. Ooo, what was it going to be? Dubai? South Africa? Tahiti?

She stalled, her eyes still reading from her computer screen, which she angled away from me when I tried to catch a peek. 'Just how desperate are you?'

'Very desperate.'

'But what's, like, the most important reason you want to go and work abroad for a season?'

'Because I have no job and no house. And I don't want to be here over Christmas.'

'You don't want to be *here* . . .' Shay mused. 'Mmm . . . oh yes, this could work.'

'You sound like a creepy toymaker in a weird play. What have you found for me? I'll do anything.'

'You will?'

'Yes!' She was being even more exasperating than usual. Maybe it was a real find. Maybe it was something like interning as a celebrity stylist in Beverley Hills. For awards season!

'Anything?'

'Oh my god, Shay, yes, I'll do anything, I just need a job and somewhere to live.'

Shay reached behind her and pulled a brochure off her shelf, shielding the front, and then looked directly at me. 'I have something. We just had somebody pull out of a placement, super last-minute, and we'd struggle to fill it at short notice. If we could get you your work permit in time, you'd fly there in two weeks, you'd be gone right through until late January, it pays well, staff accommodation is provided, it'll be a lot of fun.'

'It sounds perfect, sign me up.'

'It is a snowy destination, but it's just beautiful and there are ice hotels and husky dogs and good food and warm saunas.'

I hesitated. 'OK . . . it sounds a little "winter wonderland" but I'm sure I can make it work.' As long as I didn't have to hear thirty-year-old Christmas music blasting out of every open door for two months, or have to fight my way through ropes of tinsel to get to my desk, I could survive. 'It's nice and sunny in the mountains though, isn't it, usually?'

'Erm, yep,' she answered. 'Yep, there'll be a bit of sunshine.'

'So where is it?'

'Finland.' Shay put the brochure down on the desk before me, the page open at a pink-skied alpine forest, draped entirely with a duvet of snow.

'Finland?' What seasonal work was there in Finland?

'Well, Lapland.'

'*Lapland?* Now wait a minute, isn't that—'

'Look.' She turned the page of the brochure to show a gondola making its way up a mountain. 'A sauna inside a gondola, oooh, yummy.'

I tried to turn the page again but she clamped her hands down on top of it. We struggled with each other for a moment until I threw a jelly baby at her face and snatched the brochure.

I knew it! Pages and pages of the most Christmassy place on earth were surrounding the two non-festive photos she'd shown me. Long-bearded Santas smiling from within log cabins. Rosy-cheeked elves playing in the snow. Twinkle-light-covered trees in front of dark, Northern-Lighted skies. Reindeer hanging out in furry clumps wearing jingle bells on their harnesses. I started laughing. 'Good one, Shay.'

But she wasn't laughing. In fact, she had her hands folded in front of her and a 'take it or leave it' expression on her face. 'I'm not joking, Myla.'

'I can't go to Lapland. The whole reason I'm here is to find something to help me *escape* Christmas.'

'Actually, you said the most important reason you were here was because you wanted to have somewhere to work and live. You can have that, in Lapland.'

I shook my head. No way. No. Flipping. Way.

'Listen,' Shay said. 'The job is for an Adventure Guide, which means you'd be mostly out and about in the gorgeous countryside showing holidaymakers a great time doing all the activities not even related to Santa Claus. Much.'

'I mean, it feels like you're lying through your teeth to me.'

'I'm not.' She shook her head. 'Look, you've never been there, this could be a lot of fun, a real adventure. And yes, you won't be able to completely avoid Christmas, but what's the worst that could happen?'

I let out a scoff at that, and she waved her hands in the air. 'Just think about it, OK. You came to me wanting to get away, this is your chance, handed to you on a silver platter.'

Watching as she popped three more jelly babies into her

mouth, I said, 'As a pregnant woman, do you not feel at all bad eating jelly babies?'

'Nope.'

I looked back at the brochure. 'I can't do this, Shay. Thanks for your help, but I'll find another way. This wouldn't be good for me.'

'Maybe it could be.'

'Stop forcing it, please. Thank you, and everything, but I can't even commit to working down the road planning a Christmas party. You know I can't commit to this.'

'So what are you going to do? Go home and live with Dad?'

'No, I'll just get another job. Find another house. It might take a minute but I can do it.'

'And then something will happen in that job, like they'll ask you to help decorate the Christmas tree, and you'll run away again,' Shay countered.

'No, I won't. I'll stay if I have to – I just didn't realise this last job was a make or break for the agency.'

'All right, listen,' Shay said. 'You came to me because you need help and I want to help you out. How about this for an idea, sister. How about we make a bet?'

'What kind of a bet?' I asked, intrigued.

'I bet you can't make it through twenty-four hours without complaining about Christmas, without so much as leaving the room at the sound of a Christmas song.'

I snorted. 'I bet I can't either, so I shall not be taking this bet.'

Shay smiled, slowly, Cheshire Cat-style. 'I think you'll take the bet. If you win, if you make it through that time without complaining, I will pay for your flights to take you away somewhere over Christmas. Wherever you want to go. Within reason.'

'I couldn't let you do that—' I started to protest. 'What, for the whole of Christmas?'

'For whatever amount of time this imaginary job you're going to go and get, and stay in, will let you take off work. You can go somewhere sunny. Somewhere without even a flake of snow.'

I stared at her. 'Somewhere where I wouldn't have to think about Christmas?'

'Somewhere you wouldn't even have to *think*,' she soothed, and in my mind I was already there, on a sun lounger, with a pina colada in each hand.

'And if I lose?'

'If you lose, if *I* win, you have to take this job.'

I gulped. '*This* job? In Lapland?'

'And you have to enjoy it, and be a part of it, and jingle those bells like your life depends on it, because it would, because I will kill you if you mess it up, and I won't ever let you meet your new niece or nephew.'

'Well now, that's a little unfair,' I grumbled. 'Why would you even want to put me forward for this if you have so little faith in me being able to make it through anything Christmassy?'

'Because I know if your hand is forced, which I would be doing, you wouldn't let me down.' Shay gave me a hard stare. 'And I think this could get your Christmas mojo back.'

Staring back at her, I ate another of her jelly babies,

my mind processing. Twenty-four hours. Maybe that was doable, after all. Of course it was. 'This is going to be so easy. You might as well just give me the money now. I'm thinking somewhere really long-haul.'

'Oh, sister dear,' Shay said, shaking her head. 'I won't be giving you any money. I have a baby on the way. Don't go tricking yourself that I'm going to make this easy.'

Chapter 4

'So you actually agreed to this?' my friend Willow said as we sat in the pub that evening, after I'd called an emergency council with her and our other friend, Max.

'It'll be fine, it's one day. I go plenty of days without complaining about Christmas . . . out loud.'

'I don't know, man.' Max shook his head, staring down into his G&T. 'Your sister can be savage; I think you need to believe her when she says she's not going to make it easy.'

'I think it'll be fine,' I repeated.

Willow shrugged. 'OK. When does the twenty-four-hours start?'

'Tomorrow. She says I have to spend the day with her so she can make sure I don't cheat, so I have to be at her house at seven a.m., with an overnight bag.'

'Will you go into work with her?'

'I guess so. Or maybe she's working from home.'

Max started chuckling. 'I can't believe you agreed to

do this on her turf. I bet she's going to have you singing Christmas carols out the window for ten hours straight or something.'

'No, she won't . . . ' Would she? No, surely not. But if I had an all-expenses-paid trip to a tropical island over Christmas I would do it. She'd said all expenses paid, right?

'You are definitely going to Lapland, mate,' said Max, cheersing my glass in commiseration.

'Agreed,' added Willow. 'Though I'd happily take your place. I've always wanted to go there, it looks beautiful.'

'It does,' I agreed. 'Lapland itself sounds amazing, and Finland has been on my bucket list for years, but this is just not how I want to do it. This is literally working with Santa as my manager. Or something like that.'

I changed the subject and we spent a while talking about their jobs, good TV, gossiping about other friends. When Max mentioned something about them all hanging out recently to meet his new boyfriend, Tim, I stopped him.

'Everyone met Tim? I've been dying to meet him – he was in London?'

'Yeah,' Max said, swallowing. 'We just had a quick catch-up since a few of us were around.'

'When was this?' I asked, looking between their faces, neither of which were now looking towards me.

'Pardon?' Max leaned forward as if he couldn't hear me over the roar of the three other people in the pub or the barely-audible Adele album playing.

'I said, when was this?'

'It was just . . . a weekend,' said Max.

'Which weekend?' I asked.

Max swirled his drink, extremely interested in the trails it left inside the glass. 'This weekend, just gone.'

'When I called to see if any of you wanted to hang out and you said you couldn't? You were hanging out without me?' Wow. I swallowed and tried to laugh it off like I didn't care and was just making a joke.

'Myla, it wasn't like we didn't want to hang out with you, it's just that we were going ice skating, and it was going to be really festive, and we just . . . didn't want you to come.'

Willow shot him a look and said quickly, '*No*, it's that we didn't think you'd like it.'

'That's what I meant,' agreed Max.

'I like ice skating, just not all the Christmas music and Christmas decorations and all that that goes with it.' It was true. I like a snowy mountain and a winter-themed hot chocolate as much as the next person. Shove me atop a ski slope and I'll laugh my way to the bottom (I've never actually skied but it looks great fun, laughs aplenty). But add a length of tinsel or a Little Drummer Boy or an ugly Christmas sweater – basically anything that screams *Christmas* itself – and it causes an instant stress-headache.

Max and Willow exchanged another look and I wanted to knock their stupid heads together. Max said, 'Well, exactly. You can be . . . '

Willow put her hand on his arm. 'Don't.'

'What?' I asked.

'It's hardly a secret,' Max protested to Willow.

'Fine.' Willow reached across and grabbed my hands.

35

'Myla. It's not that we don't *want* to invite you to stuff around the city over the Christmas period, but you don't ever seem to really enjoy being there, and it can be kind of . . . a downer for the rest of us.'

Of course. I sat back in my seat. 'But I never make fun of any of it, I try hard to just be neutral.'

Max sipped on his drink. 'Neutral company is what everyone craves. What? I'm joking.'

Willow continued. 'I know, honey. It's not that you're horrible about us having a good time, but it's just clear that you aren't. It radiates off you. In a nice way.' She winced.

It sucked to know they felt that way, but I couldn't argue. They were right. I was a buzz-kill. 'You guys, I really need to win this bet. Can you imagine big fat buzz-kill me in Lapland? The kids would run a mile.'

'No, that's not true,' Willow soothed. 'Maybe if you're more aware of it you'll be able to mask it better?'

'But I don't want to have to hide myself for over two months.'

Willow shrugged. 'Maybe you'll come around.'

Max laughed loudly at that. 'Maybe you'll come back full of the spirit of Christmas and desperate to sing Mariah all year round.'

Maybe I needed to do everything I could to win this bet.

Chapter 5

In anticipation for Shay pulling a few tricks from up her sleeve over the course of the next twenty-four hours, I showed up on her doorstep at the crack of dawn wearing my sunniest, summeriest clothes.

She opened the door and squinted at me. 'Are you in a Hallowe'en costume?' she asked.

In fairness, it was the end of October and I was wearing a bright yellow sweatshirt with a sunshine face on it and cloud-print leggings. Nevertheless, I barged in, and with a smile on my face that said, *you think you can outsmart me?* I dropped my bag and announced, 'Merry Christmas!'

From somewhere upstairs I heard Tess groan.

'Merry Christmas to you,' Shay answered, her smile sweet. 'Can I get you a drink?'

She led me to the kitchen, and so far, everything seemed normal. I was expecting Christmas decorations up, festive music playing, every trick under the sun to try and get me to slip up. In fact, I'd been awake half the night worrying about it.

Shay boiled the kettle and I asked, 'Are you staying home today?'

'Nope, we're going into work. You're temping for the day, with me.'

'Wonderful. Paid?'

'Of course. Here you go,' she said, putting a mug down in front of me.

Spices rose, filling my nose with citrus, cinnamon and nutmeg. 'What's this?'

'Just a herbal tea.'

'What flavour?'

'Hmm, let's see . . . ' Shay read the front of the box. 'Christmas Blend.'

I rolled my eyes and Shay threw down the box. 'Ha! You rolled your eyes!'

'That was at *you*, not at Christmas, that doesn't count. I was rolling my eyes at you and your tactics. It doesn't. Count.'

'Fine,' she replied. 'I'll give you that one, but so there's no confusion, no more complaining about my tactics because it could turn into a big grey area. Just accept that I have a few . . . *tactics*. Which is well within my rights under the terms of the bet.'

Nothing else sneaky happened during breakfast, nor on the Tube ride, nor on the walk to Shay's agency. Nothing untoward in the lift. No brass band meeting us as the doors opened. Hmm, what was she up to?

In fact, it took precisely one hour and forty-five minutes of me temping for Shay for her to spring another surprise 'tactic' on me.

'Myla, can you come here a moment?' she called. I was mid-yawn, hunched over the shredder with snowflakes of chopped paper all around me and the instruction manual in my hand.

'Something's up with your crap shredder,' I commented and looked up to see she was standing beside a big green wall with her colleagues. 'What is it?' I said, edging over.

'We need to send a photo over to our marketing department so they can create an e-Christmas card for us to send out at the beginning of December. I thought you might like to be our model?' She held out a Christmas jumper for me, big, bright red, woollen and covered in dangling baubles.

'Did you, Shay?' I asked with a sweet smile, taking the jumper in my hands. 'Thank you, I'd love to.'

Five minutes later, I was standing in front of the green wall in the jumper, with antlers on my head, a red nose and holding a sign that said, *Thanks to all our workers for sleigh-ing it this year!*

'Oh, wait a minute.' Shay leaned forward and pressed something in the sleeve of the jumper, and all the baubles began to twinkle and flash.

I smiled wide for the camera, even when Shay put on some Christmas music and encouraged me to 'dance about a bit to get in the mood'. Even when her colleagues started draping me in tinsel and shouting Christmas phrases for me to say into the camera instead of saying 'cheese', I got through it.

I got through it later that morning when Shay sent me out shopping for Christmas decorations for the office. Even when I trapped my life-size cardboard cut-out of Jack Skellington from *The Nightmare Before Christmas* in the Tube door and everyone laughed at me. I got through it when, after lunch, she asked me to kick-start the Secret Santa by coming up with theme ideas and I kept getting interrupted and flustered by the phone ringing and not knowing what I was doing.

In the afternoon, as Shay was setting me up on her computer to go through the travel itineraries of the Lapland recruits against a checklist, to make sure everybody's work permits and flights were accounted for, and I was mopping the tea I'd just spilled on myself, I said, 'Can I ask you a question? Not a grumble, just a question, I'm genuinely interested.'

'Go for it.'

'You know Christmas is painful for me. Why are you making me do this?'

Shay softened. 'I don't want to make you relive bad memories, that's not fun for me. But this wall you've built against this time of year is affecting your life. I want you to be able to cope with it. I'm not saying you *have* to then celebrate it; I'm just saying I don't want its presence to stop you living your best life.'

'All right,' I answered. It was a fair point. As mentioned, I knew I wasn't fun to be around. I opened the Lapland itinerary and scanned down the details. The workers (which wouldn't be me) would be flying out in about ten days from their various points across the world, arriving over forty-eight hours into Rovaniemi airport in Finnish Lapland before heading to a secluded area a little outside Luosto, the area that Love Adventuring Lapland – the company my sister's agency were recruiting for – worked out of.

There was a big list of things everybody ought to bring, from base layers to thermals to thick socks. Quite the adventure.

'You're doing well, you know,' Shay said to me at the end of the day as we were packing up to head back to her house for the night. 'I'll break you yet, but you're doing well.'

'Then why are you smiling?' I asked with suspicion.

'Because for every minute you hold it together and smile and allow yourself to enjoy the festivities, it's another minute you're proving to me that you'll cope in Lapland just fine.'

Hmm. Should I be purposefully *not* holding it together? But then I'd lose the bet. My damned sister had me in a right catch-22.

I was quiet on the journey back to Shay's, exhausted from a day working for her (perhaps I shouldn't have been so quick to run out of some of those other jobs) as well as a bit crabby from my lack of sleep the night before. I leant my head against the Tube window and closed my eyes, picturing falling asleep to the sound of sea waves under a warm December sunshine, far, far away.

Shay thwacked me. 'Wake up, and please don't put your face against things on public transport. This is our stop.'

When we arrived back at Shay's, I opened the door to the scent of roast turkey. 'I knew it!' I said. 'I knew you'd have something like this planned.'

Shay raised her eyebrows. 'Don't fancy turkey tonight?' she dared me.

'It sounds perfect,' I demurred.

Walking in the house, my heart sank. Tess had gone *all out*, having had the day off, and had transformed the house into a cosy Christmas abode that could rival Santa's grotto. Scented candles were lit, not just one or two – *all* of them, filling the house with a fog of gingerbread and fir tree and cinnamon. A tree was up in the corner, covered in at least two strings of manically flashing multicoloured lights. Trimmings were toasting in the oven.

I could feel myself getting scratchy when, during a large, full, Christmas dinner, Band Aid finished, and then started up, yet again, on the stereo.

'Shall we put some different music on?' I asked in my most pleasant voice.

Shay put down her fork and started to smile.

'Other Christmas music I mean, of course,' I said quickly. I stuffed a sprout in my mouth, having helped myself to more than a bit of everything just to show I could.

When dinner finally finished, I was feeling pretty glum, especially listening to Shay and Tess compare the turkey to the one they'd had last year, and Shay trying to coax me into discussing how, as kids, we sometimes had goose instead. I didn't want these memories dredged up; this wasn't fair.

Think of the sun. Think of the sun.

I stifled a yawn. It was only coming up to nine p.m. but I was ready for bed, and was about to say as much when Shay said, 'Right, let's cap off this wonderful festive celebration with a festive romcom double-bill, shall we?'

I felt a lightning bolt of annoyance flash through me, which I pushed down. 'I'm quite sleepy actually – much as I'd love to.'

'Nonsense, it's Christmas,' Shay said.

I climbed onto the sofa and settled down, while Shay found the most sickly-sweet offering available on the TV.

After what seemed like at least three hours of a movie, I pulled out my phone to check the time. Nine thirty?!

Tess paused the film. 'Aren't you watching, Myla?' she said, even though I knew full well she was playing a game on her iPad over there.

'Just thought I'd check out some destination ideas for my big, tropical holiday in six weeks' time,' I smirked. 'What do you guys think of Bali?'

'I think you're wasting your time,' Shay retorted. 'Now put that phone away and watch the movie.'

But my eyelids were not playing ball, and they drooped further and further . . .

'Deck the halls with boughs of holly!' Shay and Tess suddenly sang in extremely loud unison, starting me awake and giving me hiccups. I rubbed my eyes, *hic*, and looked around me. I was still on the sofa, the sickly candles still

burning, the technicolour movie still playing, the tree lights still flashing, the sharp taste of brandy butter still in my mouth. And now my sister and her wife were standing over me hollering Christmas carols at my face.

I felt myself beginning to blow. I just wanted to go to sleep. I just wanted it to stop. I just wanted to not have anything to do with any of this, any more.

'What are you doing, *hic*?' I asked.

'Keeping your Christmas spirit alive,' answered Shay.

'*Hic*, stop it.' I put my hand over my chest, painful from the hiccups.

'If you want it to stop, you know what to do,' she sang, and launched into a series of fa-la-las. Tess put her hand on Shay's arm and looked at me.

A tear escaped. *Hic*. 'I said stop it,' I said louder.

'Make me,' Shay dared, and then her smile faded a little. 'Are you OK?'

'No! No, I'm not OK, I don't want to do this, I can't do this. You win! OK? You win. You were right. I can't go twenty-four hours without complaining about Christmas, because it makes me miserable, *this* makes me miserable, *you* are making me miserable. Are you happy? So now I guess I'll be going to Lapland and be miserable for the whole winter, thanks a lot. Now, I'm really grateful for the job today and for the food and the hospitality but please, please, please can we blow out these candles—' I blew out five candles in one huffy huff. 'And turn off those lights that are killing my eyes—' I yanked the plug from the wall. 'And switch off that movie and pleeeeeease stop singing and let me go to sleep?'

Well, that got rid of my hiccups. I stood, panting, while Shay and Tess looked at me with wide eyes. I blushed and sat back down on the sofa, wiping away the tear.

Tess picked up the remote and turned off the TV, and then quietly went around the room blowing out the remaining candles. Shay sat down beside me.

'Are you OK?' she asked again.

After a couple more calming breaths I said, 'Why on earth would you make me do this if you know I can't handle it?'

She propped a cushion behind her back and laid a hand on her pregnant belly. 'First of all, I'm not making you do this. Nobody can make you do anything. If it bothers you that much . . . well, it's just a bet.'

'No,' I sighed. 'A bet is a bet, I agreed to it and I'm not backing out. I just feel like you're making a massive mistake sending me,' I grumbled.

We were both quiet for a minute, though I didn't feel like sleeping as much as I had before.

Eventually Shay said, 'I want you to go because I think you can handle it. I think you have to learn how to start handling it.'

'Why? What's so terrible about me not celebrating Christmas? An awful lot of people in the world don't.'

'I know. There's nothing wrong with not celebrating Christmas, but like I said before, you let avoiding this season rule your life these days. This past year especially. Nobody needs you to love Christmas, but I think *you* need to not have to go to such great lengths to avoid it. It makes me sad that you've started to hide yourself away every year.'

'Not . . . not every year.' She was right, though. 'But this is still hiding away, just all the way in the North Pole.'

'It's not the North Pole, did you even read the brochure? Anyway, there was a time you didn't hate it. I'm curious if that version of you is still in there.'

'People change, Shay.'

'They sure can,' she agreed, and smiled. 'So . . . what's it going to be?'

'You won,' I sighed. 'I'm going.'

'It's a yes? You're sure?'

I shrugged and muttered, 'Sure.'

'Good.' Shay looked relieved and I furrowed my brows at her. Looking a little bashful she explained, 'I already got the paperwork started on your Finnish work permit in the hope it'll be completed in time.'

'I can do those things; you don't need to stick your neck out for me.'

'I already kinda have,' she replied. 'A lot of people apply for this opportunity, Myla. A lot. It's possible we could have filled it elsewhere, but I wanted you to have it.'

'I thought you'd lost somebody last minute, and needed to fill the place?'

'That's true but . . . '

'What are you saying?'

'I'm saying that I had to do some serious begging to let my sister fill the place without so much as an interview.' With a satisfied nod, my sister stood up. 'I think it's bedtime, for all of us.'

I made my way to their guest room, where I stood for a

moment, before giving the two-foot-tall singing Christmas tree she'd left on the floor a kick, tipping it onto its side.

I lost the bet. And I don't want to talk about it.

Chapter 6

Winter

I must be heading to hell, and it's actually frozen over. How did I get myself tangled into the position where, instead of closing the door on all things Christmas and hiding out until it was over, I'd actually *agreed*, *willingly*, to go for an extended sleepover at the literal home of Santa Claus?

'*Daaaaaaaad*,' I shouted down from the loft at my dad's cottage in Yarmouth on the Isle of Wight. He lives alone, has done since I left home a couple of years after my sister, but he says he's happy.

'Yeeeeeees?' he called back up.

'Do you think it could be inside the disgusting old trunk?'

'It's worth a look.'

Hmm. He wasn't going to come up and help me, so I used my sleeve to wipe dust and cobwebs off the latch of the disgusting old trunk, trying not to be perturbed by the long-dead flies lying in rigor mortis around the surface like they'd made a suicide pact back in the hot summer.

My dad, apparently, had a super-thick and toasty Gore-Tex down jacket stored in the loft from his days working as harbour master. Considering these coats are way way way *way* out of my budget, but also supposed to be amazing for Arctic climates which is where I am, apparently, jaunting off to, I don't even mind if it smells musty and is a bit on the large side. I'll take it.

Heaving the lid off the trunk, I pushed past some photos of Mum and Dad's wedding without looking at them, and found the parka, big, squidgy and maroon-red, underneath. 'Yes,' I whispered into the attic, and pulled it out, wrapping myself in it. It did smell musty, but also a bit of Dad, which was nice, and speak of the devil, he poked his head into the roof and handed me a cuppa.

'Ah, you found it!' He smiled and climbed up, carrying his own cup of tea, and took a seat beside me on one of the old dining chairs we keep up there for some reason.

'I did. I like it. You sure you don't mind me taking it?'

'Not at all, I'd be honoured. Besides, a coat like that deserves to go on adventures.'

'It probably deserves them more than me,' I commented, taking off the coat and setting it aside carefully.

'Why would you say that?'

'Because Shay is doing me a massive favour by setting me up with this job, and I've not been very grateful. I don't know if I really want to do it, still, to be honest.'

Dad nodded and sipped his tea. 'I know it's not very *you*,

but there was a time you quite liked Christmas. Maybe this will help you find your festive spirit again.'

'I'm not really looking to re-spark the magic, though. I just want to get away, and make it through to the end unscathed.'

'That's all you want from this? For it to be over?'

'No, that's not quite what I mean. I want to enjoy it – the snowy, new location side of it, anyway. I just don't want anything bad to happen while I'm out there. I don't want it to be a mistake.' I paused, studying my mug, a gnawing worry in my tummy.

It was early November now, and I had come around to the idea since losing the bet, and I was excited to finally visit Finland. But I wanted desperately to come away from it having had a good experience, and although I nearly made it through Shay's twenty-four-hour challenge, I worried that being out there surrounded by Christmas all the time could bring me really down.

'Hmm,' Dad said, 'I understand. I can't predict the future, love, but I don't think it'll be a mistake, I really don't.'

'It's going to be so freezing, though,' I sighed, but with a smile, ready to lighten the mood.

'I think I have some long johns I could lend you.'

'Dad, I do not want to borrow your thermal underwear.'

Good old Primark. Although I nearly wept on the shop floor as shoppers smacked their enormous gift bags against me to the tune of the third rendition of 'Jingle Bell Rock'

I'd heard in as many shops, I managed to escape with a haul of thermal base layers and undercrackers. Now I was back in my flat, which looked even emptier since most of my own stuff was packed and I'd taken Jamilia's bags to a charity shop. I sat in the living room surrounded by my large backpack, and all my Lapland gear around me, plus a glass of Pimm's because I would hold on to my fantasy of it not being Christmastime for as long as I possibly could.

'Thermals, check. Coat, check. Toiletries, check. Finnish phrase book, check. Avalanche kit, check.'

What was I doing? I should not be going somewhere where I'm planning to take an avalanche kit. This was just so beyond what I could cope with, even without the Christmas element.

My phone rang, my sister telepathically herding me forward all the way away in Wimbledon.

'Hey, you all packed?' she asked, when I connected the call. She sounded false-chirpy and I was immediately suspicious.

'I'm getting there . . .'

'Oh that's good, great, let me know if you need a hand. I could help you clean your place. Or take you to the airport?'

'Shay, you're a million months pregnant.'

'*Six* months pregnant.'

I paused. OK, just tell her. Just say you're having second thoughts. Sure, she would get in a grump and be disappointed and give you a tongue-lashing, but Shay was used to you flaking on jobs; she'd get over it. 'Shay, I was thinking—'

'Nope, no you don't.'

'But—'

'Stop right there. You are not pulling out of this.'

I sighed. 'I am grateful, Shay, really, but it just feels too hard. I think I made a mistake saying yes.'

'But you didn't say yes, you lost a bet, and you can't back out on that.'

'I mean, you're right, a bet is legally binding in both the UK and Finland.' I laughed, but she didn't laugh back. 'What if you have the baby while I'm away? I could come back early for that, couldn't I?'

'You won't need to. This little one isn't due until after you're home.'

I fiddled with the fluffy collar of Dad's down coat. 'Promise?'

Pausing, Shay added the disclaimer, 'I mean, I won't be shoving the baby back in if it starts to show up to the party early, but as much as I can: I promise.'

'Deal,' I said, and shook myself out of my funk. 'Look, I said I'd go, so I'll go.' *I'll go.*

Shay let out a relieved laugh. 'Yay! I really think this will be good for you, My.'

'I'm sure you do.'

'Just enjoy it, enjoy the scenery and the change of landscape and the different sights. And don't spend your whole time waiting for it to be over or worrying about bad things happening.'

'I won't.' *Yes I would.*

'Great. So you're definitely going?'

I looked at my belongings scattered on the floor, clothing

I'd never needed before, books in languages I couldn't speak, socks so thick they could be sleeping bags for kittens. And then I looked at the walls of my living room, bare of pictures and memories, my stuff in boxes, my flatmate gone, my rent drying up. 'Yes, I'm going to Lapland.'

'All right, so that's settled. There's one more thing.'

Narrowing my eyes at the phone, I asked, 'What?'

'To get you the job, I had to kind of "sell you", as it were.'

'OK . . . '

'And to do seasonal work like you'll be doing, one of the requirements is that, well, you're really into Christmas. Like, *really into Christmas*.'

'Oh my god, what do you mean?'

'Nothing. Well, just that. I needed to make out like you loved Christmas, and I'm going to get into a lot of trouble if you walk in there and declare your status as the UK's least festive woman. So you just need to keep your miserable yuletide melancholy to yourself, all right?'

'You've got to be kidding.' I mean, I wasn't about to march in and start kicking plastic elves across the log cabins, but surely I wouldn't have to be non-stop merry and bright? 'Fine.'

'And don't quit early.'

I was about to stand up for myself, but you know, fair point. Instead, I just repeated, 'Fine.'

What else could I do? I didn't want to let Shay down or get her in trouble, especially after she stuck her neck out for me. And she was about to have a baby so I didn't want to cause her any more stress.

Later that night, I begrudgingly put on *The Polar Express* to try to force myself to get in the zone. But I had to turn it off halfway through and binge-watch *Love Island*.

Chapter 7

Remember when I thought I'd be able to run away from Christmas rather than right towards it? Laughing face crying face.

No, it was going to be fine. All I had to do was make it to the end of the season without another traumatic life event and it would be worth it. I was still escaping. I was still going somewhere new. I was still being given somewhere to live and a job. I was grateful.

Did there have to be Christmas trees every ten metres throughout the airport concourse though? Standing there, all uniform and Dalek-like. I get it, *'tis the season*, blah blah blah.

'Please can I have a latte with full-fat milk?' I asked the barista at the Starbucks counter. My first flight to Helsinki would be about three hours long, so if I had a tasty drink now, I could keep the flight for chucking back the mini bottles of booze.

Oh bollocks, I probably shouldn't actually. I only had

a brief stopover before switching to my short flight to Rovaniemi, and one of the company reps would be meeting me the other end. Even I knew showing up to day one smelling of alcohol isn't the done thing.

'Would you like regular or Christmas blend?' the barista asked me with a smile, pointing at the two coffee roast options. She had tinsel around her ponytail.

'Regular, please.'

'Sure. And do you want any of our festive flavour shots?'

'No, thanks.'

'The gingerbread one is amazing.'

'I'm good.'

'And so is the eggnog one?'

I pulled my gritted teeth into a smile. 'Just a regular latte, to take away, thank you.'

'Coming right up. What's your name?' Peppy Barista asked me.

'Myla.'

'I love that name!' She wrote it on my cup, along with a drawing of a holly leaf, and danced down the queue to the next person.

Oh my god, I am such a grinch. If I couldn't even get through an interaction with a joyful barista, how would I cope when confronted with an adult pretending to be an elf?

I took my coffee towards one of the Christmas trees and forced myself to stare at it until they called my flight number.

You WILL go into this with a smile. You WILL be merry and bright, or at least not miserable and not a grumpy bitch.

*

My flight to Helsinki was smooth, and instead of slurping alcohol I filled up on way more than my share of peanuts. After a brief wee break, or 'layover' as some people call them, I was back on an aircraft again and about to begin the one hour, twenty minute final leg to Rovaniemi.

On the plane, I found my seat, sat down, clipped in, unclipped because I was already boiling in this crazy-big coat of my dad's, stuffed it into the overhead locker, clipped in again, unclipped to take it out because nobody else around me could fit their suitcases in, stuffed it under my seat where it spilled out under my legs, and clipped myself back in. I had a window seat this time, which was nice, so I should be able to see Finnish Lapland in all its dazzling snow-covered glory when we arrived.

'Hi,' said an American voice beside me, and I turned. Before me, leaning to put some headphones and a book down on my neighbouring seat, was a guy around my age. His hair was dishevelled and the colour of roasted chestnuts, with matching dark brown eyelashes that framed slightly bloodshot navy blue eyes, and he had a little light stubble. I guessed this wasn't his first flight today.

'Hi,' I answered, and turned back to the window. I then took another sneaky look at him as he reached up to help shuffle some cases around with a family, and caught a glimpse of his stomach as his crumpled, red plaid flannel shirt lifted a little.

I caught the eye of a woman across the aisle who motioned to licking her lips and I flicked my eyes away, embarrassed, and focused again on the runway beyond the window.

When the plane began to taxi, the man beside me said in a soft voice, his accent straight out of a late-night coffee advert, 'Here we go! Next stop Lapland!'

'Yeah,' I said back, wondering how convincing I sounded, and he flashed me a small grin before looking past me out of the window.

'Have you been before?'

'No. You?'

'No. I'm excited.'

I nodded, studied the side of his face for a second longer, and then looked out the window myself, as the plane made its way down the runway.

The plane swept off the ground and up towards the clouds, and I realised I'd better get on board with this trip once and for all, because it was official now, I could no longer cling on to my 'least festive girl in England' title.

Beside me, American Guy had begun watching *Elf* on his phone through headphones and chuckling to himself every couple of minutes. Before that, he'd been watching the end of *It's A Wonderful Life*, which presumably he'd started back on his previous flight. This man was really getting into the spirit of Christmas.

At the fourth chortle in about as many minutes, this time he caught my eye. Looking up from my book, I politely smiled back at him and then, facing my novel again, said quietly through gritted teeth, '*Haha, yeah, you're so annoying . . .*'

'Oh, I'm sorry,' he said immediately, and removed his headphones. 'Am I being too loud?'

I looked at him for a moment, frozen. *Busted*. 'Oh, what, no, I love your laugh,' I covered up, in a really smooth way.

'I think I'm being . . . *annoying*?' His eyes twinkled at me.

'No! Why would you? *No!*' I flustered. I mean, yeah, he was dressed like he'd stepped out of a Gap Christmas advert and was watching back-to-back festive films beside me and laughing at them, then looking at me to see if I was having as much fun. He wouldn't be at all considered annoying to most people, but to me, he was like nails on a chalkboard.

'I'm pretty sure you said . . . '

'No, I didn't.'

'OK. It's just that I'd just paused the movie, and I thought—'

I'd been caught. I gave him a bashful shrug. 'I just don't personally find that movie *that* funny, I'm sorry if I was a dick about it.'

'You weren't a dick,' he laughed. 'You don't like *Elf*?'

' . . . Or *It's A Wonderful Life*.'

'Wow.'

I shrugged. 'Sorry again.'

'It's fine. I'll try to keep it down.'

'No, you really don't have to. Please, enjoy yourself, I'm just going to look out the window and wish I could crawl out of it.'

American Guy grinned again, meeting my eye, and put his headphones back on over his ears.

A short while later, the plane began its descent to Rovaniemi airport, and as we broke through the clouds my first view of Lapland opened up before me. Snow covered the ground as far as I could see, with dark forests poking up into the air. Being late afternoon, the sun was now below the horizon, and had been for a couple of hours, so the whole vista of Lapland was bathed in a steely-blue light over the top of the white.

The plane descended like a feather landing on a duvet. The ground temperature outside was minus thirteen degrees, according to my on-screen flight map, and I squeezed my dad's coat between my calves, thankful to have it to wrap around me when we exited.

As the plane bump-bumped onto the runway, my arm bump-bumped into American Guy's arm, and I felt the warmth of his skin reach through his shirt and my jumper to meet mine.

'Sorry,' I said.

'No problem at all,' he replied, and just for a second our arms remained together, before he broke away to start collecting his stuff from his seatback pocket.

After the pilot pulled to a stop and made an announcement in Finnish, she said, 'Ladies and gentlemen, boys and girls, welcome to Lapland. And if you are here to meet Santa Claus today then on behalf of the cabin crew and myself, Merry Christmas!'

'Merry Christmas,' I wished back, in a whisper. I think I was mainly wishing it to myself.

Chapter 8

With the seat-belt sign switched off, I scrabbled to drag my coat out from under my seat and legs, trying to put it on me without clubbing the guy next to me in the face. From behind the small window, I could see it was looking pretty cold out there.

My neighbour, American Guy, was one of those people who wanted to let everyone else go first and help with everybody's luggage, but eventually we made our way off the plane and onto the air-bridge, and then into a glass corridor, where I caught my first panoramic view of Lapland.

'Wow,' I breathed against the glass, fogging it up and wiping it clean again with the sleeve of my coat with a squeak. Despite the dark, I could make out white ground with white aeroplanes that swirled grey where the wheels had waltzed through the snow on the runway.

And look at that … I don't know what I'd expected, exactly, but it wasn't like we touched down to the Rockettes and Santa Claus guiding the plane in with marshalling wands. *This* – snow and serenity and all the best bits of winter – were A-OK with me.

Realising I was now alone, I scuttled to catch up with my fellow passengers.

As I waited for my backpack, I spotted American Guy across from me, and when he turned I gave him a goodbye wave and our eyes met again for a moment. He smiled, and though I knew nothing about him and would probably never see him again, for a tiny moment in time it was nice to have somebody smile at me with a modicum of familiarity in a place a million miles from home.

I'd been told a rep from Love Adventuring Lapland would be meeting me at the airport, and we'd be heading to a hotel on the edge of the city of Rovaniemi for two nights before travelling deeper into the Arctic Circle, to an area nearby the village of Luosto, which was tucked within the border of Pyhä-Luosto National Park, that would be my new home for the next two and a half months.

So when I entered the arrivals terminal, feeling almost lost inside my huge coat with my enormous turtle-shell of a backpack heavy on me, I looked around for the rep. It was a small airport, neat, signs in Finnish as well as English, and big windows that showed the muted white sky and white ground outside. Then I saw a sign being held in the air, a little way back from the barriers, beside a coffee cart. *Welcome, Love Adventuring Lapland Santa Helpers!*

I shuffled over and joined a small gathering of people, perhaps around fifteen of us, adults of all ages, all looking a touch nervous, like me, but the key difference being that despite the nerves, they had big, excited smiles on their faces. The rep was smiling and greeting everyone as they walked over, ticking people off a list.

'*Hei*,' I said, practising my 'hello', my voice coming out more timidly than I'd intended, since this was hands-down the easiest Finnish word to attempt as it basically was me just saying 'Hi'.

The rep looked up at me and smiled kindly. '*Hei*, my name is Daan, I'm the head of operations for Love Adventuring Lapland. Welcome to Rovaniemi, the official hometown of Santa Claus in Lapland. What's your name?'

'Myla Everwood.' I watched as he ticked me off on his list.

'All right, we just have a couple more people to come through on this flight and then we'll make our way to our hotel.' His voice was gentle and slow, instantly soothing like one of those stories you listen to in order to fall asleep.

I shifted the weight of the backpack, heavy on my shoulders, and lifted the corners of my mouth at the people around me.

I began to remove my scarf when Daan said, 'You'll probably want to keep that on. When we leave the airport to walk to our shuttle bus it might feel very much colder than you're used to.'

'It's true,' said a British girl beside me who looked athletic and outdoorsy. 'I came here once with my family for Christmas and it really makes you appreciate that "cold" in the UK is actually pretty mild, comparatively. Have you been to Lapland before?'

'Never,' I answered.

'You must be *so* excited,' the girl enthused.

'Yeah,' I said, hoping it sounded genuine.

A couple more people joined the group and Daan was introducing himself to them. 'And what's your name?' I heard him say from the other end of the group.

'Josh. Josh Roberts.'

I knew that voice. Turning my whole body as best I could in my Iron Man-like get-up, there he was, American Guy, standing with our group. He'd layered up since I last saw him, now in a thick coat also, plus gloves and scarf all covering over the flannel shirt. He had a woollen hat pulled over his thick hair but his dark eyelashes were still prominent. *Josh.*

At that moment, Daan found his name on the list, and Josh looked up and around at the rest of us, catching my eye though I looked away quickly.

'All right, everybody, follow me,' said Daan, putting away his clipboard and pulling on his own humungous mittens. We shuffled along behind him; the straps of the backpack pressed into my shoulders and I hooked my thumbs under them to try and relieve some of the weight.

As the airport doors slid open, a rush of cold air hit my face and immediately froze me like Bette Midler in *Hocus Pocus* (sorry for the spoiler, but also, that movie has been out for thirty years). My eyelashes all fell off like icicles and my breath stopped in the air like a dying wish.

Lapland wasn't joking around, this was *cold*. The chill air stroked my cheeks, tracing its way over my lips, looking into my eyes, running its fingers through my hair and I wished I had a hat. It was icy and eerie and freezing, but also fresh and invigorating. Under my feet the snow was thick and compressed, crunching with all our footsteps.

And before I could get used to it, we were at a shuttle and my rucksack was being lifted off my shoulders by maybe a guardian angel and I was following the group into the warm sanctuary of the minibus and sitting down.

With the bus door closed, the heating blasting through, it was like those moments of frozen silence had never happened, and we pulled out of the airport to head to our hotel. I was on a single seat, so I spent the journey peering out of the window. At this time, in November, I'd read that 'daylight' was between about nine and three. It was soon after six p.m. now and the dark denim blue of the sky told me we'd already moved through 'civil' and 'nautical' twilight, and were now in 'astronomical' twilight. By six-thirty-ish it would be night-time until all the twilights started again come the morning. Who knew there were three types of twilight? Stephenie Meyer could write a whole spin-off series . . .

It took me five full minutes to ponder this, and then we pulled into the parking area of a hotel called the Christmas Claus Lodge, which was all wooden frameworks and fairy lights and snow-covered rooftops. Stepping from the bus, I was reading a signpost that spoke of a Santa Claus Village – whatever that was – a kilometre away, when somebody yelled a jovial 'Ho! Ho! Ho!' and a photo-fest ensued.

A large wooden Santa Claus was waving at us while we hauled our bags from the bus, and I tried to join with others but couldn't quite bring myself to snap a selfie with him and instead released a slightly maniacal laugh. *I can do this. I can get through this.*

Just don't dwell on the past for the next six weeks and then the big day will pass.

And don't get trapped in a frozen lake or get eaten by a reindeer or anything.

We traipsed through the snow up the path towards the lodge, three storeys tall and with a chocolate-box roof. It was surrounded by trees on each side, and had smoke curling from a chimney in the centre, the aroma of a log fire present in the cold air. Daan, leading the way, held the door open for us and we stepped inside, treading snow through the reception area, and one by one we were given keys to our rooms and told to meet back beside the large Christmas tree here in the lobby in half an hour.

Taking the stairs and nearly toppling backwards thanks to my already-damp fake-Uggs sludging down below my heels and the weight of my backpack, I found my room on the first floor. I opened the door with caution, half expecting it to be like entering Santa's workshop, but it was actually very calming, decorated in blues and nutmegs. Big windows looked out across the snowy clearing at the back of the property, though the sky was darkening more and more now.

I removed my coat and my boots and sat down on the bed, taking in the view before me. Wow, this was comfy.

And it looked so cosy. And mmmmm, this furry blanket felt nice under my hands. And as the light snowflakes drifted by outside, I thought that maybe I'd just lie down for a quick relax . . .

Chapter 9

I woke to an insistent knock on the door.

'Myla Everwood, are you all right in there?' came Daan's voice.

I leapt out of bed and ran to the door, checking my jeans and jumper were all decent and not bunched up weirdly. 'I'm so sorry, I fell asleep,' I cried, mortified. Oh God, I was already messing up and I'd been in Lapland less than two hours.

'It's OK, I'm rounding people up, I think quite a few travellers have experienced the same thing.'

He was so nice, thank God. Promising I'd be down in less than a minute, I yanked open my case and threw my belongings around the room, looking for my hat, then swiftly pulled on my boots, coat and scarf, and after a quick check of my appearance, added a little dab of glittery highlighter to my sallow cheeks, and raced down to the lobby, just in time to hear Daan explain what we were doing this evening.

My tummy growled. I hoped we were going for food. I bet Lapland had great food.

'Tonight, we're heading over to have some fun at ... Santa Claus Village,' he proclaimed. 'Tonight is, drum-roll, the official opening of this year's Christmas season!'

I gave a gasp of joy along with the others while in my mind I wondered how the Venn diagram of Fun at Santa Claus Village would intersect with Myla Needs Some Grub. I gave my tummy a little rub right at the moment I met Josh's eye, who was standing the other side of the Christmas tree. I dropped my hand and looked away, a little concerned he might think I was signalling I was either planning to eat him or have his baby.

There were more people here now than I'd arrived with, additional staff members who'd reached the hotel at different times during the day, so our little group was perhaps around forty, forty-five strong? This suited me just fine. The bigger the crowd the easier it was to get lost within it.

It was a ten-minute walk to Santa Claus Village, a park which held Santa's Main Post Office, various shops and cafés, and amusements, and as we neared, I was kissed from all sides with air chilled to minus fourteen degrees Celsius – colder than I'd ever experienced at home – plus falling snow, twinkling lights and Christmas music coming from speakers. I really didn't think I could be anywhere else on earth than in Lapland right now, especially since I was about to witness the opening of Christmas. Officially.

I couldn't *wait*.

No, sorry, I promised Shay I would give this a good go and so I had no choice but to embrace all the magic of the season. Sigh.

When we stepped over the threshold into the central square of Santa Claus Village, my heart had a battle with my head. The old me, the child version of Myla who still sparkled when the days counted down towards Christmas, felt her eyes widen and a smile twitch the corners of her mouth. She felt a rush of deep-down excitement and belonging and familiarity and wonder because this place was beautiful, *magical*. But the grown-up Myla, the Myla I was now, wanted to turn and run all the way back to London because I didn't think I could handle this overload of the senses, these overwhelming reminders of what Christmas has become for me.

From where we stood in the square, I was surrounded by wooden cabins, their roofs sloped and trimmed with fairy lights, some with steeples rising into the night sky. The dark night air was cold, but warm lamps of green, red, purple and pink pooled at the bottom of the large pine trees and around the footprint of the buildings. Soft white snow slept upon the buildings and the ground. Christmas trees with tiny white lights dotted the edge of the square. A trombone solo of 'Jingle Bells' floated through my consciousness.

'OK, first thing is first,' Daan said, clapping his hands together in the manner of a school teacher who drew the short straw and had to take out a group of unruly teens. 'The celebration will be busy, lots of people arrive from all over the world to witness this evening, so out of courtesy for the holidaymakers we ask that, even though this will be a very special evening for you too, please stand back and enjoy from a distance. You can still join in all the fun, but don't, what is the phrase, hog the limelight.'

We all nodded dutifully and I looked around me at the shops and cafés that made up the surrounding buildings. The pièce de résistance appeared to be a larger building constructed of wood and stone, with an arched entranceway and a big illustration of a smiling Santa. This was the Santa Claus office, and I wasn't sure what went on in there but other people from my group were excitedly trying to edge towards it.

I spotted a series of tall, red pillars with stone bases, all in a line, with ARCTIC CIRLE written down the length of them. Now, that looked a little more my scene. When Daan gave us the OK to explore, I made my way towards them, blowing into my hands as I went.

This was pretty cool. I stood a step back between two of the Arctic Circle pillars and knew that at this point, I was crossing the line to where I would experience polar nights, known in Finland as *kaamos*. I closed my eyes for a moment to let this sink in, the sounds and smells of Santa Claus Village, of music and chatter and laughter and aromatic mulled wine being pushed away from the forefront. Tomorrow I'd be heading further north into the Arctic Circle, further into Lapland, further into the dead of winter and away from England, from my family and friends and my cosy flat that was no longer mine anyway. There was no turning back after this point.

With my eyes still closed, I took a deep breath through my nose, filling it with Arctic air, and stepped over the line.

And squashed my nose against someone's back.

I opened my eyes in time to see Josh step away in surprise, and then turn to me with that big smile of his.

'Oh, I'm sorry,' he said. 'I shouldn't really walk backwards in a crowded place, I guess.'

'I shouldn't walk with my eyes closed,' I admitted, rubbing my nose.

'How cool is this place?' Josh asked, putting his gloved hands in his pockets. 'It's winter wonderland!'

'Yeah!' I tried to match his enthusiasm. 'I'm looking forward to seeing Luosto the day after tomorrow though; it looks beautiful in the pictures.'

'So beautiful,' he agreed.

'Hey, um, sorry again about the plane, I didn't ...'

'... You didn't think we'd be colleagues for the next two and a half months?'

'Yes. Sorry.'

'It's totally fine, it's funny really. So what job are you going to be doing?'

'Adventure Guide.' I nodded, even though it felt extremely strange to my ears still, considering it was only two weeks ago I was sat in my millionth office block of the year. Now my office would be outside. I gnawed on my lip for a moment, wondering if I would cope with the lifestyle change.

'That sounds fun, you'll probably get to see and do so many things. Maybe we'll even work together some days.'

He looked hopeful, but I'm sure it was only because I was the only person he knew here, so far. 'What job are you doing?' I asked.

'I'm going to be an elf.' He said it with such pride, and such a wide grin and twinkling eyes that I couldn't help but laugh.

I tried to turn it into a cough. 'I'm sorry, I'm not laughing at the job, or at you doing the job, it's just ... I'm laughing because you just don't hear it a lot, you know? *What job do you do? Oh, I'm an elf.* Like, it would be a funny thing to hear on a date or something. Or not a date, just getting to know a person.' Oh God, shut the hell up, Myla. 'So an elf, hey?'

'Yes,' he laughed, a friendly laugh that put me at ease a little.

'This is probably a really silly question, but what exactly does an elf do here in Lapland? Are you going to be making presents?'

'No, it's not really about making presents, more about making memories. We're here to make everyone's vacation even more magical. From what I can tell we'll be there on the tours or hanging with Santa, playing games, joking with the kids, singing carols, throwing snowballs. It's all about being energetic and fun and Christmassy, I guess.'

I nodded. In an alternate universe, I would love to have had the personality to suit being an elf, but as it is, mine is quite possibly the exact opposite. 'Have you, um, always wanted to be an elf?'

'You know, I have actually. I've played an elf at a mall and at a hospital before, back home, but coming to Lapland is pretty amazing. I'm big into Christmas. Obviously.'

'Obviously,' I chuckled with faux-concurrence. 'What do you do at home when you're not elfing it up?'

'I'm a surgical nurse in Seattle. How about you?'

At that moment, a peal of jingle bells rang out, and visitors to Santa Claus Village began making their way towards the stage in the centre of the forecourt. I was pleased, because I didn't fancy telling my new friend Josh all about my year of fannying around on the job front, especially when he clearly did something as honourable as nursing, and being an elf for kids in hospitals.

At home, I tried to make a trip each year to the hospital I went into as a kid. Just to bring some gifts for the children who had to spend the holidays, and often beyond, there. Dad knew I went, but I didn't tell anyone else. It was just something for me, really. I wonder if I would have ever done that without having had that experience as a child. Maybe. But knowing how I avoid Christmas at all costs, it probably wouldn't have occurred to me.

We stood near the back, joining the rest of our group though I was still just getting to know their faces, Daan being the most recognisable thanks to his height and big beard. And suddenly, it was like I was in Disneyland. The stage came alive with red-coated, pointy-hatted dancers who twirled and gasped and smiled and waved in time to the jolly, accordion-led folk music. I happened to glance at Josh, who was now a couple of bodies away from me, and he mouthed '*Elves*' at me.

Around me, people were swaying to the music, bouncing children on their shoulders, holding phones up to take photos and whooping into the night air. I kept my smile frozen on my face, jiggling up and down a little, feeling so very out of place and wondering how soon I could run back under the blankets in my hotel room. You know the feeling I mean ... when no matter how much you try and force your body and mind to join in, no matter how fabulous you can see that something is, you just feel wooden and awkward.

Don't get me wrong, the celebration was incredible, the music lovely, the dancers great, the atmosphere happy and alive and wonderful. But my heart was heavy because this was everything I'd been trying to avoid, and as much as I tried to stop it the train of thought had left the station and I just kept reliving flashes of those past memories of Christmases gone by. As the show continued, I felt the loneliness of waiting for nobody under the mistletoe at the school dance, the sadness at my sister's place at the table empty on Christmas Day and knowing she was struggling on her own in rehab, the sense of loss after my dream job was taken from me, the confusion at my mum not being around over the holidays when I'd thought everything was fine. I couldn't stop the thoughts, and so although my smile remained on my lips, I knew it didn't reach my eyes.

A cheer rose from the crowd, and people began stamping their feet on the snow and I brought myself back to the present, just as Santa Claus himself stepped on the stage. Dressed in a long red robe with a white furry collar and wide sleeves, a droopy red hat and a beard so long it quite covered up any hidden belly full of jelly, he was clearly the star of the show, and checking the faces of those around me – both adults and children – I knew I was very much in the minority here. In fact, I think I was probably the only one not going wild. So it probably looked a bit suspect. I let out a '*Woooooo!*' for good measure, a microsecond too late, and then caught Josh giving me a slightly bemused, slightly interested look.

Had I blown my cover already, before even the first night in Finland?

I kept my eyes forward, focusing on my smile, listening to Santa greet the visitors in jovial Finnish and English.

When he declared the Christmas season as now open, here in Lapland and all around the globe, ending with a heartfelt, 'Merry Christmas,' in his warm-as-a-fireplace voice, a cheer rose high into the night sky.

I refused to look over at Josh again, and after the ceremony, when the music turned into a festive, outdoor disco, I made the conscious effort to leave the group and explore the village before he could catch up with me.

Stopping at a stall selling gingerbread cookies and *glögi* – a Finnish mulled wine – I stocked up and let the sweet aromas drift into my nose and the fiery cinnamon spices fill my mouth. Standing on the compacted snow with warm steam making its way over my face, I followed the edge of the office until I was behind it and the music from the square was fading into the background. I was now alone under the falling snow, so I gave myself a minute to breathe.

I should never have taken that bet. I should have just joined another temp agency, found a random room in some random house-share, and kept my head down over Christmas. I should not, under any circumstances, have willingly agreed to enter the lion's den.

The air remained cold, perhaps colder even now than before, and I could see my breath being picked up by the chill breeze while I munched on the gingerbread cookies. My god, these were incredible ... I was just breathing out audibly when I heard someone else do the same, and noticed a creature plodding lazily in the paddock beside where I stood.

Behind the slanted wooden slats, the reindeer who had wandered over lifted his great head and antlers and looked at me with large, glossy eyes the same colour as the sky. His fur was the colour of a creamy latte that hadn't been fully blended, his coffee-toned antlers raising high into the sky like branches looking for the sun. His nose had dipped into the snow, giving it a sugar coating. I wanted to reach over the fence and give him a stroke, but didn't really want to start my new job having had my hand chomped off so thought better of it.

'Hello,' I whispered, and edged towards the fence. I don't know a lot about reindeer. Did they spit, like llamas? Could they kill me, like elk? This one seemed pretty friendly though. 'How are you?' I asked him.

'I'm fine,' the reindeer answered.

Just kidding. He snarfed at me and wiggled his antlers from side to side.

'I hope you understand English because my Finnish isn't very good,' I said.

The reindeer blinked, which I took as a yes, and I lowered my voice to a whisper. 'I don't know what I'm doing here.'

Chapter 10

Back in my room at the end of the evening, I realised the hotel had done a turn-down service that I hadn't been expecting when I'd left my underwear and toiletries scattered all over the floor when I'd been yanking thermals from the depths of my rucksack.

Part of the service appeared to have been to prop a plush Santa on my pillow, as if I hadn't seen enough of him that evening, and feeling a tad claustrophobic (Claus-trophobic, ha), I picked up the Santa and stuffed him deep under the bed, and then changed into my thick PJs and fell onto the mattress.

During the night, my brain struggled to absorb the polar twilight concept. I was well aware of the theory of how it would be dark from about four p.m. to nine a.m. here in Lapland in mid-November, but for some reason the reality had me waking up every hour and looking out the window to see that yes, it was still dark out. Perhaps it was just nerves.

At five thirty a.m., I knew I wasn't going back to sleep, so slipped out of my hotel room dressed in my dad's coat and several layers, and padded down the silent corridor and past the reception. Waving at the concierge, I heaved open the door of the lodge and stepped out into the cold air.

Holy moly, I pulled my coat tighter around myself, tugging the sleeves down over my gloves to avoid any unnecessary exposure. I walked the path of the hotel to the back, where a wide expanse of snow-covered field led towards a pine forest. There was a snow-dusted dock that sat above a pond, or maybe a small lake – I couldn't tell under the cover of ice and twilight and small pools of illumination from the lamps dotted about the hotel's exterior.

But I could see that someone had beaten me to it, and when I saw who it was, I had to laugh. 'You again,' I said into the quiet, not meaning anything bad by it.

Josh, standing on the dock, turned in surprise, and then laughed at seeing me. 'Are you following me?'

'Definitely. I just can't keep away from you,' I joked. 'Mind if I join you?'

'You can't sleep either?' he asked.

I shook my head. 'New job nerves, I think. You?'

'Jet lag.'

'Ah.'

'I thought that after three, no, four flights, changing in New York and then London, then Helsinki, before reaching Lapland, I'd be dead to the world, but after I'd, say ... two hours of sleep I just woke up again. Wide awake.'

'That sucks,' I said, and looked across at what I could

80

see of the dark view, a secret winter wonderland stretched before me. I could be on another planet; I'd never woken up to a scene like this in my life. 'Does it snow a lot, back in Seattle? It looks cold there on TV.'

'Yeah, Washington State doesn't have the warm ambience of, like, California, but I love it. We get some snow, though it's nothing compared to this. You know, I fell over on my way back here.'

I chuckled. 'You did?'

'Yep. Stepped on what I thought was a solid verge, and my foot sunk two feet. The rest of my jet-lagged body toppled over in surprise, and I face-planted a big mound of snow.'

'That's one way to make sure you're awake.'

We were silent for a moment, looking out at the view, until I blew breath upwards onto my nose in an attempt to warm it up.

'Do you want to go inside?' Josh asked, and I met his eyes and tried not to laugh inappropriately because he was hardly asking anything saucy, I was just feeling awkward.

Controlling myself, I said, 'Yeah, I think I might. Perhaps this will look just as nice from within a warm room, looking out of a window.'

'With a coffee?' Josh looked hopeful.

'The lobby had a coffee machine for guests to use, if you want . . . ?'

'Yes.' Josh seemed genuinely enthusiastic – he was such an elf. 'Yes, let's go. Unless, of course, you think I'd be too annoying?'

'Shut up.' I gave him a soft thwack with my thick gloves.

Back in the warm of the hotel, Josh and I fiddled with the coffee machine until two steaming cups had churned out, and helped ourselves to a few foil-wrapped *lusikkaleivät*, or 'spoon cookies'.

We took them to a couple of lounge chairs beside the floor-to-ceiling windows to watch, well, not really to watch the sun come *up* but to watch the colours begin to change from dark-dark to cornflower-blue-dark.

As I bit into the sugary little blob with a layer of tangy jam in the middle, Josh told me a bit about his life in Seattle, about how he lived in a studio apartment in an area of town with a lot of art, music and coffee. How he was an only child and his mum lived with his grandfather across the bay.

'Are you close with your mum?' I asked.

'Yeah, and my grandfather. We all lived together while I was growing up. How about you with your mom?'

'I'm close with my dad,' I sidestepped. 'And my older sister. Dad'll be spending Christmas with my sister and her wife, as my sister will be only a month or so away from popping. From being pregnant, I mean, in case that's a very British thing to say!'

'Will you miss being home over Christmas?'

'No,' I answered, truthfully. 'I think being out here will be a really new experience. I've never been to Finland before, let alone Lapland. Did you say you hadn't been before either?'

'Nope. But it seems pretty good so far,' he grinned.

'Do you know what the plan is today? Are we going into Rovaniemi?'

'I think we're heading back to Santa Claus Village, Daan said.'

'Oh. Good. That's great.' I sipped on my coffee and gazed back out of the window. 'Ten weeks,' I said.

'What's that?'

'Ten weeks here in the Arctic Circle. Do you think we'll make it?'

Although Josh answered with a confident, 'Sure,' I think I was asking myself, more than him.

Chapter 11

Later that morning, after a buffet breakfast of porridge, rye bread and omelettes, we employees found ourselves back at the Santa Claus Village once again.

Daan explained that the morning was ours to explore, to help us really get into the Christmas spirit that would be invaluable for us over the next couple of months. And then, he said, he had a surprise for us in the afternoon.

Uh-oh.

The group split into smaller gatherings, and I latched onto the one that included Josh for no reason other than he was the only one I kind of knew.

First, we went inside the Santa Claus Main Post Office, open all year round.

'Look at this,' said Josh, stopping in front of a chalk-board sign after we stepped into the cosy-warm log cabin building. 'Santa can get thirty thousand letters a day at

Christmastime. He has about half a million sent to him here from all over the world.'

'No wonder he needs elves to help him,' I quipped.

Our group was recommended to write cards for loved ones back home that would then bear the special Arctic Circle postmark. So, to get into the spirit of things, I picked a large card with Santa's smiling face on it, and settled onto one of the benches, the scent of wood all around me, and wrote a quick note to Shay.

Dear Sister,
    Merry Christmas from the most festive place on earth. I can't believe I'm here.
    Love from,
    You know who.

One of the Post Office elves kindly helped me as I stood hovering beside the two post boxes, trying to decide which to put my card into.

'The yellow ones will be sent off today, they are like normal post, but if you put it in the red box your card will be held until Christmas and sent then. Which would you prefer?'

'I think ... I think I want to send it to my sister now,' I replied, and stuffed it into the box, offering a thankful smile to the lady. *Everyone is so kind here.*

From there, we crunched back over the snow and went inside Mrs Santa Claus' Christmas Cottage, where the lady herself was inside and fed us gingerbread. Her cottage was beside the reindeer, so I waved hello to the friend I made last night as I passed. Or at least, I waved at a reindeer that looked a lot like the reindeer from yesterday. As did they all.

We then found our way to a tiny cabin called Roosevelt Cottage, which was the very first building at Santa Claus Village and contained photos and memorabilia from when Eleanor Roosevelt visited in the summer of 1950.

And finally, we crossed back over the square, wide and open and empty of the stage that had been there the night before, and entered the Santa Claus Office.

'Hello!' Out from behind a corner sprang a man. Sorry, an elf. He was dressed in green and red felt, with a pointed hat and a smiling face. I glanced at Josh, and wondered if this was what he would look like soon. 'Would you like to meet Santa Claus?'

'Yes!' the others chorused just as I said, 'No, that's OK.'

Everyone turned to me so I added, flustered, 'I just mean, not if he's busy, or if we'd be making any little kids wait around in the cold or anything.'

'Santa is never too busy to meet with his friends,' the elf said, and beckoned us to come with him.

We followed a series of darkly lit corridors and stairs decorated with clocks and decorations and gift-wrapped presents, a chart explaining the Earth's Rotational Speed Regulator, a Wall of Fame showing Santa hosting some well-known guests. I could well imagine that seven-year-old me would have felt her excitement growing with every step. Even late-twenties me could feel the intrigue, though I hated to admit it.

But when we rounded the corner and met Santa Claus himself, I felt like a fraud. My heart was thudding and I stayed at the back, and I'm sure you could one hundred per cent tell from the group photo that there was panic in my eyes. As my colleagues chatted to him and laughed and posed, I focused on my breathing, a fixed smile on my face, forcing myself to remember in intricate detail the plot of *Pretty Little Liars* instead of letting my thoughts spiral elsewhere.

'You know,' Santa was saying to our group, 'here in Finland, Santa leaves the presents for the children to find on Christmas Eve, not Christmas Day. So Christmas Eve is a very exciting day here in Lapland. But then, so is every day.' He laughed with a *ho ho ho* and caught my eye. 'But no matter how exciting, everybody can feel a little nervous meeting Santa Claus.'

I blinked and smiled, and with the tiniest nod he moved on to asking questions from the others.

As soon as I feasibly could, I broke from the group and headed for the gift shop, where the wooden walls were painted red and the big man's face emblazoned everything from ornaments to socks to sweatshirts and chocolate bars. It was so warm in here I almost didn't want to leave, but also, the extreme festiveness was making my head hurt, so I ventured back outside into the frosty air.

A short while later, Daan had us pile onto a bus, and when we stopped again five minutes down the road, outside a place called SantaPark, he looked extremely pleased with himself.

'OK, I know only some of you will be working as elves

over in Luosto, but I have arranged for something special for everyone this afternoon.'

Uh-oh, where was this going?

Daan continued. 'Now, this isn't formal training, but ... this afternoon you are all going to elf school!'

Nope, I signed up to be an adventure guide, not an elf. I can't be an elf. Elves are kind and happy and fun and make the world sparkle, whereas I'd make all the children miserable! As we piled off the bus, I cursed my sister under my breath, and wished I could go back and get that card I'd sent her and chuck it away. No I didn't; calm down, Myla.

Entering through a giant archway, we seemed to be going inside an indoor theme park. Shows and workshops, ice galleries and underground tunnels, bakeries and magic trains, it was all go here.

Inside the Elf School, we took our seats in front of the stage, which was covered in props and had a huge blue and gold world map covering one wall. For the next twenty minutes I listened to two elf women give us a talk, alternating between Finnish and English, on the skills and secrets of being a good elf. The women were great, and I had a lot of respect for them, but that persistent feeling crept back in, like it had last night at the Christmas season opening. The one where I felt visibly out of place. My heart thudded in my chest, again, like it was claustrophobic, and I felt myself getting hot and sweating.

As music played and bells on toes jingled and everyone laughed, I was right back there again in Shay's home, two weeks previously, just before my, ahem, meltdown. This was overwhelming, and memories pushed and shoved, trying to make their way to the front of my mind, distracting me, vying for attention, and I could tell I was glazing over.

I couldn't do this. I couldn't put myself through months of this. I had to get out of here.

Excusing myself, I left the room and stumbled my way back through the corridors and out into the open air again, the snow compacted under my feet, the air so fresh and clear it felt life-saving to breathe.

Look around you, Myla! And it hit me like a snowball in the face. This wasn't torture, not even close; how ridiculous of me to act like it was. This place was ... magical. The people ... nothing but kind. Sure, I didn't feel the magic, not yet, but that was *my* problem. And I didn't like who I'd become.

Wouldn't it be nice to not quit something? Wouldn't it be nice to prove I *could* do it?

I took another big gulp of air. And vowed to pull myself together. This wasn't a question of could I get through this; I *had* to get through this.

Chapter 12

After a better sleep than the night before, I was up and packed the next day, ready to board one of what was – thanks to some extra arrivals late yesterday, many of whom were Finnish seasonal workers who'd come up for the winter – now two Love Adventuring Lapland-branded buses to take us away from Rovaniemi an hour north towards Luosto. We wouldn't be living in the small village of Luosto itself, but a remote area to the side of the National Park, surrounded by forests and fells. I half expected the drive to be slow, crawling over snowy roads and fighting our way over snowdrifts, but of course, Lapland is pretty used to the white stuff so we glided up there without a problem.

My solemn mood was all but gone, for now at least, thanks to the stern talking to I'd given myself the day before.

Josh, with all his festive fervour and impending elf-ness, might not have been my obvious choice for a new friend but he was easy to talk to and had a certain infectious enthusiasm. He and I sat a seat away from each other on the bus, and I was definitely teetering back on the 'new adventure' side of being in Lapland again.

'I nearly forgot!' he said, reaching into his pocket and pulling out an envelope and handing it to me.

'What's this?' I asked, ripping into it before I gave him a chance to reply. 'A diploma?'

'From Elf School,' he laughed. 'I picked up one for you, as you had to leave early yesterday.'

I studied the piece of card decorated with two smiling elves, and couldn't help but unleash a little smile myself. Who'd have thought it? 'Thank you.'

On the bus I made small talk with those around me, but when the Christmas song-singing started up with gusto I became very interested in photographing the view outside.

Beyond the window the road was bordered by endless pine trees rising from the snowy verge and dusted with their own icing sugar toppings that twinkled in the light of the low, mid-morning sunshine. Occasionally we passed a frosty lake, some wooden barns and cottages painted an earthy red, or the road carved above a river, babbling over the rocks and stones below the surface. It was almost hard to imagine that only about forty-eight hours before, I'd been navigating my way through the rain and London Tube to get to Heathrow airport.

'When we get to the Love Adventuring Lapland base, the first thing you'll see is the activities lodge,' said Daan, standing up and addressing us all when the singing stopped. 'That's where all guests arriving by coach will be taken to check in for their booked activities, making any changes or book more things, and to borrow their clothing, plus there is a big hall because we sometimes have indoor workshops and things. Behind the lodge is the staff chalet, where you will live. And nearby is the husky farm and the reindeer farm.'

He paused to let the excited murmurs die down again before continuing. 'We're a little more spread out than some of the operations here in Lapland, but everything is walk-able. Through a lot of snow and trees. But there's plenty of room to explore and have fun with the guests. Lapland is the best part of the world, in my opinion.'

Daan sat back down for a while, until the trees began to part to show glimpses of cabins. 'This is the village of Luosto,' he called back. 'Which means we're not too far from your new homes now.'

And before I knew it, we were pulling onto a track that wove inside a pine forest, and into a cleared car park, coming to a stop in front of a large wooden building tucked in between a forest of trees, which said Love Adventuring Lapland – Activities' Lodge on the outside.

Daan stood up at the front of the bus, spread his arms wide, and said, 'Welcome! To your most wonderful Christmas ever!'

My coat was the best. *The best*. After trekking from the bus through the forest to the staff accommodation chalet, I was toasty warm even though the temperature outside was minus seven, I think, today. It also helped that my backpack was giving me back-sweats like I was in a weights class, or hauling one of those reindeer around with me, and that my knock-off Uggs were really no match for the thick snow so every step felt as tough as, well, wading through three-foot deep snow. Anyway, by the time I reached my room I'd pretty much had a full workout.

The staff housing consisted of a two-floor wooden chalet, tucked between the trees at the foot of a fell, a few minutes' walk from the activities' lodge. I'd learned that a 'fell' in Lapland, aka *tunturi* in Finnish, was basically similar to those in the UK, in that it's a hill with its top above the trees, and in Lapland, that can actually make them even more accessible in the snow because you could walk over them. We were given our room numbers on the bus and told that, by tonight, all staff members would have arrived so we'd have our orientation then.

Climbing the steps to the second floor, I followed a wooden corridor where the scent of pine trees was baked into the walls, emitting the aroma and feeling of being outside, even when you were warm and within.

My room was number sixteen, and I put my wrought-iron key in the lock, unsure what – or who – to expect on the other side.

But it was just me. At least for now. Inside the room was a bunk bed against one wall, red covers neatly made up, and a pine ladder propped between the two bunks. The walls were a continuation of the rounded logs, and I ran my fingers over the smooth, hard wood, feeling the dimples beneath. A small, square window with red curtains looked out across the white fairy-tale forest. Two chairs, a chest of drawers, a desk, a mirror and some shelves were the only other things in there. We'd been asked to hang our coats and boots on the warmers in the 'boot room' just inside the main door, so I padded around in just my thick socks, wondering how long to leave it before venturing to find the toilets, since I guessed everybody else would be forming a queue outside them right about now.

I wasn't in a rush, so FaceTimed the mastermind behind this whole operation.

'Myla!' Tess's face appeared on Shay's phone. She looked behind her. 'Shay? Shay! Your sister is on the phone. Myla, how are you doing, are you still in Lapland?'

'Of course I'm still in Lapland,' I laughed. 'Did you think I'd give up that easily?'

'Yep.' Tess nodded.

'No way, you know how scary Shay can be, I'm under strict instructions not to come home.'

'Fair point,' agreed Tess, and lowered her voice. 'She's in such a mood today. She threw an avocado at the wall.'

'Why?' I laughed.

'Because I said the one she'd picked wasn't ripe yet and she wanted to prove me wrong.'

At that moment, Shay appeared in the background, brandishing a knife. 'Hey, I told you that was just pregnancy hormones and I was sorry, and now I'm making you a fancy dinner to make up for it so shut your mouth.'

'Put the knife down, Shay,' I called. And then wondered how soundproof these walls were.

Shay laughed and squeezed her head in next to Tess. 'So how is it? Are you full of festive spirit yet?'

I rolled my eyes at her. 'Yesterday I met Santa Claus at Santa Claus Village, so I'm not exactly able to hide away.'

'Where are you now?'

'We just made it to Luosto, and I'm in my new room. Do you want a tour?' I flipped the camera round and showed them my bedroom while they ooohed at the wooden walls and ahhhed at the cosy decor.

'Bunk beds?' asked Tess. 'Do you have a room-mate?'

'I don't know yet. Nobody so far but I think some people are still to arrive.' I didn't know how I felt about a room-mate. I mean, I'd liked living with Jamilia (though I now wondered if the feeling had ever been mutual) but we were never room-mates. In fact, the one time I'd asked if I could sleep on her floor because the curtain pole had fallen down in my room and it was the middle of summer, she'd politely reminded me we had a sofa that was only slightly uncomfortable. 'Do you want to see out the window?'

'Yes!' cried Shay and Tess in unison.

When I angled the camera out to where the snow drifted down and I was level with the trees, I felt a tiny swell of peace. Because this *was* very lovely and different, and just because it was a winter wonderland didn't mean it was *entirely* Christmas focused.

'That view is so gorgeous, Myla, I'm jealous,' said Shay when I turned the phone back to my face.

'It is,' I admitted. 'How is everything at home? Apart from exploding avocados?'

'Everything's fine. Now go and enjoy yourself, OK? And, Myla?'

'Yes, boss?'

Shay smirked. 'Stay present, OK? Don't get sucked into stressing about Christmas pasts. Or Christmas yet-to-comes. Not to sound all Dickens on you.'

'Yes, boss.'

'All right then.'

I hung up the phone, visited the bathroom, and was contemplating where to put my things when I didn't know if I had the room to myself or not when that question was answered for me by my door being swung wide open, and a woman clomping in wearing enormous, fur-trimmed snow boots that trailed wet patches across the flooring.

'*Wau, on kyl ihan huippuu olla kotona! Tää huone on kyl tosi kiva!*' She looked up at me for the first time, sizing me up, her ashy-blonde hair sticking in snowflake-wetted tendrils to her face. '*Hei*. You look English.'

'Uh, I am. Hello.'

'Hello,' the stranger replied with a wide beam on her face, and stomped to the bed where she sat on the bottom bunk and began pulling off her boots. 'I'm Esteri.'

'Hi, I'm Myla. I think you can leave your boots at the front door; they have those boot warmer things to dry them out,' I said, watching her.

'No way,' she said. 'These are extremely high-quality boots; they go wherever I go until we're all issued with our Love Adventuring Lapland ones. Besides, some people here brought suede boots, can you believe? In this snow?' She laughed her head off and managed to release one of her feet at the same time while I blushed. 'Could you help me with the other one, I just don't have the energy.'

Esteri lay back on the bottom bunk while I started pulling on her boot, which seemed oddly intimate considering all I knew about her was her name and that she was going to laugh at my shoes if I ever left the house at the same time as her.

When I managed to drag the boot off and it thunked me on the head, I asked, 'So, do you prefer the top or bottom bunk?'

'No preference,' she answered. 'You?'

I eyed the wet snow-angel she'd left on the bottom bunk and said, 'I'll take the top?'

'Perfect.' Esteri stood up and without her big boots and coat on I realised she was about my height with grey eyes and a big smile. Her hair was long and unruly, but it looked perfect against her round face and outdoorsy cheeks. 'Now, who are you?'

I stuttered. 'I'm Myla. Your room-mate.'

'No, I know that much,' Esteri chuckled. 'But who ARE you? Tell me about yourself.'

'Oh, OK.' I took a seat on the floor and started unpacking my rucksack while I told her about my life in England, glossing up the part about not having a home or job any more, and glossing over the massive-dislike-of-Christmas thing. She listened, giving me her full attention, and asking me to explain further on any detail she thought I was missing.

When I wrapped up, she said, 'Yes, you sound like a good

room-mate. My room-mate last year was the absolute worst person in the world.'

My eyebrows shot up. I didn't think Lapland would even allow the world's worst people to enter. 'Why?' I asked, and then, 'You were here last year?'

'This is my fourth year,' Esteri said with pride, holding up four fingers. 'But last year, my room-mate quit her job after two weeks and then she just hung around, getting in the way, trying to get the company to hire her again but not in a customer-facing role, and in the end I had to drag her outside by the hair.'

Bloody hell. 'Really?'

'Well no, not really, but I did lock her in the sauna.'

'*Really?*'

'No,' Esteri laughed and booped me on the nose. 'What do you think of me?'

'I – I don't know,' I replied.

She continued. 'The truth is, eventually she left, but she was such a downer because all of us are here for fun, you know? And work, but the work is fun and the guests want fun, and she was just not a good fit. Plus, her socks smelled.'

'Wow, that sounds awful,' I laughed, and kept laughing all the way out the door and to the bathroom to sit on the loo for a minute and make sure my hands weren't shaking. A million voices in my head were cackling about how I wasn't a good fit either, and how I possibly should avoid trying out the sauna with Esteri in tow. Plus, those eyes, those grey eyes, they looked right into my soul, you know? It felt like she could smell a faker from a mile off.

Back in the room, Esteri had stuck washi tape down the centre of the desk and piled her belongings on one side. 'This just avoids arguments, but by all means if you need to sit at the desk and write a postcard or whatever I don't mind you using the whole desk.'

'Thank you,' I replied, and went back to my unpacking while Esteri stretched out on her bunk. 'So tell me about you, where are you from?'

'I'm from Helsinki,' Esteri declared, and then added, 'No I'm not, I'm from Turku, but I usually just say Helsinki to people from other countries as it's easier. Have you been to Turku? Or Helsinki?'

I shook my head. 'I've never been to Finland before.'

'That's nice, welcome to Finland, *tervetuloa*! That means welcome. Turku is a couple of hours from Helsinki and it's on a river. I grew up there, and my immediate family were all from there, but my parents have both passed away now as has my brother. So now my only family, apparently, is actually up here in Lapland.'

Whoa, that was a lot of information. 'I'm so sorry about your parents, and brother,' I said.

'Thank you,' Esteri smiled. 'But it's OK.'

'Do you know the family you have up here?'

'No, they're distant family. But I am going to visit them this year. You can come with me.'

'Oh, OK,' I agreed, not quite sure what I was agreeing to, but I was all for seeing more of any parts of Lapland that didn't directly involve the C-word.

(Christmas. I mean Christmas.)

'What else about me ...' Esteri mused, moving the conversation on and staring up at the top bunk. 'I like reading, I like quiet time, I like being outdoors and of course, I love Christmaaaaaas,' she sang.

'Me toooooo!' I joined in the song for good measure.

She stopped abruptly and sat up. 'All right, we have orientation in twenty minutes, and then, I will show you a real orientation.'

Chapter 13

I wasn't quite sure what Esteri had in mind for me after the 'official' orientation, but I noticed she kept catching my eye and winking at me at various times during the talk led by Daan.

For orientation, all the new seasonal employees gathered in the large living room of the staff cabin, after being told to help ourselves to drinks that had been laid out in the kitchen. Esteri sat next to me, her arm pressed against mine which felt both reassuring and territorial but also, I didn't mind one bit because it was like I was new in school and had made friends with the coolest girl here.

I found myself looking around for Josh, just out of curiosity, and saw him chatting and laughing with a group at the other end of the room. He was in another flannel shirt again, and his hair was swept to the side, looking wet from the shower. Or the snow. Or whatever. He laughed loudly and jovially and I was reminded of my journey next to him on the plane. Contemplating him, I decided that even though I now knew him a little better, he'd still be kind of annoying to sit with for *too* long.

'The elves,' Esteri murmured quietly next to me. I caught her eye and she motioned towards Josh and his group with her head. 'Extremely confident, extremely fun to be around, but good luck having a conversation with them.'

'What do you mean?' I asked.

'After training is done and the guests begin to arrive, they're to stay in character *at all times.*'

'*All* times?'

'As long as guests are around, they are living and breathing their elf-selves.' She caught me staring over again. 'It keeps the magic alive for the visitors. A big reason they come is to see Santa and his elves so how would you feel if you'd just been playing snowballs with lumberjack-shirt there,' she pointed at Josh, 'and the next minute he's leaning against the wall behind the reindeer paddock playing on his phone.'

'Gotcha,' I said. *Wow.*

She moved her attention to a couple of guys on the next sofa over, mere metres away, and whispered, 'Bet they're on the husky team. Sexy mother—'

'Hello, everyone.' Daan clapped his hands together, appearing at the front of the room. 'I know we have a lot of people from a lot of places around the world joining together as a family for the Christmas period, but just to check, are you all OK with me speaking English?'

A general chorus of yeses came up, before Daan added,

'And in case you aren't, and that made no sense . . . ' He then rattled off, in a string of languages, what I assume was *Please let me know if you don't understand English.*

Daan proceeded to introduce us to the various members of the management team, including the adventure guide lead, Zoë, and the owners of the reindeer farm, Kirste and Johánná.

Kirste, who, like her sister, was Sámi, stepped forward. Her fingers were wrapped around a cup of steaming coffee and her grin was wide as she regarded us. 'Hello, everyone. We're looking forward to getting to know you all over the coming months, and for you to get to know our reindeer, and us.' She proceeded to explain a little about both the traditional and modern indigenous culture in Finnish Lapland, and how the Sámi homeland, Sápmi, crosses areas of Finland, Sweden, Norway and Russia.

Zoë followed Kirste, the women exchanging warm smiles as they swapped places, so our adventure guide lead could give a few more details about my new job.

As Shay had described back when we first 'discussed' the job in her office, I was to be an adventure guide. This meant I'd be taking people out on snowmobile-, snowshoe- and reindeer trips, and I'd also be trained on – and sometimes run – husky sled trips, though there was a separate group of husky guides who would do that the majority of the time. The actual tour I gave would depend on the excursion the guests had booked, be that following trails through forests to our hidden Santa cabin, travelling over a frozen lake at night to look for the Northern Lights, climbing up to the top of a snowy hill to see the view, or simply hanging out in the minus temperatures and learning about Lapland.

It all sounded extremely outdoorsy.

In addition to the guides, and the husky team, the other job roles were filled by elves and guest reps. We were to work five days a week, where we'd be on our feet pretty much all day and working hours to suit the excursions we were leading. We'd be busy – we could guide anywhere between one long and a lot of short excursions in one day, and so Daan was really encouraging us to use our days off to explore Lapland and make the most of activities on offer.

I mean ... this was kind of cool. I know there was a general air of festivity, but right now, among these happy faces and with the snow falling outside the window, I could just as easily be in the Alps, or the mountains in Canada. Really, I was just working in a winter resort. I could probably pretend it wasn't even Christmassy ...

'OK, now, all together,' Daan suddenly said, and, raising his arms in the air, he began singing 'We Wish You A Merry Christmas' at the top of his voice. And the whole room joined in. Beside me I felt Esteri's arms shake as she banged on the coffee table, the elves were up and dancing around each other, the two supposed husky men were singing heartily and I watched in gory fascination, having spoken too soon inside my mind. This was my actual nightmare. I hadn't sung Christmas carols in ... I don't know ... five years? A flash of my sister came into my head, saying, *'Don't bugger this up!'* which I'm not sure she actually said in as many words but was what she would be saying now, if she were here.

My mouth moved with the words, but no sound came out. Luckily, everybody else was making enough racket that my bad lip-syncing went unnoticed. I hoped.

Oh Myla, we're definitely not going to be able to pretend our way out of this one . . .

As orientation concluded, following health and safety guidance and information about local amenities, we were dismissed. Most people stayed though, including Esteri and me, to tuck into the delicious buffet put on by the leaders of pies, cheeses, fish, all sorts of yum.

I'd barely finished my main course when Esteri said, 'OK, let's go.'

'Where?' I said, slurping down the rest of my Lapin Kulta, a Finnish beer.

She beckoned me to follow her, and led me down a corridor, then another, then to a side door that led out into the snow.

'Wait,' I said, 'I need to go and get my snow boots,' (I hadn't confessed to owning the non-Ugg-Uggs yet). 'And my coat. Where are we going?'

Esteri smiled and pulled two towels and some slide-on sandals from behind a counter. 'Get ready to take all your clothes off, you stuffy little Brit.'

Um.

'Excuse me?' I stopped short.

'I'm going to show you the best thing about coming and living in Finland. The sauna.'

'Oh, we have saunas in the UK, in spas and things.'

'This is the perfect end to the day,' she carried on, ignoring me and taking off her shoes. She held the door open for me which I reluctantly entered, and found myself in a small changing room. By the time I turned back around, Esteri's right breast was in my face.

'Whoa, OK, you really meant we were getting naked.'

'Yes, calm down, it's perfectly normal. Look, there are several staff saunas here but this one is the furthest away from all the other action. Coupled with the fact most people are still eating, it should be lovely and quiet.'

Esteri was butt-naked by now, so in a way I almost felt more awkward standing there in my thermals. And a sauna did sound quite nice actually. A good way to calm me down, perhaps?

I stripped down quickly, leaving my undies on, and wrapped a towel around myself. Unwittingly, my mind flittered to Josh and his lumberjack shirt, and I asked Esteri, 'Are the saunas for all sexes and genders? Together?'

'We have female and male saunas, one mixed plus two individual ones,' she explained, now in her own towel and sliders. She led us out of the changing room and then threw open the door to the outside world. An icicle stormed through and jabbed me in the gut. That's what it felt like, at least. Actually, it was just a freezing gust of wind, but it caused me to make a '*Burrururururururur*' sound and my towel to flap around me.

Esteri strode out like she was in Marbella heading for the best sun lounger, and I tottered along next to her resisting the urge to complain like hell, until we reached a small wooden hut and she stepped inside.

Ahhhhh. That was more like it. Instant warmth had me feeling like I'd never even been cold, as steam rose from hot rocks in the corner. The air was scented with pine and as I was closing the door behind us I gasped at the glimpse of a billion stars above the treetops.

Esteri got naked again and lay down on the bottom bench, meaning I had to climb over her to the top, but all my insecurities drifted away with the steam within moments.

'Thanks for bringing me—' I started.

'I like quiet times in the sauna,' Esteri said. 'But you're welcome.'

I smiled to myself. She wasn't so bad, at all. *This* wasn't so bad.

Chapter 14

This was so bad. I had never felt more out of depth in my life. And while my fellow guides were standing tall in the snow, confident postures and big smiles, I was dying from nerves on the inside.

'So that's all there is to it, really,' Zoë stated, releasing the handle of the absolutely massive snowmobile in front of her and it shuddered into silence. 'Does that all make sense?'

'Hahaha, yes,' I said, trying to sound as oomph-ful as the others. My stomach churned and I looked at the vehicle.

'When you take out the guests, they'll each be on either their own vehicle, or two-person ones where they share the driving, so you might have someone travelling behind you. Or perhaps you'll pull children along in a sled, if they aren't tall enough to travel in the back of the adult snowmobile,' Zoë said, patting the small seat at the back of the main one. 'You need to make sure the snowmobiles are all good to go before you head off, with enough fuel and drinks and snacks to see you through the day.'

In case we crash and stare death in the face.

'You'll talk to the guests through your microphone, and you'll tell them all about all of the beautiful nature and wildlife you'll be passing. Don't worry, thanks to the snow coming in nice and early and deep this year, you will learn all of this during practical training over the coming days.'

It would be different if I were here on holiday and just having a simple snowmobile lesson to then putter about on for a few hours. But I was expected to have *passengers* with this thing. Children, even. People who came here to have a Very Merry Christmas, not a Very Messy Catastrophe.

'Who wants to try first?'

Almost everybody shot their hands into the air, including Esteri, though she must have been on these a lot if this was her fourth year in Lapland. Not wanting to stick out like a sore thumb, I raised my hand too, but deliberately avoided eye-contact with Zoë.

'Great, let's start with you, Myla.'

Damn our name tags!

'No,' I said, almost reflexively.

'Come on, everyone has to start somewhere.' She beckoned me towards her so I crunched my way over, the snow creaking beneath my feet, cursing my sister and all of Christmastime.

Flakes started to drift down from the sky, which made everyone but me joyous, because now I had two words zipping about my mind: *reduced visibility*. Sliding on my helmet, I looked down at the snowmobile, dark and sleek and threatening, and everything Zoë had taught us dropped out of my head like an avalanche. I looked up at her. 'I'm a little nervous,' I admitted.

'That's OK, you can do it. You wouldn't be here if you weren't already brave and fearless, right?'

Hahaha, or had lost a bet. 'Right ...'

'On you get.'

I climbed aboard and sat down, my arms stretched out to the handlebars, my feet on the snowy ground below.

'Now, Myla, remember to relax your arms, you need to keep yourself able to move with the movement of the snow-mobile,' Zoë said.

I loosened my arms, but my nerves stayed tensed.

'And what did I say about feet?'

'Oh,' I said, bringing my snow boots into the feet trays either side of the snowmobile. That was a silly mistake – Zoë had stressed how important that was only minutes ago.

I gulped and looked at the two levers on either side of the handlebars. Left for brake, right for accelerate. 'Should I go?' I asked Zoë.

'Where is the safety cord?' she countered.

'Oh, right.' I clipped the cord to the front of my snowsuit.

'Ready?' Zoë checked, as she switched on the engine.

I nodded, took a breath, and squeezed the right-hand lever, and the snowmobile shot forward with a *vroom*, sounding to my untrained ears like an extremely angry lawnmower that wanted me to stop straddling it immediately.

'Slow down!' Zoë called, and I squeezed the left-hand

lever and the machine shuddered to a stop, my body shuddering along with it.

Zoë jogged over and checked over the snowmobile. 'OK, no damage, but remember not to press both levers at the same time because you could flood the engine and harm it.'

'Of course, I'm so sorry.'

'It's OK. You want to try again?'

I really did want to try, and try I did, but no matter how many times I started, stopped, tried to turn, or tried to give the appropriate hand signals, something just wasn't working for me. And by that point I was embarrassed and frustrated, and I think Zoë could tell things weren't going to get any better until I calmed down.

'OK,' she said, making a note on her clipboard that I couldn't see. 'Why don't you step aside, Myla, and we'll give somebody else a go.'

'I think I can get it with a little more practice,' I insisted.

'I'm sure you can.' But Zoë didn't look me in the eye again, instead gently pressing me back towards the group using her big ski mitten.

As one of my fellow guides stepped forward and managed to turn on, manoeuvre, and emergency stop all in one go, Esteri leaned over.

'So what?' she said to me. 'So you didn't get it first time. Big deal. You will.'

'How do you know?'

'Because I have faith in you.'

'I don't know why,' I protested. 'I couldn't even take my bra off in a sauna.'

'That was weird,' Esteri agreed. 'But you'll get there. Just remember how lucky you are to be here, how lucky you are to be in the home of Christmas, and you will get your Christmas wish.' She smiled.

Chapter 15

After the snowmobile disaster, over the course of the following week we underwent intensive training that left my body aching, my hair frizzing, and my brain blissfully free of having time to conjure up and ruminate on those old Christmas memories. I learned how to snowshoe (hard), lead a reindeer sleigh (surprisingly relaxing), work alongside the husky team, and the huskies themselves (lush), and how to handle my microphone and radio. I was led, snowmobiled, and pulled around the whole, snow-covered area, and was beginning to get used to the feeling of solid ground being not so solid.

Esteri and the rest of the guides were with me every step of the way, but we also regularly joined forces with the reps and elves, since we'd be sometimes working in tandem with them, depending on the adventure that had been booked.

More than once, I found my tired body and mind feeling agitated at the long twilight hours and what felt like such short bursts of daylight. We actually had about five hours with the sun above the horizon (just) but I couldn't help but long for the time I'd be used to it and not mildly bothered by it. And I had no choice – I had to get used to it. I just had to.

When the first morning came that we were to welcome real, live guests, here in Lapland for the winter holiday of a lifetime, I was brimming with confidence.

Lol.

Actually, I was bricking it, to the point that Esteri had to come and sit down in front of me in the boot-warming room to help me tie on my snow boots as my hands were shaking too much.

Luckily, my poor, damp faux-sheepskin boots had gone back to my backpack to hibernate for the season, and Love Adventuring Lapland had provided everyone with Arctic-suitable boots, snowsuits, mountain salopette trousers with braces, vests, coats, mittens and hats. I felt as snuggly as a toddler in a padded babygro but with more responsibilities than simply making snow angels.

At that moment, just as Esteri was giving my laces a strong, final tug, who should walk through the door . . .

I didn't mean to laugh. I wasn't making fun of him. It's just that up until now Josh had looked so Abercrombie-Autumn-Winter-cool in his flannel and tousled hair, and so to see him in elf regalia, complete with rosy rouged cheeks, was just a surprise. Still handsome though . . .

'OK, OK,' he said, holding his hands in the air and giving us a twirl.

'I'm sorry, I'm not laughing.'

'You're not? Not even at my hat?' Josh was wearing a berry-red tunic made of thick felt over forest-green felt trousers. Under that lot were probably a lot of layers of thermals, too. Then on his head, covering that chestnut hair of his, was a matching berry-toned velvet hat which stood straight up into the air.

'No, I'm not, you look nice.'

He raised his eyebrows at me and smiled. '"Nice"?'

'Not *nice*,' I clarified, feeling my own cheeks become rosy. 'Just, you look fine, I'm just surprised. I've not seen you in your elf get-up until now.'

'I think you look very handsome,' Esteri said, finishing with my boots and giving my shins a hard pat like you might a pony's behind.

'Thank you.' He bowed, then came up with a laugh. 'Where are you both posted today?'

'I'm heading out on the snowshoes, a private tour,' I replied. 'I don't think they want me on a skidoo with other people just yet.'

'And I am Seeking Santa Claus,' Esteri declared, naming one of the most popular excursions we run, where a guide leads a family through the forests and over fells via snowmobiles or reindeer sleigh (depending on preference), eventually 'finding' Father Chrimbo at his secret cabin hidden in the woods. It sounded extremely festive to me, so I was happy to be rostered off that for as long as possible.

'Oh, I'll see you there then,' Josh said to her.

Esteri smiled at him. 'You're with Santa today?'

'With the big man himself. Hey, shame you won't be

stopping by today though,' he said to me, and just for a moment he put his hand on my shoulder, and I felt a small pang of wishing I would be there with them too.

'Haha, believe me, it's fine.' I reached into my locker and froze, realising my slip-up. I turned back around with haste. 'I mean, because I'm looking forward to being on the snowshoes and not the snowmobile.'

They hadn't seemed to notice, luckily.

'Well, good luck today,' Josh said, chirpy as always, and off he went.

'You too,' I called.

'Right,' said Esteri, putting her hands on my shoulders. 'You come back to me, roomie, don't let yourself get lost in the snow, all right?'

'I won't. You too.'

She gave me a football-player-style high five that cartwheeled down to a bum tap, and left the staff chalet to walk over to the activities' lodge. I still had to put on a couple of layers, and decided a quick wee would be a good idea prior to that, then I'd be joining her.

Chapter 16

'Hello!' I greeted my guests, clutching my snowshoes under one arm while I waved like a children's TV presenter with the other.

I was pleased to be guiding a couple, rather than a family, for my first trip out. I was having an attack of guilts at some poor kids getting lumped with me when all they wanted was the most wonderful time of all their years.

The couple were early-twenties, and she had one of those fuzzy headbands and her pale-lilac hair in a ponytail coming out of the top. Even bedecked in our bulky onesies she looked Insta-worthy, and her partner seemed to agree as he took a million selfies of the two of them before we'd even set off.

And then, when she, Anna, was having her snowshoes fitted, he pulled me aside.

'I'm going to propose on this holiday,' he told me in a

whisper. His name was Alexander, and he had a lovely rich Scottish accent which combined beautifully with her bubbly, pretty, Welsh voice.

'You are?' I asked, a genuine smile spreading across my face. 'Where? When?'

'I don't know, I can't wait, I want to do it right now!'

'Well, maybe wait until somewhere a little more romantic than the boot-fitting room. But we'll be visiting some pretty spectacular places today so let me know if the mood strikes and I can go off and hide behind a tree or something.'

'Actually, if I do it today, I wondered if I could ask you to be the photographer?'

'Oh, of course!'

'Of course, what?' asked Anna, stepping over to us, snowshoes on, beaming away.

I faltered for a second. 'Of course, we'll see lots of snow,' I said.

Anna laughed and caught Alexander's eye, who let out a big fake laugh but gave me a secret thumbs-up.

Leaving the activities' lodge, I led the two of them away and into the forest, smiling to myself as they giggled and slipped and marvelled at the thickness of the snow under their large metal shoes.

Once we were in a little secluded patch where the trees rose tall around us and the only sound was the patter of snow dropping from higher branches, I turned to tell them about their upcoming walk.

Taking a big, deep breath, and using my best big-girl

voice, I said, 'All right, how are you both feeling so far? Shoes feel OK?'

Anna lifted one leg in the air, sending a sprinkling of snow fluttering to the ground from the wide, tennis-racket-like base of the shoe, which strapped onto the underside of her boot. 'Feels good,' she said. 'It's harder than I thought it would be though.'

'It is, and just wait until you feel your leg muscles tomorrow. But I think you said in the morning you were going on a reindeer sleigh ride, right? Now that's relaxing.'

'I can't wait for that,' said Alexander. 'But I think this will be really fun.'

I nodded. 'It will. So today, I'll be taking you through the forest trail and then we'll be going up one of the fells and you'll see amazing views of the countryside plus a frozen lake.'

I looked up at the sky through the trees. On the day I'd done this snowshoe walk with the training group, it was overcast, but now I could see clear blue sky above. Even though daylight hours are a bit short at this time of year, on clear days the light can be spectacular. 'Ready?' I asked them.

Alexander seemed to hesitate on the spot for a moment, so I asked, 'Do you want me to take a photo of the two of you?'

'Oh, yes please!' said Anna, and she handed over her phone.

I stood back, snapping pictures of them in the clearing, surrounded by dark green pine needles peeping through the white snow. After a handful of photos, I got the sense Alexander hadn't quite plucked up the courage for the proposal after all so I handed the phone back and off we went on our merry way.

I peppered the walk with facts about Lapland, second-guessing every single fact I told as soon as it came out of my mouth, but I thought it was going pretty well. I mean, I was just walking. I was just regaling facts. I could do this. If tramping through the snow with happy holidaymakers each day was what would get me through the festive season, well it may not be a beach bar in Bali but it was better than organising a Christmas party and having to spend all day deciding between turkey menus and festive playlists.

Besides, like I mentioned, I was just walking, so nothing could go wrong with this, surely?

The three of us started to incline and though Anna and Alexander were ploughing along like mountain goats beside me, I needed a break, so chose the moment we exited from the trees to stop for a snack. And actually, I couldn't have timed it better.

Stretched before us was the most beautiful vista I'd ever laid eyes on. It looked like a winter screensaver, the kind of ones you get with a new laptop to show off the colours. The sky's blue melted into lemon yellow, lilac and lavender. The untouched white ground glowed a reflection of the colours, with the palest purple tint. The trees up here were coated in thick, blobby snow, the weight causing the tops of them to furl over and give the appearance of tall, white Santa hats, rising from the ground. And this view seemed to go on for ever, like we were on top of the world.

'Wow,' I breathed into the cold air.

'Wow,' echoed Anna. 'I can't believe you get to work here.'

'Yeah, me neither,' I replied.

Beside me, Alexander gave me the smallest nudge and when I met his eye, he nodded. He looked nervous, but sure, so I leapt into action.

'The light is ever-changing up here,' I said, pulling off my thick mittens where underneath I wore fingerless gloves. 'Let me take some more photos for you while you're here, so you can always remember this moment.' All right, Myla, let's not give the game away . . .

Alexander handed me his phone and took Anna by the hand to stand a few metres away, the stunning background behind them, the snow pure and lilac-toned around them. The colour of the snow matched her hair, actually, which was a cute touch.

'Photos, or video?' I asked Alexander.

'Um . . . photos, I think.'

I took a couple of snaps, and then a couple more, sneakily, when Anna thought I was done and turned away to open her arms wide in front of the view. Alexander took the opportunity to yank off one of his mittens with his teeth, which he then flung in my direction, and reach inside his onesie to pull out a ring box.

Oh my god, oh my *god*! I couldn't believe I was about

to be part of a proposal; this was so cool! I hoped she said yes. If she wanted to, of course. I hoped this didn't end up being a horrible Christmas memory for both of them which came back to sting them every year at the first sign of a snowflake.

Snap, snap, snap, I was snap-happy over here, and told off my wandering mind, forcing it to bloody well come back to the present.

Here we go . . .

As Alex got down on one knee in the snow, and opened the box, Anna turned around. It was all very fairy-tale. Then Anna shouted a gleeful, 'COCKING HELL!' and I was glad I was on photos not video.

I couldn't hear exactly what he was saying to her, but she was happy laugh-crying and he was grinning and she was nodding so it all seemed like it was going well. I took photo after photo, feeling like maybe I could try being an event photographer when I got back to the UK because I was getting some lovely images and it wasn't just because Alexander had the latest iPhone with a million lenses and a billion pixels. No, no. It was because of ME and my artist's gaze.

Gosh, it was nice to be being artistic out in nature. It had been a minute.

Anna removed her left mitten, and I hoped neither of them developed frostbite on my watch with all these mitten-removals, and Alexander held the ring out and I was about to let out a whoop when –

He dropped the ring into the powder-soft snow.

'Bollocks!' I heard him say, and Anna dropped down to her knees in front of him.

I lowered the phone. 'All right over there?'

'Erm, yep, nobody move!' he called back. He and Anna stayed still as statues while he peered down into the tiny hole made by the ring. 'I see it, give me a mo.'

I walked over, stepping carefully as if I were navigating the surface of the moon, afraid of dislodging any snow clumps. Alexander was very carefully digging with his fingers and Anna was trying to look concerned about the ring but couldn't keep the big, giddy grin off her face.

'Use this,' I said, handing him my pole, worried again about that frostbite becoming a reality.

As Alex scooped out snow and the ring wriggled tantalizingly further out of sight, I whispered to Anna, 'Did you say yes?'

'Yes, absolutely!'

'Good, just checking. The photos are lovely.'

'You took photos?' She seemed over the moon, which was nice because I guess it meant she'd been so in the moment she'd forgotten I was there.

'Any luck?' I looked down at Alexander while simultaneously awarding myself the Stupid Question of the Year award.

'How thick is this snow?' he commented. Then looked up at me.

Oh, it wasn't rhetorical. I had no idea. 'Ten foot?' I guessed.

'Ten foot?!' Both Anna and Alexander exclaimed in unison.

'Oh, you mean this snow, sorry, probably only two or three feet.' I don't know why I was even talking, to be honest. 'Shall I have a go?'

'OK.' Alexander sat back, so slowly it was like he was doing tai chi.

'Right.' I shuffled forward and looked down to where he'd dug.

'It just keeps slipping further down,' he explained.

Digging my bare fingers into the snow, I pinched them around as carefully as I could, while Anna and Alexander snogged above my head. Eventually I gripped something small and hard, and pulled out my arm like I was King Arthur himself, holding the snow-covered ring high.

'Oh, it's *beautiful*!' Anna exclaimed, holding her hand out to me. I shuffled on my knees to face her and started to place the ring on her outstretched finger when Alexander cleared his throat.

'Oh, um, maybe I could do that?'

'Gosh, sorry,' I said, scrambling up and handing him the ring, regaining my place as official photographer instead.

And returning to the serene silence, with the lilac light glinting off the snow, I snapped away as Alexander placed the ring on his bride-to-be's finger, and they kissed, and hugged, and squealed, and then all of us quickly put our gloves back on.

That was pretty special. Not a bad first day of work.

I was feeling good. Today was a good day because:

1. I made it through day one on the job without losing anyone, losing myself, breaking anything, or ruining anybody's holiday.
2. I spent the whole day in Lapland and managed to avoid all hints of Christmas.
3. Oh, other than my brief encounter with an elf first thing.
4. And the fact Anna and Alexander asked my opinion on which engagement photo they should have printed into two hundred Christmas-slash-announcement cards for all their friends and family.
5. Two hundred, though??? If I did that, I'd have about one hundred and eighty-four cards left over.
6. We found the ring! Thank GOD.
7. I also made it through the day without dwelling on past Christmases too much, which is a good sign of things to come, I think.

Back in my room, I sat on Esteri's bed wrapped in a towel, having just treated myself to a sauna in our secret sauna, and a hot shower to boot, and I was now inspecting my feet for blisters but they seemed to be OK.

I checked the calendar on my phone. Roughly five and a bit weeks to Christmas. I wonder if I could speak to Daan and ask to be put on snowshoe tours all the time. I mean, I was basically a pro now I'd done it once. Though ... I only had one tour to give today, and judging by the fact everyone else was still out, the staff lodge seeming almost deserted, I think most days I might be much busier. But think of the thigh muscles I'd go home with at the end of January! That would show Shay.

Five weeks to Christmas. Could I stay in one piece until then?

Chapter 17

Wish me luck, I might die today, I texted to Willow and Max on a group chat a little over a week later.

I was lying awake in my bunk, listening to the creaks and shuffles of the staff chalet waking up around me. In the bed below, Esteri was gently snoring, a noise which I liked a lot (I'm not being sarcastic) because it was like listening to one of those soundscapes on the Headspace app that help you relax.

I reached my arm out from under the covers to lift the curtain while I waited to see if anyone would text back. It was sometime around seven a.m. here in Lapland, which meant it was only five a.m. back home, so they might be fast asleep.

Outside the window, the world was black. Tiny outdoor floodlights lit the paths from the chalet to the activities' lodge, and the chalet to the saunas. Lights also sat nestled under the nearby pine trees, with their beams pointing upwards, and I could see the snowflakes falling to the ground thanks to them. All was calm.

Out of the corner of my eye I saw my phone screen light up with a message from Willow.

So dramatic. See ya then.

Charming.

She followed it quickly with, Just kidding, don't snuff it. What are you doing today?

> I'm heading back out on the snowmobile. With a family. With kids.

> Oh god.

> I know.

I was making light of it, but I was a bit nervous. Today, for the first time, I was running a Seeking Santa Claus day tour. The adults would have their own snowmobiles, the children would be in a sleigh pulled along by me. Lucky them.

What are you doing awake? I asked Willow.

I've been checking out the Black Friday deals online. Christmas shopping!

It was Friday? Well, there we go.

Ooo, gotta go, Willow wrote. Just made it through the virtual queue onto the Boots website. Happy snowmobiling! Don't ruin it for anyone.

Thanks, I won't, I replied, hoping that were true.

It turns out I needn't have worried, because when I arrived at the activities' lodge a while later, I was told my family had changed their minds, and wanted to switch to the reindeer Seeking Santa option instead. Now that was more like it. I was saved from the snowmobile for another day!

While I waited for them to arrive, I searched the faces of my elf colleagues who were milling around the lodge to see if any of them were Josh. I hadn't talked to him in about a week, only seeing him in passing across the chalet. I mean, we were hardly best buds, but still, I wondered how he was getting on.

He didn't seem to be here though.

All of a sudden, a shuttle bus from a nearby hotel pulled up and a tumble of little limbs and bobble hats came out, two of whom ran straight over to me, hand in hand.

'We want to find Santa! Where is Santa? Where is Rudolf?' cried one little girl, looking up at me with a toothy smile.

I was about to answer when the other girl, younger, with braids that stuck haphazardly out from under her hat and big eyes behind her spectacles, shouted 'Merry Christmas' up at my face.

'Girls,' called the dad in a British accent, a tall man with a gingery beard. 'Come on, we need to go inside first and find out where to go.'

'Hello,' I replied to the younger girl. 'Come with me and we'll get you put in special clothes so you can keep toasty warm while you look for Santa.'

The girls stuck their hands out immediately, so I checked in with the dad, who smiled, and I took hold of the little hands, leading them back to their parents and inside the lodge. At this point I had no idea if they were *my* guests, but then the mum said to me, 'We were booked in for a snowmobile tour today but called ahead to see if we could switch it to reindeer instead?'

'Oh, then you're with me!' I said. 'I'm Myla. Welcome to Lapland.'

'Great,' said the mum. 'I'm Aubrey. This is Greg. And this is Briony and Leah. Thanks so much for letting us change at the last minute. The girls are so excited, they can't believe they're actually here, in the most Christmassy place on earth.'

Join the club, I thought, but led them to the counter where they checked in and then were shown to the shoe and outerwear room to get them all kitted up.

Briony and Leah came running out first, straight back over to me.

'So do you actually *know* Father Christmas?' Briony, the older girl, asked, taking my hand again.

'Sure,' I said. That wasn't actually true . . . today was going to be my first time meeting him at his cabin too, though I'd been there during training. 'He told me he can't wait to meet you both.'

Leah screamed up at me in delight. 'He is my FAVOURITE, I like him even more than I like Daddy because he gets us all our presents.'

Briony tugged my hand. 'Are the reindeers we'll ride on today the ones Santa uses on Christmas Eve?'

'Some of them. Santa has lots of reindeer friends.'

'Are we actually sitting on the rains-dears?' Leah asked, her little face concerned.

'No, they'll be pulling us on sleighs, just like how Santa rides.'

'Do you know any Christmas songs?' Briony asked.

'Yes, I love Christmas songs. Do you?' I deflected.

'Can you sing us one?' she asked, the wily little rascal.

Nooooooo, don't make me do this torture. I opened and closed my mouth a few times, looking around to see if anyone was in earshot, and sadly, they were. This meant a) I couldn't refuse and say it was against company policy or something, and b) now my colleagues would hear me sing, badly, to songs I don't even know.

Racking my brains for a suitable Christmas song – it had been a long, long time since I'd listened to or sang such things, I started to sway from side to side, like I was working up to a melody.

Briony blinked at me. 'Can't you think of one?'

'Of course I can, I'm just trying to come up with the perfect one, that's all.' I began with a tuneless murmuring of 'Frosty the Snowman', but forgot the second line, so faltered out after I'd replaced it with, 'Hmm-hm-hmmhmm-hmmhmm-hmmmmmmm.'

'Do you know Britney Spears?' Briony asked.

'Yes!' I grinned. Now we were more on my kinda turf. 'My favourite is "Slave 4—"'

'So do you know "My Only Wish This Year"?'

I felt my mouth dry. 'The Christmas one?'

Leah nodded, staring up at me, and whispered, 'I love that one.'

'Oh good . . .' I did know it, because Britney gets my love even if Christmas doesn't, but I wouldn't say I knew it well enough to sing. 'What about "Baby One More Time"? I could sing that?'

131

Briony and Leah both shook their heads, and Leah laid down the law. 'A Christmas song. Please.'

'Please,' added Briony, all fluttery eyes and cold nose. God, it was like they were a couple of poor little street urchins at the beginning of *A Christmas Carol* and I felt like the biggest Scrooge ever.

Fine. *Fine.* I looked around for inspiration and then it hit me, as I saw the sleighs, it was so obvious. I launched into a rendition of 'Jingle Bells' because even that was lodged into my memory from primary school days, although the Batman-Smells lyrics were intertwining with the real ones in my mind.

By the time I hit the second verse, with a few dashes of poetic licence thrown in, Leah was tapping me on the arm.

'Yes?' I asked, stopping my awkward, swaying dance and pretending not to notice other guests and my workmates giving me Looks.

'Shall I sing instead?' Leah asked.

Ouch.

'Um, OK, go ahead.'

I didn't want to sing anyway, but I was still a little affronted. Never mind. This just proved that I was right to not go to all those Christmas sing-along concerts with my friends over the past decade.

Leah started singing a soft little version of 'Away in a Manger', so Briony joined in louder, and just as they were about to get in a scrap – they so reminded me of Shay and me – Aubrey and Greg reappeared.

'Time to go!' I said, and led them the short walk towards the reindeer farm.

I waved to Kirste, who was checking the harnesses as we neared.

'Well, do we have some people very excited to meet Santa Claus today?' she asked, to the shrieks of the children.

Each sleigh could hold two guests, plus I would be in the front one, guiding along with Kirste today. When everyone was snuggled into their seats, and I'd shown Aubrey and Greg how to handle the reins, we took off on the most relaxing thing, in my opinion, that Lapland has to offer.

We bumbled through the snow for some time, watching the reindeer's bottoms as they walked and sometimes trotted, their brass cowbells making low tinkles with each step. We paused for hot chocolates and warm fresh blueberry juice that I'd made back at the activities' lodge and brought along with me in flasks. We fed the reindeer snacks of lichen, which apparently they love, though I had to stop Leah from giving it a try herself. And eventually, I signalled for the reindeer to pause at the edge of a section of forest.

To Briony and Leah I said, 'Do you think Santa might be in the forest?' and they both stared at me in wonder.

Briony, with her dad in the sleigh, whispered, 'I think he might be.'

'Shall we find out?'

We walked the reindeer slowly through the forest, soft snuffles and grunts emitting from them, until we reached a clearing. I drew my sleigh to a slow stop, the others following suit, and even the girls paused for a moment of silence while we were awed at the sight of Santa's log cabin. Nestled among the trees, its sloped roof was under a weighted blanket of snow, and candles in ice lanterns dotted the ground around the entranceway, giving a twilight effect to the dim daytime air. The forest seemed still, save for the mellow shuffling of our reindeer.

'Is that where Santa lives?' Briony whispered to me, her face full of awe.

'Is he in there now?' Leah added.

At that moment, the door to the cabin opened, and we all held our breath, even me, but I exhaled into a smile when I saw who was at the door.

There was Josh, his big grin and rosy cheeks, that cosy felt costume and big pointed hat. He caught my eye for a second, before pointing at the girls and hurling himself face-down into a snowdrift, much to their squeals of delight. Leaping up and shaking himself off, he then scampered away behind the house, only to then throw a snowball in their direction (but deliberately not getting anywhere near them).

I caught myself laughing for a moment, more because the kids were in hysterics. While Aubrey and Greg climbed from the sleigh and helped down the children, who went zooming after Josh to have a snowball fight with him, Kirste and I stayed behind to keep our reindeer company.

Josh was doing a great job of being fully in cheeky Christmas Elf mode; he was a natural. At one point he looked over and gave me a wave – large and exaggerated and in character, before singing 'Rudolph the Red-Nosed Reindeer' at the top of his voice and encouraging the family to do the same, while they marched around the circumference of the cabin.

'He's funny,' Kirste laughed, before making her way towards the other sleighs while I stayed up front. 'I'm going to check on the other reindeer.'

'All right,' I said to her, watching her go before turning to my nearest fuzzy friend. 'What do you make of all this, Rudolph?' I asked my reindeer, quietly, patting his furry side with my thick mittens. He snorted into the cold air, his shiny black eyes on me. 'Do you ever get tired of all the Christmas spirit?'

He probably loved it. The reindeer here were so well treated, and guests were instructed to only pet them gently and if they came to them. In fact, I think I read that it was against the law in Lapland to scare or disturb reindeer, in any way. Besides, we weren't even in December yet – that's when the real crowds would get here. He couldn't be sick of it all yet.

I couldn't be sick of it all yet. I wasn't allowed to be.

'Who wants to meet Santa Claus?' Josh's voice sang out and I looked back over.

Briony got a bit overwhelmed with emotion all of a sudden here and had an impromptu cry, but before I could go over and help, Josh was sat in the snow building her a small snowman and making her giggle through her tears. Leah was fascinated as he whipped up a second, even shorter, snowman and then declared them called Briony and Leah.

I took a moment to release my cheeks from my perma-grin, and let my brain come down from the sugar-rush of enthusing about all things Christmas, which did not come naturally to me, as you can imagine.

With dry eyes and excited smiles back in place, it was time for the family's private meeting with Santa, their reward for completing the Seeking Santa Claus day, and likely, the highlight of their trip. Josh led the family into the cabin, and I watched him leave.

Chapter 18

'Is that Santa calling?' my dad chuckled down the phone when he picked up, all the way over in the Isle of Wight. I couldn't help but smile, sitting down heavily on the ground, thankful for the super-thick padding of my snowsuit. It was my day off, and despite my exhausted body, I'd grabbed some snowshoes and taken myself up to the top of a fell the other side of the forest, so that I could call my dad for a check-in without risking being overheard.

Now, sitting here, with the white-duveted world stretched far before me, the sky violet and the air – some of the cleanest air in the whole world – lightly scented with pine, I'd actually forgotten some of the grumbles I'd been planning to offload. The world was so silent, all I could hear was my own breath, and the soft crunch of the snow beneath me when I pushed out my legs. I couldn't even hear many of my thoughts, which was nice, it was like they'd drifted away, snowflakes picked up by the breeze.

'Hey, Dad, how's home?'

'Home is home,' he replied. 'How are you? How's my coat?'

'Your coat is wonderful,' I said. It was around me now, actually, over my snowsuit, as the temperature had dropped again and was now at a late-November minus eleven degrees. 'Thank you for letting me bring it.'

'You can take it on all your future adventures. How are you coping?'

'I'm OK ... well, actually, I'm not very good at all this,' I confessed. 'I still haven't led a snowmobile trip, and I don't feel like I have the natural gung-ho that the other guides, that *everybody*, else has here. But!' I added, chirping up. 'It's now only four weeks until Christmas, so not long to go!'

Dad was quiet for a minute. 'Please don't wish your life away,' he said. 'Enjoy yourself out there.'

'I am,' I said quickly, feeling bad. 'I love Lapland. It's just ... you know I don't cope well with the Christmas stuff—'

'Any more,' he interrupted.

'—*Any more*. So I'm just trying to make it to that point, that's all.'

'All right. Shay told me that if you rang, I had to tell you you're not allowed to quit.'

'I'm not going to quit. I know I've said that before, and I know I don't have a good track record, but I'm going to stick this out, you don't need to worry.'

'I'm not worried,' Dad said. 'I know you're going to be just fine, and once you get on that snowmobile they'll be wishing they'd put you on one sooner.'

'Thanks, Dad,' I said.

'What do you actually think of the job itself, and the people? You know, all the non-Christmas things?'

I sat up straighter and breathed in the fresh air, feeling my heart instantly lift. 'I like being outside, it makes a nice change from office jobs, actually. And the people are great. I have a lovely room-mate and there are some other staff members I get on well with. There's someone I met on the plane on the way over who's friendly, but his job is as an elf and he's almost always in character, so I'm avoiding hanging out with him, hahahahaaaaaaa.'

Dad paused. 'Well that all sounds very positive.'

We chatted for a while more, before I thought I'd better get moving again so I hung up the phone.

Sticking my poles in the ground I heaved myself up to standing, catching the branch of a tree to steady me when I wobbled and causing a rain of snow to thud its way down onto my head and into the powder below. Hmph. I'd still meant what I said, though. Working outdoors all day every day wasn't exactly what I thought it would be back when I first went to Shay, asking for seasonal work – I wasn't getting very sun-kissed, for a start – but I did feel like the endless sights and smells and sounds were keeping me in the moment, and that could only be a good thing.

Chapter 19

I wish I'd not been such a massive chicken, and taken the snowmobiles out earlier, back in November when there were fewer visitors to our little part of Lapland. Now, with December under way, we were working full hours outside and running several trips each per day. The company did a great job of making visitors feel like they had all the space and time in the world, and thankfully my muscles were beginning to adapt to hiking through these conditions, which was kind of cool. Also, hooray for saunas! They are just so bloomin' lovely after a day on the snow. Esteri and I were regular end-of-day visitors to our secret sauna in the staff chalet.

Now, finally, I was on snowmobile safari duty. I was leading a group of six on an all-day adventure, and as they were getting kitted out, I was wandering back and forth along the line of skidoos I'd be in charge of and running through the emergency procedures in my head.

'Good luck today, roomie!' Esteri called, whizzing by me on her own snowmobile, on her way to help out with husky puppy meet-and-greets at the farm for the day. That job is the best.

'Thank you,' I called to the spray of snow she left in her wake.

Guests were milling around, getting ready for their various excursions, sitting beside one of the many small campfires that dotted the ground, taking photos, marvelling at just how snowy it was. I was using a large brush to sweep snow off the seats and handles of the snowmobiles when some jingle bells caught my attention.

'Hello!' said an enthusiastic voice.

Turning, I faced Josh, in full regalia again, waving at me like a panto performer.

'Hey, Josh!' I felt like I'd barely seen him since we started, and now he was right there I couldn't help but smile.

'*Elf* Josh, silly.' He wagged his finger then laughed and leapfrogged over one of the snowmobiles. Ah yes, *Elf Josh* had to stay in character at all times. How could I forget. I stifled a sigh.

'I'm coming with you today,' Josh said in his children's performer voice, leaning beside me with his arm resting jauntily on my shoulder. He grinned widely but this close up, my face directly looking into his, I saw the twinkle in his eye, not of Elf Josh but of real Josh. Surgical nurse Josh. The Josh I'd met on the plane, and who'd picked me up an elf diploma.

I blinked and turned my gaze towards my group, happily

waddling through the snow like a gaggle of teddy bears. 'What do you mean?'

'I mean, I'm coming on the snowmobile safari.'

'Why?'

'Why?' he laughed, then waved a big hello to the group. 'I'm joining in because I heard someone in this group is very excited about Christmas.'

'That's me!' A bubbly Australian girl stepped forward. 'It's my birthday month and I love Christmas so much.'

'Me too!' shrieked Josh, taking her hands in his and spinning her in a circle while she laughed her head off.

Our snowmobile safaris can be really tailored to what the groups say they want when they book, so if they want quiet and wilderness, we'll offer them a trip to unspoiled fells with magnificent views. If they want to try and spot the Northern Lights, we'll suggest one of our evening tours, where we head to the best locations as predicted by our managers. If they want a romantic trip, we'll take them to beauty spots with good photo ops. And if they want Christmassy, we'll provide gingerbread and mulled wine and tell tales about yuletide. So in this case, I had the snacks and drinks sorted, and it looked like Josh was bringing a dash of extra festive joy.

Speaking of, he now had the whole group lying on the ground making snow angels.

'All right, shall we get going?' I said, and they all began to try and get up again in their padded onesies, meaning Josh had to run around and every time he'd pull one of them up he'd theatrically fall back onto the ground himself, then ask *them* to pull *him* up. What a palaver. 'Everybody gather around, I just need to tell you a few health and safety things before we start the tour today.'

As I was giving my talk, cold, wet dust hit my face with force and I gasped involuntarily, sucking some of it in as I did so, and coughing as it turned to water at the back of my throat.

There was a pause while I stood in shock, and then I heard a loud, jovial-though-minutely-less-than-usual, 'Uh-oh, I'm sorry Adventure Guide Myla!'

Wiping the snowball from my eyes I glared for a second at Josh who, with his back to the others mouthed 'Sorry' to me.

I slapped on a smile before the guests saw any break in service. 'You cheeky elf,' I laughed loudly.

I liked Josh, I really did, but yeah ... he could be pretty annoying.

Nevertheless, the group, Josh, and I, set off on our snow-mobile safari without incident. My hands were shaking inside my merino wool gloves, which were inside my mittens, and I concentrated as hard as I could on not cocking up. The snowmobile, which seemed loud, heavy and hard, carved through the snow without effort, spray pluming out beside my legs, and after a while, I let my breath out, a white cloud into the blue cold, and began to chat to the group via my microphone.

Josh, who had no clue how to drive a snowmobile, rode with me on mine, and the feeling of him against me – of somebody familiar quite literally having my back – allowed my wobbly voice to settle, and my confidence to up. Just a notch. I was still weeing myself a little bit.

We drove in a line over hilltops and fells, around frozen lakes and then circled back to the reindeer farm for our warm drinks. All was, actually, going fine.

Until ten minutes after we'd left the reindeer farm to explore the other direction, and had pulled to a stop near the top of a fell which had a spectacular photo op.

'Let me take some pictures with you in,' I said to the group, and we spent a while with me swapping between different cameras and phones and them swapping between different poses.

Climbing back on the snowmobiles, I motioned to the group to wait for my signal to get going ... and then my snowmobile wouldn't start.

Through a fixed grin, I said into the microphone, 'Just a moment!'

Behind me, Josh shifted in his seat, turning his head towards me. 'You all right, Adventure Guide Myla?'

'Yep, no problem!' I sang back, trying to match his sing-song voice.

I pulled the handle and nothing. I rattled it ... nothing. I'd checked the fuel, I'd checked it was all in working order ... what had I done wrong? Shit shit shit.

'Wait a minute!' said Josh, leaping back off the snowmo-bile. 'We didn't take a jumping photo!'

With cries of, 'Oh my god, yes,' the whole group scram-bled off the snowmobile train again and ran back up the fell, with Josh leading the way.

I breathed a sigh of relief, and sent Josh a silent thanks for buying me some time. Hopping off the snowmobile, I checked the fuel levels, but they were all fine.

A few minutes later, Josh appeared at my side again, the group still at the top, just starting to make their way down.

'How are you doing?' he asked in a whisper.

'I don't know. I don't know what's wrong.' My eyes searched his, my breathing shallow.

'It's OK, we'll fix it.'

'You can fix it?'

'No, I have no idea how snowmobiles work,' he shrugged. 'But you're not alone. Just breathe.'

At that point, the group arrived back at the snowmobiles, and Josh plunged back into Elf Josh mode. He kept them entertained while I phoned the activities' lodge and explained what happened. I could hear my voice shaking. I could hear the panic seeping out. What if Daan or Zoë were angry at me? What if they made me pay for the snowmobile? What if they realised I didn't belong here and fired me and my sister then got fired and—

'Myla?' said Zoë's voice coming onto the line. 'They told me what happened, are you OK?'

'Yep, great, well, stuck actually.'

'All right, don't worry, let's talk through what could have gone wrong and how to fix it.'

With my heart racing and my brain trying to focus on the task ahead instead of zooming off into panic mode, I followed her instructions, and was a little incy bit proud of myself for sitting here in the snow cleaning fuel lines.

A short bit of tinkering later, Zoë said down the phone, 'That should do it. Try the on button again.'

I took a breath. *Please work, please work, please work*. Oh, I was going to look like such a massive twat if it didn't.

For one second that felt like ten hours, nothing happened after I flicked the snowmobile switch. And then, suddenly, thankfully, the machine roared back to life. Catching Josh's eye as I exhaled, I took my seat on the snowmobile again, relieved but shaken, and confused at my reaction. Was what happened really that much of something to panic about? Or had I just so conditioned myself to expect the worst at this time of year I'd jumped forward in time before the situation had even caught up with me?

'All right, adventurers, let's see if we can get this thing going,' I said, as jovially as I could. I was more on edge now, more convinced something else would go wrong.

I inhaled deeply, and that's when I felt Josh give my padded arm a squeeze, leaving his hand there until I'd exhaled slowly. It was a simple gesture, but a kind one, one that made me feel like we were in this together. One that kept me present. And with the final thought that maybe he wasn't too annoying after all, even in elf mode, I turned the handle of the snowmobile, and we were able to pull away.

Chapter 20

Ahhhh. I lay back in the sauna for the first time completely in the buff, my towel resting at my side. I needed this, I thought, as the heat circled my body like cigarette smoke in a romantic bar from the nineteen twenties. I let my limbs and flesh and boobs melt onto the warm, wooden bench and breathed in the scent of birch wood, switching all my thoughts off so all that I heard were the sizzles of the water baking the rocks.

I wondered if I could find a new flat back home that had a sauna inside it. If not, how likely was it that I would cause a massive mould problem if I blocked off ventilation to the bathroom and let it steam up every day? Hmm, no, that wasn't a good idea at all. There's a reason that saunas don't have loos in.

In here it was quiet. There was no Christmas music. No elves. No images of the man in red. Not even any snow. In fact, with my eyes closed, I could almost, *almost*, pretend I was lying on that sunshine-soaked beach somewhere, that I thought for a hot minute I could spend the Christmas season in.

Bang. 'Hello!'

My eyes flung themselves open at the same time my hands went to cover my bits.

Esteri plonked her fully naked self on the bench below me. 'Don't cover up, you silly thing, let it all relax, won't you?'

Tentatively, I removed my hands, but even though Esteri couldn't see me from where she was lying I still found it hard to relax quite in the way I had been. Especially when she then sat up, eye to eye with my left boob, and said, 'Good news, I found them!'

I shuffled myself upright and wrapped the towel around me like the big prude I was. 'Found who?'

'My family, my Lapland family.'

'Oh you did! That's amazing!' I was pleased for her. 'Are you going to go and see them?'

'Yes, we're going tomorrow.'

'Who are you going with?'

'You!'

'Me? But I'm working tomorrow.' I wondered if Josh would be joining me again.

Esteri was shaking her head. 'Nope, you're coming with me. I have two days off, and I have spoken to Daan and now your two days off this week are also tomorrow and the day after. We will stay overnight.'

'Oh. Thanks,' I said. Wait a minute, a chance to get deep into non-Christmassy Lapland for two days? That would take me two days closer to the big day, and two days closer to no disasters happening. 'Are there any disasters that could befall us?' I asked, super-casually.

Esteri laughed. 'You're so weird. This will be a lot of fun. You'll come with me, right?'

I could tell she was nervous, even with a dash of excitement. This was a big deal, meeting her only remaining relatives. And in a place, Lapland, that she loved enough to keep returning to year on year.

'Of course,' I said, and gave her sweaty shoulder a pat.

'Urgh, you are all clammy.' She shook me off, but also gave me a small smile and nod.

'How do we get there?'

'I'll drive. I'm hiring a car. So be ready to go tomorrow morning quite early, OK?'

'OK,' I agreed. Esteri lay back down so I did too.

Chapter 21

The following morning, bright and early, as per Esteri's command, we found ourselves in a chunky hire car with heated seats. Or, not-so-bright, but still early. It was just gone eight and the sun here wouldn't poke above the horizon for another couple of hours, and even then it would be so low that shadows would be long and the snow would be bathed in amber sunrise light until it went back down again a short while later.

We'd begun the three-hour drive north towards Inari, the district of Finnish Lapland known as the heart of Sámi culture, with the aim to first visit the village of Inari itself to meet with Esteri's mum's cousin, who worked in the museum there, within the Northern Lapland Nature Centre. After that, said cousin would take us back to her home for the night, and we'd drive back to Luosto tomorrow morning.

I took a sip of my coffee, watching the morning twilight

pines rush past the car window. 'So you've never met this cousin of your mum's before?' I asked Esteri.

'Nope,' she said from the driver's seat. 'I don't think my mum knew her very well, they lived so far apart when they were kids, but they would exchange Christmas cards, so that's how I knew her address after my parents passed away.'

'What's her name?'

'Kalle.'

'Are you nervous?' I asked, sneaking a look at her.

'Yes, a little bit,' she admitted. I liked how honest and authentic Esteri always seemed. She wasn't afraid to admit vulnerability. 'They are the only family I have left, you know, so I hope they are nice. And I hope they like me.'

'They will.' I nodded, my gaze falling back out of the window.

'What makes you so sure?'

'I like you. You're a nice person.'

'So I have your stamp of approval and therefore everyone else will feel the same?' Esteri cast me a sideways smirk.

'Exactly. Seriously though, you're very easy to talk to and you're kind, if a little intimidating, so I think this will go well.'

'Intimidating?' Esteri laughed.

I chuckled. 'Just a little.'

It was nice to be out here on the open road. It felt like we'd left Christmas behind us for a couple of days, if that made sense. We were taking a break from tourists and responsibilities and festive cheer and elves.

We travelled a little further in easy silence, watching

151

as Lapland slowly, slowly had the brightness turned up, a notch at a time. Sometimes we passed lakes, sometimes the road took us right over them, but they were almost always frozen over; vast, flat vistas that looked like they begged to be skated upon.

'It's pretty cool, huh?' Esteri commented as we drove the low road over one of the frozen lakes.

'Lapland is *actually* incredible,' I replied.

'You sound surprised?'

'I guess I didn't quite know what to expect. I feel like I didn't know much about Lapland beyond trips to meet Santa Claus, before I came here.'

'Ah, but Santa Claus is only *one* of the best bits.'

I turned in my seat to face my friend. 'You said this was your fourth year here. What keeps bringing you back, do you think; is it the Christmas stuff or Lapland itself?'

'That's a good question,' Esteri answered and looked thoughtful for a moment. 'For a long time I thought it was the Christmas stuff, because I just love the lights and atmosphere and the faces of the tourists and the fun everyone has, and, oh, the Christmas Eve party – I love it.'

'Christmas Eve party?'

'You didn't know about that? Love Adventuring Lapland puts on a Christmas Eve party every year in the activities' lodge for both guests and staff. There's food and dancing and Santa comes. Not all companies offer a party on Christmas Eve, so it's quite popular.'

'I can imagine.' My first thought was, *oh no . . . a Christmas party*. And then it occurred to me – maybe it wouldn't be so bad this year. Being right on the night before Christmas held a certain significance, like a celebration that I would have made it all the way to the big day without the 'curse' befalling me. That is, *if* I made it that far.

'Anyway,' Esteri interrupted my thoughts. 'So I love all of that, but actually, the more I come here the more I just think I love the place itself, you know? The scenery, the peace and quiet, the people, the light.'

'The light?' I looked out at the cornflower-blue sky.

'Yep. Light doesn't have to be "light" to make you happy.'

Hmm. I realised in that moment that the darker days weren't actually bothering me any more. I'd struggled in that first week, craving bright blue skies and earlier dawns and later sunsets. But even though the days had got even shorter, I no longer minded. In fact, when the stars and the moon were out in all their bright glory, the reflection on the white-coated world I now lived in wasn't all that dark after all. Dare I say ... I was beginning to appreciate the natural hygge-lighting of Lapland. 'Have you ever come in the summer? I read it's nothing but "light" light then,' I asked Esteri.

She glanced at me, her eyes twinkling like the sun was already behind them, and said enigmatically, 'Not yet.'

'Do you think you'd like to?' I pressed.

'For sure. I think I really would. How about you? What attracted you most to this job – Lapland or Christmas?'

'Lapland,' I answered, which was, actually, the truth. 'I love Christmas, of course—'

'Of course.'

153

'—but Finland was somewhere I always wanted to visit, and when I looked at the brochure and saw a photo of, um,' I hastily thought back to the month before when Shay had pressed the brochure in front of my face, 'a sauna inside a gondola, I was like – now that's the place for me.'

'Oh yeah, the Sauna Gondola at Ylläs; that's pretty nice.'

'You've been?'

'No – it's pretty expensive, but I've heard about it. Maybe one day. So you like it then? Finland?'

'I do. I feel . . .' Hmm. How do I describe this to Esteri without sounding like a knob? 'I feel kind of safe here. Everyone here in Lapland is kind and friendly and it's not that I expected anything else, but it's just . . . My favourite thing is the people.'

Esteri reached over and booped my nose. 'Ahh, you softie little Brit.'

A while later, after we'd travelled north enough that the bright gold of the sun on the horizon had disappeared, the scenery began to change, from snow-covered roadsides to crops of buildings.

'Here we are,' Esteri said, leaning forward in her seat. 'This is Inari. Keep an eye out for signs for Siida, that's the name of the Sámi Museum and Nature Centre where Kalle works.'

I did as I was told, and shrieked out, '*There it is!*' when I spotted a road sign directing us towards a modern, low building encased in glass and red-slat panelling.

We parked, and Esteri sat for a moment.

'You OK?' I asked.

We were quiet for a moment longer, until Esteri turned her grey eyes to me, and searched mine. 'This is a good idea, right?'

'Of course.' I squeezed her hand. 'They will love you.'

'Thanks for coming with me.'

'Thanks for bringing me.'

She exhaled slowly, then undid her seat belt. 'Right, come on, you silly Brit.'

With a smile, I hopped out of the car and stretched my legs, tightening the laces of my snowboots as a gust of chilly Arctic Circle wind said hello.

Esteri locked the car and strode ahead into the museum, seeming like she'd given herself a pep talk and was now marching towards her destiny. I tottered and skidded a little to keep up, and welcomed the blast of warm air when we entered the building.

As Esteri spoke in Finnish to the reception desk, I hung back to look at a museum display about traditional Sámi clothing, known as *gákti*, tailored to each family and region. I was admiring a risku, a circular silver brooch used to hold scarves in place and as part of wedding day traditions, decorated with small, tinkling silver disks which represented the sun, when a voice cut through the quiet.

'Esteri?' a woman said, tentatively, coming around the corner.

My friend turned, and the women looked at each other. A generation and a life apart, but they shared the same grey eyes, the same ashy-blonde hair. Esteri smiled and stepped forward, and I don't know what they were saying, and I tried to not stare and instead read the information on the display, but by the way Esteri was smiling and gesturing at the woman I was guessing it was something like, 'Bloody hell, you look like my mum.'

'Kalle, this is my good friend, Myla. She's from the UK,' Esteri said, coming over to me. 'Myla, this is my mother's cousin.'

'Hello,' I said, giving a small wave. 'Thank you for letting us stay with you tonight.' I spoke carefully and clearly, not sure how much English Kalle spoke.

Turns out, she was great at English. Her voice was soft and lilty, her smile wide, her tone kind. She welcomed me alongside Esteri, who she linked arms with the whole way around the museum, telling us (in English – so so kind!) all about the museum and background of the area, inviting us to learn more about the Sámi heritage from the museum staff. Afterwards, she took us for lunch in the museum restaurant and I ate a ginormous croissant filled with nutty cheese and salty ham. Yum yum. Ginormous anything always gets my vote.

After noshing, we went into the gift shop. I picked up a smooth wooden cup, *kuksa*, a traditional craft about the size of a coffee mug sometimes given as a gift, which stated it had been made by a local Sámi artisan. The lines and detail were beautiful, it was authentic with deep historical roots, and I thought I could gift it to Shay and Tess, a keepsake for their new baby, perhaps. I picked up a small wooden reindeer, painted red, to give to my dad and a book on Sámi culture for me and paid for my purchases, clutching them tightly and carefully to my heart.

Kalle had taken the afternoon off work, so after lunch she told us to follow her in her car, and we drove another twenty minutes away from the village and into the wilderness, stopping outside a beautiful blue-painted wooden home with a sloped roof that was piled high with snow. It was nestled in a forest, and before I got out of the car, I spotted a reindeer slowly wandering past the front door.

Seeing my face, Esteri said, 'Still not used to seeing the reindeer everywhere, are you?'

We stepped from the car and onto the snow at the same time as Kalle did from her car, and she beckoned us towards the house just as the front door opened. Out stepped a woman about our age, holding a little girl on her hip, long hair straggling down her back and cheeks a rosy pink.

'Who is this?' Esteri asked.

I put my hand on her arm and said quietly, 'Esteri, don't feel you all have to speak English for me. You all just get to know each other, I'll be fine.'

She just smiled at me in return.

Kalle reached forward and the little girl clambered from one set of arms to another. 'Esteri, Myla, this is my daughter, Sade, and *her* daughter, Taimi.'

Esteri's eyes grew wide. 'I have a cousin and a niece too? Well, second-removed-whatever version of a cousin and niece?'

'You do,' said Kalle.

Sade stepped off the porch into the snow and pulled Esteri into a hug. 'It's so very, very nice to meet you,' she said with a warmth to rival a summer midnight sun.

I let a sun beam smile dance across my face, happy for my friend.

That evening, having spent the afternoon drinking coffee and being shown around Kalle's peaceful and quiet homestead, we sat down to a dinner with Esteri's new family. Over a delicious dinner of delicate salmon soup, and tangy and sweet cloudberries to nibble on afterwards (which looked like orange blackberries and tasted a little sweet and a little sour), Kalle, her husband Onni, and Sade told us all about their lives, and Esteri told them about hers, and about her parents and brother. There were some tears, but a lot of laughter, and that night, before we went to sleep in our beautiful guest room, Esteri tempted me outside where we wrapped ourselves in colourful blankets and looked up at the stars, dazzling thanks to so little light pollution.

Kalle and Sade stood beside us, and Sade said, 'Have you seen the Northern Lights yet?'

'Not yet,' I replied. 'I'm hoping to see them at least once before I leave Lapland at the end of January.'

'I'm sure you will,' Sade replied. 'Do you know the Finnish myth for how the aurora borealis originated?'

'I do, but I would love for Myla to hear it from you,' said Esteri, tearing her eyes from the stars to look at Sade with interest.

'Well, as you know, Esteri, in Finland our word for the aurora is *revontulet*, which translates as "fox fires", right?'

Esteri nodded.

'The story goes that the Arctic foxes run over the fells and

158

through the sky, and when their tails brush against things it sends colourful sparks into the air, and that's what causes the phenomenon.'

'I love that,' I said, turning my gaze back upwards in the hope of seeing sparks.

Sade and Kalle took their leave back inside and left Esteri and me standing there. It was absolutely freezing, but too beautiful to feel the frost.

'You've had a good day, haven't you?' I asked my friend.

'One of the best days,' she confirmed. 'I have family again now. It's the best Christmas present ever.'

That knocked the wind out of me for a moment. Family. I had my family at home, preparing for Christmas, with a new addition on the way. Even with my mum all the way over in Malta, she was still my family.

'It's nice when Christmas can be about family, you know?' Esteri added, and I just nodded, because somewhere, somehow, very very deep down – like, the bottom of a frozen-over lake deep – I thought maybe I did know that.

We drove back to Luosto the following day, after a deliciously silent sleep in the wilderness, and a morning of more great food.

In the car, as we neared our Lapland home in the late afternoon, Esteri said, 'I want to go back up there again, you know?'

'Of course,' I said, totally getting it – it was gorgeous up there. 'Kalle said you were welcome back anytime.'

'And you too.' Esteri smiled. 'I feel like … I don't know …'

'What?' I prompted.

'I feel like I want to go back properly. There's so much I still don't know about Lapland, so much to explore. I mean, just take the North of Lapland … the history and culture. I don't know.'

'You want to move there?'

'I don't know,' she repeated, and then went quiet, lost in her thoughts. She didn't speak again until we turned into Luosto village to drop off the hire car, where Daan would pick us up if we called him. When she turned off the engine, Esteri spoke. 'It just feels like change is on the horizon, you know?'

Chapter 22

We walked back into the chalet that evening, kicking off our snowboots with a series of thunks and then padding our way over the wooden cabin floor into the living room. I was mid-yawn when somebody thrust a bowl under my face with two scraps of folded up paper inside.

'Great, you're back!' said Jens, one of the elves.

'Hello,' I replied, suspiciously.

'We decided to do a Secret Santa, since we'll all be away from our families this Christmas,' he said, his happy elf grin plastered across his merry face.

'Oh, that's OK,' I replied, my usual response over the past few years to what seemed to be the obligatory work-place Secret Santa.

Jens lowered the bowl, and the corners of his smile a bit.

'You don't want to do the Secret Santa?' he asked.

I hesitated, looking at the faces of my workmates, who

looked over at me while I stood there, gormless, holding my overnight bag. 'I mean, yeah, of course I do, I just meant, you know, don't worry if everyone else is already sorted, hahaha.'

Jens' smile returned, full-width. 'Great. We've already all picked, but you two need to select your names.' He shook the bowl and the two papers flittered about in the bottom.

'What kind of thing are we giving? It's just, I didn't bring anything very gifty.'

'We're doing home-made,' he answered.

'Greeeeeat.' I grinned through gritted teeth. Home-made *what*? I could make someone a spaghetti bolognese if they wanted? I'm sure that would be just the gift to find under the tree on Christmas morning.

I picked a name from the bowl and unfolded it, keeping it hidden from Esteri and Jens beside me. My eyes widened. Now this was a stroke of luck.

Myla

Jackpot. I can easily make something for myself, because what do I care if it's crap? Ha, Christmas was maybe, just maybe, throwing me a bone this year after all.

Beside me, Esteri folded her own paper back and put it in her pocket, then took me by the arm. 'Come along, let's put our stuff back in our room and then we'll make some dinner.'

I followed her up the stairs and along the corridor to

our room, and when inside, she closed the door and faced me, her eyes narrowed. 'You picked your own name, didn't you?' she accused.

I gasped in the manner of a Victorian woman being accused of showing her ankles. 'No!'

'Yes you did.'

'Fine, then yes. But how did you know?'

'Because your face went from, "I don't want to play" to "Sure, I'd love to" in zero-point-five seconds.'

'It's just because I'm no good at handicrafts, so if I have me then there's no pressure.'

'If you have you, there's no fun.' She snatched the paper from my hands and tossed me hers instead.

'But, if you have me then it's not secret anyway,' I protested.

'Maybe I'll swap with someone.'

'Oh.' I sighed, and unfolded my paper.

Angelique.

Well, at least she was a guide so I vaguely knew her and what she might like. I wasn't sure about her spag bol preferences though.

'What shall I make?' I whined, which I immediately regretted because Esteri didn't seem like she'd be one to tolerate whining.

But she merely laughed, patted me on the back, and gathered up her toiletries bag to leave the room. 'It's Christmas, use your imagination, and remember that everything is magical at Christmas so sprinkle on some love and it will be loved.'

'It will be loved,' she said. Hmph. Not likely.

I was standing in the forest behind the chalet a couple of days later, making the most of the light late-morning while I had a break in work. And in my hands were some sticks.

I held them together, a scrunchie hairband wrapped around their lower halves, trying to figure out why a bunch of twigs looked like a classy bit of room decor when it was bought in a department store, but just looked like the Blair Witch's pitiful cousin when I tried to do it. I couldn't give Angelique this. I added one more stick. Nope, definitely not.

Sighing, I took back my scrunchie and dropped the sticks to the ground. Everyone here took Christmas so seriously, how was my gift going to compare? I could just picture it now, Christmas morning, and someone will have knitted someone else the softest sweater. An elf will have created, from scratch, a gingerbread house for one of the guides, a perfect replica of our staff chalet with working lights inside. Another guide will hand-cure some dried reindeer meat for one of the reps, seasoned with their family's secret recipe. And then I shall present Angelique with the inside of a toilet roll that I'll have drawn eyes onto.

I wondered if I could cut the Topshop label out of my scarf and pretend I'd crocheted it myself...

Then an idea began to form. I was actually good at one thing, thanks to my degree and previous job. I did have a good eye. And I knew a little about photography, and had a decent camera on my phone. And there was a printer in the activities' lodge, albeit a black and white one. A sparkle of excitement ran through me, one I hadn't felt in a long time. Could cold-hearted me be actually looking forward to making somebody a Secret Santa gift after all?

Over the next couple of weeks, as December stretched on, Christmas drew closer and the daylight hours grew shorter, I counted down the days. Not in anticipation of the big day, but more a private Advent calendar of when I could stop holding my breath and waiting for something bad to happen. I figured, if Christmas Day arrived with no disasters, I could consider myself safe this year.

That was my goal: make it to when the clock passes midnight on Christmas Eve night without throwing in the towel. And so, I kept my head down, my work schedule busy, and my sleep restful. I had days where I worked with Esteri, and days when I only saw her when we both crashed onto our bunks at the end of a long day.

Being outdoors all day, every day, was doing something to me – it was opening up my artistic side again. Little flecks of nature would catch my eye or inspire me. Plus, whenever I had the chance, I snapped a candid photo or two of Angelique. Not in a creepy, hiding in the bushes way – I always made it known to her that I was there taking pics, I just didn't tell her some of them were specifically of her. And one day, while she had one hand on a reindeer and a low sunbeam was just streaming on her from between two trees, and she was laughing her head off at something Esteri was saying, I got my photo.

'Yes,' I whispered to myself. 'Take that, Christmas.'

Converting the picture into black and white on my phone, I was pleased to see it looked even better. I printed it out that night, laminated it (hey, this was home-made) and then stuck it in a cardboard frame that I nicked, also from the activities' lodge. I hoped she liked getting a picture of herself, and didn't think it was a bit odd, but I did think it captured a nice moment, a nice memory, if I do say so myself.

During this time, I found myself crossing paths with Josh more and more, each time feeling a flutter of pleasure at seeing him, and then each time getting irritated with him and the lack of being able to hold a proper conversation due to his always being in elf mode.

In fact, it wasn't until the middle of a mass snowball fight in the forest beside Santa's cabin – a large group of guests vs their guides and the elves – that he suddenly broke character for a minute.

We'd just ducked into a small, snow-covered wooden *kota*, a Lappish hut. It was a permanent shelter not far from the Love Adventuring Lapland activities' lodge which, thanks to the firepit in the centre, was sometimes used to make guest dinners or to host speakers.

Inside, Josh and I huddled together, the smell of woodsmoke within and sounds of muffled shouts and laughter now outside. We caught our breath, ready to run our separate ways and grab new ammunition at any moment. Then he turned to me, his face close to mine while we squashed together, all damp and panting and peeping through the doorway, and he said, 'Having fun?'

'What?' I asked, surprised to hear his normal voice, albeit as a whisper, and not 'performer Josh'. 'I mean, yeah.'

He frowned a little. 'Are you sure?'

'Yes, totally. Snowball fights are fine.'

'Snowball fights are fine?'

I laughed, quietly. 'I just mean ... ' I trailed off, but he didn't look away from me.

'I think I know,' he answered.

I searched his eyes, a snowball dangling from my upturned fist. 'You know what?'

'How you're feeling.'

'You do?' Did he feel the same?

He looked serious for a second, like he was worried that I was worried. 'I wouldn't tell anyone, you know that.'

'What is there to tell?' I asked.

He leant closer and whispered in my ear so only I could hear, as if while he was there the rest of the world wasn't. 'I don't think you're quite as into Christmas as the rest of us.'

I pulled away, and my heart began to race. *He knows, oh God he knows.* 'No,' I stammered. 'That's not true.'

But his arm stayed on mine. 'It's OK. If you want to talk about anything, I'm here.'

I swallowed, searching his eyes with mine, wanting to ask him a million things like, How did he find out? What did I do wrong? Was he going to tell anyone? Did he think I was a horrible person? Instead, I ran my eyes over his elf costume, and said, 'You're not often here just as *you*, though.'

'That's a fair point.' He was interrupted by a snowball soaring over the tree trunk and landing in front of the open doorway. 'We've gotta go. Do you want to hang out tonight?'

I paused, mid-scoop of a pile of snow. 'What? Like a date?'

Another two snowballs pelted the ground before us. Our opposition were drawing in.

Josh stumbled over his words, checking back over his shoulder, keeping his voice low. 'I, uh, I was just meaning we could grab a beer at the chalet, but, yeah—'

'Oh, yeah, sure, let's do that. That would be nice.' I was so embarrassed, of course he hadn't meant a date. I didn't even want it to be a date, for God's sake.

I reached out and grabbed an armful of snow, avoided his eyes, and whispered a final, 'See ya,' and left the *kota* to take off in the other direction from him.

That evening, after I'd showered, I resisted the temptation to crawl straight into bed and instead went down to the lounge, where Josh was waiting with two beers.

'Hi,' I said, joining him, curling into one of the tartan felt-covered armchairs while he occupied the corner seat of the sofa next to me.

He handed me a beer. 'Hi. Any bruises from the snowball fight?'

'Nothing to write home about,' I laughed. 'You?'

Josh shook his head. 'No. I'm sure I left some on other people though.'

'Of course you did,' I snickered.

He leant forward, dropping his voice, and said to me, 'Listen, I'm sorry if I put you on the spot before or made you feel uncomfortable—'

'No, no, it's fine,' I said quickly, glancing at our fellow Love Adventuring Laplanders scattered around within earshot. There could be no gut-spilling tonight.

'OK.' He looked like he wanted to say something else but was trying to choose his words carefully. 'You know, though, I'm not going to . . . '

'I know,' I said. I knew he wouldn't tell anyone, I trusted him.

'And not just because, you know, I wouldn't, you know, *expect* anything—'

'Oh God, no, Josh, I know, it's fine.' I couldn't help but chuckle a bit. It was kind of sweet how much he was trying to get his point across. But I did need him to shut up now, so I changed the subject. 'Tell me about working as a surgical nurse in Seattle. Is it just like being in *Grey's Anatomy*?'

'Just like it. I've not personally been on shifts during quite such dramatic stuff, but I did get to help pull glass out of a guy who streaked through a movie set once and crashed into a prop window.'

'Whoa.' I raised my eyebrows. 'Was the glass . . . ?'

'Oh, it was *everywhere*.'

'Being an elf in Lapland sounds a million miles away from your usual job.'

'I don't know,' he replied. 'There's definitely less blood and cursing, but probably about the same level of dancing.'

169

I laughed, which made him smile though he tried to hide it with a sip of his beer. 'Tell me about you; what did you do before you came here?'

'I did . . . a few things. I used to have a design job I really liked but there were redundancies, so, you know. Since then I've not really landed on anything. I'm trying a bit of everything, I guess.'

'Like what?'

'Like . . .' I thought back over the previous year. But, if I was honest, I'd been pretty passive. I couldn't really claim I was 'trying' a bit of everything, it was more like I was 'agreeing to' a bit of everything. 'Mainly office jobs, a bit of retail.'

'Does it feel like a big change now to be working outdoors all day?'

'It does. It took some getting used to, but I do quite like it,' I admitted. 'It feels . . . hmm. Creative? Is that the word I'm searching for?'

'I get what you mean. I've always worked shifts so it's not like I switched from the office nine-to-five but it was definitely an adjustment. Especially the polar nights.'

'Yes!' I cried. 'At first I was like, I don't think I can live without more daylight, but it's amazing how quickly you adjust.'

'We're about to hit true polar nights, too. The sun won't rise above the horizon at all for a little bit. But it's kinda nice, now, right? Everything seems permanently . . . um . . .'

'Calm?'

'Calm,' Josh agreed.

'Plus, low lighting is flattering anyway,' I added.

'That's true.'

The conversation paused, and we both took sips of our beers, our eyes trailing around the room while we thought of what to say. I wondered if he felt the same as I did right now – like we could talk for hours if only we could be totally open and relaxed with each other. It was an odd feeling, one I hadn't had for a long time with a guy, and I liked it, but it caused my mouth to feel constantly dry and my mind to go blank, and a hummingbird to hover in my stomach.

Not literally.

'You said your parents are close by, near Seattle?'

'My mom and grandfather, yeah.'

'I bet that's nice.'

'It is,' he said, smiling. 'My grandfather is in his late eighties, but he still wants to go and do water sports every weekend.'

'Like, wakeboarding and things?' I asked, enjoying seeing Josh's face light up talking about his grandfather.

'Well, not quite that extreme, but his favourite thing in the whole world is parasailing. You know, when you're like, sitting in a parachute and being towed by a boat?'

'That sounds fun,' I said. I wondered if I could get my dad to do that on the Isle of Wight.

'Yeah.' Josh went quiet for a moment. 'I hope he's able to keep doing it for a long time.'

'Do you have a reason to think he won't?' I asked gently.

Josh looked down at his beer bottle. 'I don't know. He's just getting older, you know?' He paused, and then stood up. 'Another beer?'

'Sure.' I smiled. I watched him as he strolled to the kitchen, running his hand through his hair.

It was nice to get to know Josh a little more. And as he got me a beer, holding both in one hand between his fingers so he could also grab us two cookies from the stack on the side, he looked back and caught my eye and smiled, and I admitted to myself he wasn't *entirely* super-annoying.

Chapter 23

Christmas was fast approaching, only a few more Advent calendar doors away, and the excitement in the air was becoming harder and harder to ignore.

Guests seemed to be arriving in their hundreds every day, and we all worked hard to make sure every one of them left smiling and with a little extra magic in their hearts than when they arrived. Yes, even me. With not long to go now until Christmas was behind us, I was clawing my way to the finish line.

Even though Josh now knew my secret, I wasn't worried. I trusted him. And besides, despite my internal screaming at times, I was doing nothing to give away that I wasn't equally full of Christmas spirit as the rest of 'em.

Just sometimes, I had to work a little harder to keep up the show ...

'Esteri,' I called, jogging over the snow as best I could dressed like the Michelin man. I'd just finished for the day after doing four consecutive snowshoe tours, and was heading back to the staff chalet from the activities' lodge, where Daan had released the next week of rotas. And something was concerning me.

'Esteri?' I called again, and this time she heard me and turned.

'Oh, hello!'

Catching up with her, we walked through the pine trees to the chalet together. 'How was your day?' I asked.

'Great, as always. I was with a group over in the National Park all day, so a lovely mix. You?'

'Snowshoeing.'

'All day?'

'Yes, but that's fine. It's my favourite, actually.' Because there wasn't a jingle bell or Santa suit in sight. 'Esteri?'

'Yes, Myla?'

'Just wondering . . . You like cooking, right?'

'Yeah?'

'Do you fancy baking some gingerbread tonight, and maybe decorating it together?' I was being totally casual so she wouldn't suspect a thing.

'Do you not know how to decorate gingerbread?' she asked, seeing right through me like some kind of detective from *CSI*.

'What? No, *of course*, I just thought it would be fun. Room-mate bonding.'

We reached the door of the chalet and Esteri held it open for me, usuring me into the boot room to de-Michelin man. 'So it has nothing to do with the fact you're rostered

174

on to help with the Mrs Claus gingerbread decorating day tomorrow?'

'No, not at all. I *know* how to decorate gingerbread, believe me, I am never more comfortable than when I have a piping bag in my hand— OK, fine, I've never done it before, please help me.'

Esteri chuckled and we took it in turns to pull each other's boots off. 'All right, well, even though I was hoping to have a nice relaxing evening of sauna and reading my book, I will help you.'

'Thank you.' I smiled gratefully.

'But I doubt we have any icing in the chalet, so you and I will need to head back to the activities' lodge and do some thieving.'

'Good plan,' I nodded, 'under the cover of darkness.'

'It's dark now, in case you hadn't noticed,' she said, pointing at the Arctic night outside the window. 'We'll go back after dinner, when there won't be as many people around.'

I was ready for our heist. Dressed in my dad's bulky coat and only one layer of thermals underneath, Esteri and I snuck back over to the activities' lodge where we pilfered a tiny amount of their vast stash of royal icing, piping bags and food colouring, and stored it inside my jacket.

Back at the chalet, Esteri whipped up a batch of gingerbread and had me use a cookie cutter she found to turn it into a mixture of hearts and snowflake shapes. The scent of ginger and cinnamon was enough to encourage various other staff members out of hiding, sniffing the air.

Before long, the first batch of cookies were cool enough, and Esteri had shown me how to make the icing, put it in a bag, and how to squeeze it out ever-so delicately to create pretty loops and waves bordering each biscuit.

'Like this?' I asked, my first snowflake done. I was pretty pleased. It wasn't perfect but it was … icy.

'No,' Esteri said with that bluntness I kinda liked.

'No?'

'That looks like one of the children did it. It looks like a very sad, melted snowflake.'

'Oh.'

Around me, my colleagues were wandering in and out of the kitchen, nibbling the gingerbread dough, pulling up a chair and a piping bag to join in, making a drink and watching *my* attempt, which seemed a little unfair. Somebody turned on some Christmas music, and dammit, this was never supposed to be an impromptu Christmas party.

I splodged some more icing onto one of the hearts, trying to write my name just to get the hang of handling the piping bag.

'Mujoee?' Esteri read over my shoulder.

'I think it says Myla,' Angelique said, coming over.

'Thank you,' I said.

The door from the boot room into the chalet opened and out of the corner of my eye I spotted Josh walk in with a couple of the other elves. He had his hat in his hand, his hair a bit wet and messy, and he was laughing at something one of the others said. I looked away quickly as he started to turn towards the kitchen, so he didn't spot me staring.

'All right,' Esteri was saying. 'The next batch of cookies are nearly done so I need you to watch the oven for me to make sure they don't burn.'

'On it.' I nodded, one eye on Josh as he entered the opposite end of the kitchen and shuffled past the hoards to grab himself a beer from the fridge, checking out the cookie decorating station we'd set up over the large table on the way. I cringed seeing him studying my 'Myla' cookie with an amused smile on his face.

Esteri appeared at my side again, a bowl with bright green icing in one hand and a wooden spoon in the other. She sniffed at the air around the oven, and all of a sudden shoved me aside.

'Myla, they're burning!'

'Oh, shit, I'm so sorry.'

Esteri pulled the tray from the oven, and they looked fine to me, perhaps more of an auburn than a ginger, but close enough. I waved a little plume of smoke away from the air.

'I told you to watch them,' she said.

'I did. I was. I was just—' My eyes flicked involuntarily over towards Josh who was still hovering in the kitchen, chatting to others.

Esteri stood in my line of vision and put her hands on her hips. She whispered to me, 'Do you like Elf Josh?'

'What? *No*, not at *all*,' I spluttered. I looked around her at his elf costume. 'Believe me, he's completely *not* my type.'

She just smirked and drew my attention back to her. 'Yeah, when is a good-looking ray of sunshine anybody's type?'

'Well, he's not mine.'

Esteri shrugged and started loading the cookies onto a baking tray just as Josh looked over and met my eye.

'Oh, hey, Josh.' I waved across the room like a lunatic. *Oh, Myla*.

He raised his beer bottle in return and then one of the reps stepped in between my view of him, picking up my Myla heart and chomping down into it. Esteri side-eyed me. 'What? I was just saying hi. I barely see him out of his elf character now, that's all.' Apart from the other night, when we got to talking . . .

'Sure,' she replied, and handed me the icing bowl. 'But anyway, are you ready for round two?'

By the time I'd finished scooping the icing into a new piping bag, dropping only one great dollop on my foot, I looked up to see Josh leaving the kitchen. I saw he had icing on the back of the hand he held his beer in, and looked back at the table to see he'd left one there, decorated.

'Let's be careful this time, OK?' Esteri said, holding her hands over mine like we were in a romantic movie scene and she was teaching me how to play golf.

Over the next thirty minutes, Esteri, bless her heart, helped turn me into someone that looked like their gingerbread cookies had fallen face-first into a vat of icing, to someone whose gingerbread cookies resembled that of only a mildly intoxicated contestant on *Bake Off*. Well, if I was being incredibly generous with myself. Either way though, it was a vast improvement, and I felt more confident going into tomorrow's gingerbread decorating workshop than I would have before.

Most of our colleagues had scarpered with their own creations as cleaning up time loomed, and the least I could do was to now release Esteri to enjoy her evening.

'Are you sure?' she asked, one foot already out the door and hopping towards the sauna.

'Yes, of course. And thank you.'

She paused and looked down at the table. 'Is this the cookie Josh made?'

'Is it? I don't know,' I lied from over by the sink.

'I think it is. I saw him decorate one and then leave, back when you were throwing icing on the floor. Have you seen it?'

'No. Do you think I should go and give it back to him?'

'I think he left it for you.'

I frowned in confusion and walked over to the table. There, on the corner, was one of the heart-shaped gingerbreads, topped with white icing expertly calligraphied into the word *Myla*.

'That's your name,' Esteri hissed. 'In a heart.'

'Yes, I can see that,' I replied, looking around to check no one was watching. My own heart thudded with a sparkle of what this could mean. He left this for me. My name, in a heart.

'Do you think he likes you too?'

'No, no, of course not, and I don't like him like that,' I whispered, picking it up. And then it dawned on me. 'You know what, this is nothing. I just remembered that he saw Lumi eat the "Myla" cookie I'd made myself. He was just replacing it. It doesn't mean anything.'

But even if that were true, even if it was nothing more than a friendly gesture, I was still in trouble. Because I could deny it to Esteri all I wanted, but I wasn't fooling myself.

I had a crush brewing. On an elf.

Just my luck.

Chapter 24

Christmas Eve. Every year, I do the same thing.

On Christmas Eve, I would wake up, realise what day it was, and just for a moment let myself remember the things I quietly loved about Christmas: watching *The Snowman* with Dad; the gravy Shay made; the time Mum made Christingles with me by candlelight because we had a power cut; my secret life-long crush on Colin Firth because of *Love Actually*; the song 'Sleigh Ride' when sung by Ella Fitzgerald because it's a jam and I think it can be enjoyed any time of year; the smell of mulled wine; the feel of home and family.

Then, though I never demand they come knocking on the door, the bad memories would inevitably show up like uninvited party guests who paid for the booze so you can't turn them away.

So instead you shut down the party, and all the memories, good or bad, get pushed aside.

Christmas Eve is, however, my favourite day around this time of year. It always has been. Once, because it was the epitome of weeks of excited build-up; now, because it means I've nearly made it to the finish line! And so, I wasn't even mad when I heard Esteri's voice whisper to me while I lay in bed, awake, looking up to the ceiling, at five in the morning.

'Myla? Are you awake?'

'Yeah. How did you know?'

'You stopped snoring.'

I rolled onto my side and hung my head over the bunk to look at her. 'I don't snore. You snore.'

'Merry Christmas Eve,' she said by way of reply, an excited grin on her face. 'Did you know that Christmas Eve is more celebrated in Finland than Christmas Day? We love Christmas Eve.'

'Christmas Eve is my favourite too!' I said, then lowered my voice back to a whisper. 'It's less pressure.'

Esteri nodded. 'And more special. Good, I'm glad you feel this way. Would you like to get up with me?'

'Sauna?' I asked, with hope.

'No. I'd like to make rice porridge for everyone.'

' . . . All right.'

She stepped out of bed and pulled a sweatshirt over her PJs, and an extra pair of socks over her feet. 'It's a tradition here to eat a bowl of warm rice porridge for breakfast on Christmas Eve, with some cinnamon in. I want to make it for everyone, but it would be nice if you could help.'

182

'Of course.' I made my way down the ladder.

'I hope you like it. Maybe it could be a tradition you could take home, then every Christmas Eve I could know you're having the same thing over in England, and it would be like we're having it together. Like family.'

'Ah, Esteri,' I said, pulling her into a hug, which she reciprocated for three seconds before pulling away.

'Come along,' she instructed, and we crept out of the room and along the corridor, then down the stairs, to the quiet and dark kitchen.

Esteri pottered about, whispering instructions to me as she placed a big, heavy pan on the stove and measured out a large quantity of rice and milk. I was in charge of stirring the rice in boiling water while she opened and closed cupboards until she found cinnamon, sugar, and some hazelnuts.

'Hmm. It would be better if these were almonds, but we only need one. We pop this in the pot at the end and whoever finds it in their bowl will have good fortune.'

As Esteri transferred the rice to the milk, the creamy, sweet aroma filled the air, and I kept on stirring, methodically. This was very relaxing. And just when we were finishing up, our first few 'customers' appeared in the kitchen, padding in with messy hair and crumpled pyjamas, wanting to stick on a pot of coffee or brew a cup of tea.

Esteri doled out small bowls of the rice porridge to anybody that entered the kitchen, topping each one with a sprinkle of cinnamon and sugar, and before long the chalet was coming to life. People returned for seconds, or sat down on the sofas in the lounge. Today was, apparently, going to be our busiest day of the whole season, so we all had an early start, and were more than happy to stuff ourselves with Esteri's delicious, filling, festive brekkie.

I know I was. That was why I had two helpings.

Fine, three helpings.

Josh entered the kitchen mid-yawn, flannel PJ bottoms down below and, you guessed it, a flannel shirt slung over the top, buttoned haphazardly, and currently lifted as he scratched his toned belly.

I held a bowl of porridge under his nose and waited for him to open his eyes.

'Merry Christmas Eve,' I said when he stopped yawning, started sniffing, and dropped his hand.

He laughed in delight. 'Merry Christmas Eve to you. Did you make this?'

I could tell he was picturing my gingerbread heart situation. 'Esteri made it.'

'Great. Thank you!'

'Elfing all day today?'

'Absolutely. What are you on?'

'A bit of everything,' I said.

'OK.' He took the bowl and began heading out of the kitchen. 'Thank you, and maybe see you around today?'

'Yeah, maybe,' I replied, my conversation glowing.

'Or at the Christmas party tonight?'

The party. Of course. I was about to have an internal grumble about my dislike of festive shindigs and then stopped myself. I was actually looking forward to this party. By tonight, I would have made it to Christmas.

'See you there.' I smiled.

Before heading out to work for the day, it was Secret Santa gift opening time. Not everybody could be in the chalet at the same time as we were all on different shifts, but the general agreement was those who were here now opened their gifts, those who weren't would get theirs later, and nobody should open them alone.

Trying to keep a total poker-face, I watched as Angelique opened her 'framed' photo and laughed with delight. 'This is gorgeous!' she cried. 'I don't know which magical photographer made me look even prettier than the reindeer but thank you!'

I smiled. I'd fess up at some point and send her the pic digitally. If she really wanted it.

When it came time to open my present I winked at Esteri, since I knew she was my not-so-secret Santa. The gift was small and wrapped in red tissue paper, and when I opened it, out dropped a fabric bracelet, woven from soft emerald-green plaid. A friendship bracelet! This was so sweet and thoughtful, and I loved the colour, so slipped it on immediately. 'Thank you so much, Secret Santa, whoever you are; I love it!' I said, winning the Oscar for Best Actress.

I stayed to watch a few other people open gifts, but then really had to get to work. And nothing, not even being late, was allowed to go wrong today when I was this close to making it.

*

Esteri and I moaned as our tired bodies lay down on the warm wooden slats. We were sneaking in a quick pre-party sauna after our long, busy day of work full of different excursions and activities. Esteri told me a Christmas Eve sauna is a must-do ritual here in Finland, but because we'd be at the party the whole evening neither of us wanted to risk not fitting one in later. So ten minutes now would tide us over.

'Is tomorrow ever as busy as today?' I asked my roommate, and in reply she let out a satisfied sigh.

'Yes, it'll be busy, but we get a slightly later start. Today just feels extra-epic because of the party tacked on the end as well. Are you feeling ready for tonight?'

'Hell yeah I am,' I answered, my eyes closed. The excitement in the air had been everywhere today; on faces, in smiles, buzzing energy through the cold, dancing in the snowflakes.

'I wonder if anything interesting will happen.'

'What like?'

'Well, you know, Christmas parties, dancing, mistletoe, Josh . . .'

'Shut up.' I tried to swat her but couldn't quite move my arm.

'All right, all right,' Esteri laughed, then said with determination, 'We will have fun tonight.'

Chapter 25

I could have been sixteen again, getting ready for the school Christmas dance. Only this time, I wasn't anticipating kissing a boy under the mistletoe, I was anticipating midnight, when the clock turned to Christmas itself. Because when that happened, I would have made it. Against all odds, I would be able to say I lived in the most festive place on earth, and survived without tragedy.

Since the Christmas party was mainly for the visitors, though all the staff were asked to join in (we couldn't drink, though), the Love Adventuring Lapland workers, including management, had been issued with special T-shirts with the company name on the back so guests would know who was who. Elves had to still be elves, albeit in slightly altered costumes, and Santa would be making an appearance.

Esteri told me that it was usual practice to jazz-up your T-shirt for the Christmas party, and since I'd brought barely any smart clothes with me, I ended up being bedecked in her array of festive party wear.

'Could you tuck the T-shirt into your knickers?' she asked me, standing back. She'd manhandled me into her jade velvet floor-length skirt with a big slit up the side, but the long-length red T-shirt was visible at the top of the slit.

'No, couldn't we pin the slit at the top so it doesn't come up so high?' I was insisting on wearing tights with the ensemble so I didn't freeze my bottom off walking from the staff chalet to the activities' lodge, where the party was being held, and Esteri was making it clear I was a difficult client for her to style.

My hair was up and with a Lauren-Conrad-circa-2008 side-plait which had tinsel woven into it, can you believe it, and while Esteri was adjusting my skirt and grumbling I snapped a selfie and sent it to my sister. I hoped she didn't give birth there and then in shock.

A message came back immediately.

Is that the least festive girl in England wearing TINSEL IN HER HAIR?

I smiled. On Christmas Eve, getting ready to go to a Christmas party, no less.

Whoa. When was the last time you went to one of those?

Well, I nearly went to one last year, at my old job, but then skipped out on it. And that party of Callie's that I don't want to think about was more of a Christmas-slash-engagement thing. So ... Maybe at uni?

Shay was typing, and there were a lot of pauses so I guessed she was deciding between bollocking me or pitying me.

In the meantime, Esteri finished pinning my dress and stood up. 'Perfect,' she said, and faced me to our mirror.

I stood on tiptoe to try and get the full effect of my not-full-length reflection, and quite liked what I saw, actually. The green of the skirt looked nice against my skin, the T-shirt was cute tucked in, my hair was interesting, and, was that a smile on my face? Well, I never.

Esteri was looking very glam indeed. She was wearing a bright red, flared dress that matched perfectly with the colour of the T-shirt which she wore over the top. She'd cut the neck wider, and stretched it out, giving it an off-shoulder, classic look. She had matching lipstick and curled hair with a red ribbon in it. 'Tonight, I am kissing one of the husky boys.'

I laughed. 'You can't kiss anyone tonight, you're working!'

She just raised her eyebrows at me, smugly. 'Who would you kiss tonight?'

'Oh nobody,' I said, probably too quickly. 'I have no intention of hoping for a kiss tonight.'

I'm not waiting under the mistletoe at another Christmas party for anyone. Not even Josh. I mean, of course not Josh, why would I want to kiss Josh, he's so annoying . . .

My phone lit up with Shay finally replying. For all the time she took, it was a short and simple sentiment:

Let yourself have a magical time tonight, and a Merry Christmas xx

Thanks, sis, I wrote back. Happy Christmas Eve and I'll FaceTime you all tomorrow xx

*

'Wow,' I said, on entering the activities' lodge.

'It's good, right?' Esteri stood beside me, beaming.

Staff were to arrive thirty minutes before the doors opened to the holidaymakers, to make sure we all were in the know about the evening's plans, health and safety procedures, rules and regs, and could have a quick mingle together before we were expected to mingle with guests. We were still allowed to interact with each other during the evening, but weren't allowed to purely move around in little cliques and should instead make everyone feel part of the Christmas family celebrations.

Walking from the staff chalet to the activities' lodge had been beautiful and perilous, like Britney in her *Toxic* video. Both Esteri and I were braving wearing trainers – hardly stilettos but also not exactly designed for Arctic trekking, our coats bundled around us, gripping each other as we crunched over the snow. The temperature felt like it had plummeted, but that could have been because I was wearing less than three hundred layers for the first time in over a month. And we had to stop halfway because the sky above the treetops sparkled with a billion diamonds.

'It's a good, clear night for Santa to make his rounds,' I joked to my friend, and she smiled up at the sky and nodded. I asked her, 'Are you OK?'

'Just saying a Merry Christmas to my family, up there.'

'Oh, I'm sorry.' I shut up quickly.

'No, it's OK, they like you. They say "*Hyvää joulua*" back, which is Merry Christmas in Finnish.'

'Oh! Hoov-eye Julia,' I mispronounced back, immediately cringing at my ineptitude.

We kept walking then and entered the lodge, where I couldn't believe the transformation.

Being a large, wooden structure nestled in a snowy forest in the lead-up to Christmas, the building had always looked festive to me. Tall, decorated Christmas trees stood proudly in the entranceway, Christmas music hummed in the background, and the air of excitement was always present. But tonight, Love Adventuring Lapland had gone all-out.

Now, the large, almost sports hall-like room that was used for indoor activities (like the gingerbread decorating workshop, or sometimes weddings) had long tables that were stretched along one end, their tabletops blooming with winter shrub and berry centrepieces, accented with chunky cream candles, while strings of gold stars dangled from the ceiling. The other half of the hall was left clear for a dance floor, or for guests to mingle, and capping one end was a stage where Santa would be joining the party at the beginning to wish everyone a Merry Christmas before he had to get going on his deliveries (and younger holidaymakers would be heading to bed). He would then be replaced with a band who would play a Christmas disco.

'This is gorgeous,' I said to Esteri, breathing it all in. It was truly a winter wonderland, but not in the white crepe way my school had done, this was magical. Maybe it would be a magical night after all, just maybe ...

He appeared at the other end of the hall, Josh, wearing his staff T-shirt but with a green waistcoat loose over the top,

191

and green trousers. A slightly cooler version of his elf outfit, considering he and the other elves would risk overheating spending all evening in their big felt ensembles. He carried a box, his arms bare and just slightly muscled, his hair – currently hatless – messily swept to the side while he helped out with final preparations. As I watched he laughed heartily at something somebody said and then swept his eyes around the room. He landed on me, catching me looking, and held my gaze for a moment.

'Jackpot,' Esteri whispered beside me, and then edged away, yelling out, 'Daan, what can I do?'

By the time I looked back at Josh he'd gone, and feeling a bit lost standing in the centre of the hall on my own, I scuttled after Esteri and helped her arrange the props for the photo booth.

'Love Adventuring Lapland workers, can I have your attention?' Daan called out and we all gathered around him.

'First of all, you all look wonderful and festive, thank you for making the effort but also for all wearing your Love Adventuring Lapland T-shirts. I think you'll stand out from the guests but still look part of the party, which is what we wanted. I hope you feel part of the party too, but remember, not too much.'

A chuckle went around the group.

Daan proceeded to go through the details of the party, reiterating fire escape plans and the plan for the evening. At the end, he added, 'The party will go on until one o'clock in the morning, but if you *really* don't think you can last that late please come and see me and don't just leave.

In my experience, guests will usually leave soon after midnight, many before, but I don't want to be the only staff member here with a hundred rowdy visitors from around the world. And . . . ' he paused, 'if you make it to the end, we'll crack open a little *glögi* after we've closed the doors.'

This time, we all cheered. *Glögi*, as I'd experienced way back at Santa Claus Village in Rovaniemi, was delicious. 'What time is your first job tomorrow?' I whispered to Esteri, who was making eyes at one of the husky men.

'Ten thirty. We all get a nice lie-in on Christmas Day.'

I nodded. I hoped to still wake up early enough to call home, and then I didn't have anything until late morning when I was taking some guests out on the dreaded snowmobiles.

When Daan dismissed us, we all raced about the hall making last-minute tweaks to decor, props, outfits, before the pre-band music was switched on and the soulful sounds of Ella Fitzgerald singing 'Sleigh Ride' filled the space (yay! My favourite!), and the doors were opened.

Outside, it had started snowing, and with the music, the smells, the beautiful scenery, my one much-loved Christmas song, I felt my heart rise in my chest, and a smile spread across my face.

I was, this Christmas, in this moment, *happy*.

'Good luck tonight, you silly Brit,' Esteri said beside me, uncharacteristically pulling me into a quick hug and kissing me on the cheek (actually, right on the ear, but I think she was aiming for the cheek).

'Thank you,' I laughed. 'What was that for?'

'Just because. You've worked hard. Good luck for a wonderful evening.'

'You too,' I stuttered, not quite sure what she was meaning, but grateful for the pep-talk which was actually more appropriate than she realised.

With that, the guests started to arrive, children running into the hall with big, wide eyes, trying to jump to reach the dangling stars and hitting the dance floor with amazing moves and zero insecurities. Parents followed, along with other adults, handing coats to the front desk and shaking snow from their hair and redoing their updos, having removed their hats.

The hall quickly filled up, the staff popping in our bright red T-shirts against reams of sparkles and maroons and forest greens. The elves were a huge hit with the kids on the dance floor, and during 'Last Christmas' I noticed Josh holding the hands of a little cutie-pie boy who could almost be a small version of him, and who seemed so entranced by Josh's elfdom that Josh even let him try on his hat.

All of a sudden, the lights dimmed, and a quiet jingling of bells broke through the hush. Knowing what was about to happen, I, and my colleagues, all gasped theatrically and started whispering, 'Is that . . . could it be . . . ' and suchlike, and for the millionth time on this trip I floated out of my body to look down and not even recognise myself.

OK. I know I'm an adult. I know I don't even like Christmas and I'm just happy that I've made it through to this crucial point without any disasters, but even I could feel the excitement permeate my cold, dead heart, and I found myself standing on tiptoes to try and see the door.

The chuckle started before we even saw him. A low, approaching, '*Ho, ho, ho, ho, ho,*' and while the children, who were practically crawling their way onto the stage, nearly exploded with anticipation, in he came.

'SANTA CLAUS!' '*Joulupukki*!' '*Père Noël*!' '*Samichlaus*!' People from all around the world, uniting over tradition and fun.

Santa made his way to the stage, waving and smiling from behind his big beard, while the Christmas music swelled.

As the crowd settled, Santa gave a speech about how happy he was to have all these visitors, how the reindeer were all fed and ready to get going, how he had a big night ahead, and how everyone at the party should eat a lot and be as merry as possible on the dance floor so they were nice and sleepy come bedtime.

There were whoops and squeals of joy from guests and staff alike. And from me.

Chapter 26

After Santa had done his bit, including posing for photos and chatting to anyone who wanted a moment with him, it was time for everyone to take their seats for the big, Christmas Eve feast.

I spotted my name on the seating chart and then made my way to the furthest table, along with a few colleagues and a number of guests. I saw with sadness that Esteri was heading in the opposite direction, but I was OK making chit-chat with strangers. What did I have to worry about now, anyway? I'd practically made it to Christmas!

Then, when I reached my place, my eyes fell on the name written on the card next to mine in curly cursive font.

Elf Josh

For a second, I looked at the words, my eyes tracing the lettering. Before I could react, he was beside me, pulling out my chair for me, all rosy-cheeked and in full elf-mode. I looked up at him for a moment, and his smile reached his eyes, which twinkled at me. I think he thought this could be a lot of fun, sitting next to me, who was being a normal human while he was a non-stop elf. He already knew how maddening he could be, but I felt like he might become even more so during this dinner.

When I went to sit down, he sat in my chair. He then began to introduce himself as Adventure Guide Myla to everyone at the table while I stood behind him laughing but kind of wanting him to move.

'Elf Josh, *I'm* Adventure Guide Myla,' I said after a minute. 'And you're in my seat.'

'No,' he laughed. 'That can't be right. You look more like an Elf Josh to me.'

This went on for a bit while I tried very hard not to roll my eyes or shove him out the way until eventually all the nearby kids were shrieking at him with glee that *he* was the elf and he was in *my* seat.

Eesh, this was going to be a long meal. But when I sat down (finally), Josh's bare arm brushed against mine, and inside me a tiny flame ignited.

It reminded me of being back on the plane, before I even knew his name.

An aromatic dinner of baked ham with cloves dotting the mustard and breadcrumb coating, salty fresh fish and a rich casserole was served. The band played low Christmas classics, the dangling stars above us twinkled in the candle-light, and while I chatted to the people on my left and Josh

197

chatted to those on his right ... our arms kept touching. It was impossible not to, the table was packed, and better that we kept nudging up against each other and gave the guests a little more elbow room. But ... I know my right forearm didn't *need* to be resting on the table while we waited for dessert, with his left arm doing the same, as we both turned our heads away from each other to talk to those on our other sides.

But my skin against his, the contact, the knowledge of our fingers so close they could almost entwine, had me struggling to focus on what anyone was saying.

It didn't mean anything, I told myself, when he shifted away to reach for the sparkling water. It had just been a long time since anyone had touched me physically, in any way, as more than a friend and it was just making my hormones stir. That was all.

'Adventure Guide Myla, do you like Elf Josh?' asked the little girl in front of me, and if she didn't look like a tiny angel, I would swear she was trying to meddle.

'Um,' I hesitated, refusing to look at Josh who was theatrically leaning his chin on his hands waiting for my answer. 'Yes, of course, he's a very good elf. But he's quite a naughty elf, you know.'

'Why?' asked the little angel.

'Well once, he threw a snowball right at me.' The kids looked unimpressed. 'And another time, I'm pretty sure he laughed at my gingerbread cookie decorating.'

'You wouldn't laugh at my gingerbread, would you, Elf Josh?' Little Angel turned to him.

'I might eat your candy cane,' he said, trying to reach over and she laughed and thwacked him with her plastic spoon.

'Do you like Adventure Guide Myla?'

'I do,' shouted out the boy who reminded me of a small Josh.

'Thank you,' I said to him, and caught the eye of his mum who chuckled.

Beside me, Josh leant his head on my shoulder and sighed, and for a second I had a view of those dark eyelashes from above, of the shape of his nose, the smell of his shampoo. 'I do like Adventure Guide Myla, very much,' he replied. I held my breath. What did he mean by 'very much'?

I let out a small laugh and added, 'We're all good friends here in Lapland.'

At that moment, one of the other elves came over and tapped on Josh's shoulder. He leant around, placing his hand on the back of my chair for support, while she whispered in his ear and I tried to pretend that his arm around my back wasn't all I could think about.

'Excuse me a minute, everyone,' Josh said, placing his (clean) napkin atop my head, causing more giggles, and I watched as he and the other elves gathered on the dance floor for an impromptu dance-off to 'Santa Claus Is Comin' To Town'.

As he joked and laughed with the other elves, in full performance for the room, I shook my head. I was just being sentimental and letting all this Christmas nonsense get to me.

*

Following the meal, the Christmas party ramped up big time. The music got loud and the Christmas spirit was overflowing, in more ways than one. I spent a while going in and out of the photo booth with Esteri, other staff members, and guests of mine from today's activities, and even enjoyed a little dance on the dance floor, albeit a bit self-consciously.

When the band took a break and the playlist came back on, I took myself to the edge of the dance floor for a breather. It was after eleven, and I could see some people tiring, while others seemed on a second wind as they counted down the minutes until Christmas Day.

I, for one, would quite like to go and sit in the sauna again and have some quiet time right now, but even if I did, I knew I wouldn't wind down. I was too excited. Christmas was nearly here. I'd nearly made it.

The lights were dimmer now, with a glitter ball (had there always been a glitter ball in here?) slowly rotating and creating stars upon the dancers.

In the dark, at the edge of the dance floor, I closed my eyes for a moment. And that's when the music changed. 'Rockin' Around the Christmas Tree' melted into 'Bleeding Love', and I was right back there in my mind, aged sixteen, at my school disco, watching my first unrequited love kissing my friend.

CHRISTMAS 2007 ~ AGED SIXTEEN
The mistletoe was the first thing I saw when I walked into the school's Christmas party. A thousand thoughts and scenarios twirled through my teenage mind as I imagined how it would play out when I told Rick how I felt.

The school hall was decorated in white fairy lights, white crepe snowflakes hanging from the roof, and that all-important mistletoe. What a spot to have my first kiss, finally, under the mistletoe.

Rick was my friend, he'd been my friend since primary school, but over the past two years I'd fallen in love with him, the way he laughed and the way he and I had our own inside jokes and nicknames for each other. He called me Molehill and I called him Rinkle.

The evening flowed and my confidence ebbed, but a series of slow songs had started and the night would be drawing to a close in less than half an hour. The last thing I wanted was for the bright overhead lights to switch on, highlighting my dragged eye glitter and frizzed hair while I was declaring my love for my friend.

'Where's Rick?' I asked another friend, Sarah, trying to be casual even though my heart was thudding so loudly she must have heard it over the beat of the music.

Sarah shrugged, and went back to twirling her hair, trying to catch the eye of her own crush on the other side of the dance floor.

'Bleeding Love' by Leona Lewis was playing, the melody and bass filling me up with confidence while I searched the crowd of year elevens before me. I didn't want to step too far from the mistletoe, and I pressed my fingers to my lips, imagining him kissing me after I'd told him.

'Oh, there he is.' Sarah broke into my thoughts and my heart leapt, a smile spreading under my fingers while I tried to follow her eyeline.

This is it; I'm ready to tell you everything, Rick.

'Ah, bless, he's kissing Ashley,' Sarah chuckled.

I saw him then, his arms around one of my best friends, his

forehead against hers, his lips on her lips. She smiled into him; I could see it even from the sidelines. My heart broke in that moment.

Sarah leant in. 'She's fancied him for ages, she must have told him. They're so cute.'

Despite my throat drying, I said, 'She has? She never said.' Neither had I.

'It looks like he likes her too, yay!'

I tried to smile, but all my hope, all my dreams, were pooling in the corners of my eyes and I tried to blink them down.

School parties were always an excuse for people to kiss their classmates, but Rick rarely joined in. He must think Ashley is pretty special.

And she is. She's lovely, and funny, and pretty, and, like me, I knew this must have meant a lot to her. I took a step back.

'I'm just going to get another drink,' I said to Sarah, who gave me a thumbs up. But I didn't get another drink, instead I stepped back into the shadows, hiding in the dark, and couldn't take my eyes off Rick and Ashley as they slow-danced and kissed all while I and the mistletoe wilted away alone.

I tilted my head back, looking towards the ceiling and willing the painful memory to float away, and fluttered my eyelashes open.

My mouth curved into a smile, and then I let out a laugh. Of course I'd be standing under the mistletoe right now. It was sod's law. Poor teenage me, she was so sure her life was over in that moment.

I let my eyes close again, and to the soundtrack of Leona Lewis, I let myself, actually *let myself* be back there with her.

You know what, remembering wasn't so bad, at least that memory. I still appreciated teenage me's pain in that moment, and felt for her. But I guess one of the good things about growing up is you can look back at things in your past and tell yourself it gets better. And Christmas may have remained sucky, and maybe always will, but if Rick and I had kissed that night, he may have become my boyfriend, or broken my heart, or I might have made choices that would have affected my life because of him. He's married now. And did I wish I was with him? No.

I must have looked a little odd standing there with my eyes closed under the mistletoe, but I didn't mind. And when I opened them, like a magnet they met Josh's across the other side of the dance floor, and he looked away quickly.

Chapter 27

On Christmas Eve night, over the past few years, I've fallen asleep in bed watching something completely out of season, like a summer road-trip movie. In fact, last year, after refusing Shay's invite to spend the holidays with her and Tess, together with my dad, and still wallowing over the loss of my dream job, I'd holed up in my flat alone and cranked up the heating. With Jamilia away with her friends on a winter sun holiday that she didn't invite me on, I padded around home in shorts and T-shirt, made myself margaritas, and watched *Mamma Mia!* with the curtains closed. This year, I had anticipated doing something very similar, and had already decided that I'd do an eighties theme of *Weekend at Bernie's* as my Christmas Eve movie choice, with perhaps *Dirty Dancing* for Christmas Day.

Usually, on the night of Christmas Eve, I do not stay up until midnight to celebrate the big day. Does anyone usually do that? The point, surely, is to go to bed early and wake up with Santa having been. Or in my case, go to bed early because you've had a sugar crash from margaritas and you're furiously refusing to believe it's Christmas tomorrow.

But tonight, for the first time in years, I was excited. I was right there with the other partygoers as the clock ticked ever closer to midnight.

You did it, Myla, I told myself. *You nearly made it to Christmas unscathed!* Now I could finally start to enjoy myself.

Hmm, that wasn't quite fair. I'd been enjoying myself more than I was letting myself believe. But now the pressure was off.

'Are you really excited for Christmas Day?' Esteri asked me, looking a little bemused as I jiggled next to her while we stood at the back of the hall.

'You have no idea,' I replied.

I kept checking my phone under the guise of taking lots of pictures, and then it was only five minutes away, then two, then one. And then the room erupted in choruses of 'Merry Christmas!' before the band struck up again for their final set.

I hugged Esteri, and gave myself a little hug too, beaming with happiness. I'd made it. I'd made it!

The guests were still having the times of their lives, with the party only thinning out slightly as any last visitors with children took them back to their nearby hotels. But I was buzzing – me, buzzing, instead of being a buzz-kill, so I was willing to stick it out until the end and try some more of that *glögi*.

Separating from Esteri again, I took a lap around the

edge of the dance floor, smiling at people and wishing them happy holidays.

As I came level with the stage, I dropped into the shadows and leant against the wall, taking a breather and watching the scene in front of me. The back of the stage consisted of a tall wooden backdrop painted with a snowy scene, and it created a hidden walkway between the stage and the wall, partially obscured by lengths of material hanging from the ceiling. And that's where I spotted Josh.

He reached out to me, his fingers slipping into mine, and he pulled me into the space with him. From back here, the music was muted, the crowd disappeared, and it was just him and me.

He held onto my hand for a second longer than necessary, before dropping it.

'What are you doing?' I asked, looking up at his face, aware of our close proximity with every inch of my body.

'Just taking a tiny break.' He smiled. 'I thought you might want one too?'

His hat and waistcoat were resting on top of a wooden crate beside us, and I realised that for the first time in what felt like for ever, it was really just me and him here. He wasn't in character; he was just with me.

'Well, hi, Josh,' I found myself saying.

'Hi, Myla.'

'I didn't even know about this area back here,' I said, gesturing around, trying to keep my eyes from flickering to his face and his lips and those eyelashes.

'Yeah, I just found it,' he said, his voice caramel. 'I'm

definitely not supposed to be back here and out of my costume. Don't give us away, OK?'

'I won't.'

'I hope you don't mind me bringing you in here; if you want to get back out there—'

'No, no, it's nice. I mean, not *nice*, but it's nice to take a break from being "on", you know?'

'I do know. Are you having a good evening?'

'I am, actually,' I admitted.

'You sound surprised.' Josh leaned back against the wall and gave me a lopsided grin.

'Um, not surprised, but . . . ' I chose my words carefully. 'I'm not usually great at parties. Unlike you.'

He shook his head, glancing down at our feet. 'Nice shoes,' he said.

'Back atcha,' I remarked, and he jangled his bell-tipped boots.

'I saw you earlier standing by the dance floor with your eyes closed, and you looked kind of sad. I nearly came over to check you were OK, but I thought maybe you'd seen enough of me by then, after sitting with me during dinner.'

'Are you fishing for a compliment, Elf Josh?'

He laughed.

I put my hand over my face for a second. 'I was just remembering something. I didn't mean to be looking forlorn and dramatic under the mistletoe.' I kept my voice light but we both heard it catch at that word.

Josh put his hands in his pockets and looked down again,

a flick of his hair falling over his forehead. 'I noticed you were standing underneath it.'

'I didn't even realise it was there . . . to begin with.'

His eyes flicked up and met mine, briefly, and my breath stopped.

On the other side of the stage, the band were playing 'Cozy Little Christmas', the Katy Perry song, and as we looked at each other wordlessly, I knew I couldn't pretend it wasn't happening. I had feelings for Josh.

And I think it showed.

At that moment, movement of someone else passing by the end of the stage pulled us out of ourselves. I grabbed Josh by the T-shirt and pulled him to me so we were both pressed into the dark, hidden by the curtain-like fabric.

Our bodies close, I untangled my fingers from his shirt, and realised his hand was behind my shoulder, holding us together and protecting my back from the hard wall.

We stayed quiet, close, both pretending it was because we didn't want to be caught flaking on our jobs, both aware the jobs had nothing to do with it.

'What are we doing back here, Josh?' I breathed, not making any movements in case he moved his hand, moved himself, and right now he was everything I didn't know I wanted for Christmas.

Josh moved his hand a centimetre further around me. 'I just wanted to say, before the night was over, a Merry Christmas, from the real me.'

'And to you,' I replied. 'From the real me.'

We looked into each other's eyes, as if we were seeing

208

each other for the first time. As if we were back on the plane, meeting each other, clueless how intertwined we'd become even when we couldn't spend much time together other than in our thoughts.

When his eyes left mine for a second, his eyelashes lowering as he glanced at my lips, I knew I wanted to kiss him. And he wanted to kiss me.

There was no turning back now. Whether I liked it or not, Lapland was going to have left an impression on my heart.

But the song drew to a close, and the sound of the band telling the crowd they were finishing up meant we reluctantly stepped away from each other.

For now.

Chapter 28

I lay in my bunk that night, in the early hours of Christmas morning, feeling more excited anticipation than I had in years. Something had shifted in me; I could feel it. It wasn't just from the warm and welcome glass of *glögi* I'd had at the end of the party alongside my co-workers and friends. And this wasn't my imagination; there was something between Josh and me. Had I known ever since we sat together on the plane? Maybe.

But now there were no more maybes. It couldn't have been more obvious.

I replayed the moments leading up to our near-kiss. The eye contact, our arms touching at dinner, the smiles, the glances, and then finally being alone with him, with all of his acting put aside and it was just him, me, and that electric space between us.

And now I couldn't sleep. Unlike Esteri, who, in the bunk

below, was snoring and occasionally chatting in Finnish in her sleep.

A thought danced through my mind like the sugar-plum fairy: what if he would be my *bad* memory from this Christmas? What if, as I held my heart near his, it would soon break like a fallen icicle?

Or ... What if I stop living in the past, or the future, for just tonight?

I rose from my bed and as quietly as I could pulled a jumper over my pyjamas and stepped out of our bedroom. In the dark corridor, I didn't quite know what to do with myself. I couldn't go knocking on Josh's door because a) he had a room-mate, and b) now I was standing here in the silence I didn't know what I thought would happen anyway.

I went downstairs to the kitchen and started making myself a hot chocolate as quietly as I could. In front of the hob was a small window with short, plaid curtains, which I pulled aside and peered out, looking up towards the moon.

'Is he up there?' came a soft whisper.

Turning, I saw Josh standing against the doorframe of the kitchen, his arms folded. He wore those flannel PJ bottoms and a Seattle Seahawks sweatshirt. His hair was a mess. He looked beautiful.

'Must be still out on his deliveries,' I answered, and he smiled. 'Do you want a drink? I'm making hot chocolate and I could split it with you?'

'Um, if you're sure?' He stepped into the kitchen and pulled up a chair at the table. 'You couldn't sleep?'

I kept my eyes on the milk, warming on the hob, stirring

it slowly with a wooden spoon, the steam rising to my face. Because if I looked at him, I'd give everything away. 'Yeah, just a busy brain, you know?'

He paused and then said, 'Me too.'

Dividing the milk between two pottery mugs, I heaped in some powdered hot chocolate and then something caught my eye. I looked up and out of the window. 'What was that?'

'What?' Josh came over, his body beside me, and he looked out of the window with me.

I pulled the curtain further aside. 'I thought I saw something, in the sky.'

Our eyes met and in a flash I was back in that cramped position behind the stage. 'Was it being pulled by flying reindeer?'

'No,' I laughed and peered back up at the sky. 'It was green.'

'The Northern Lights?'

'It could have been.'

'So let's go out and see.'

We scrambled ourselves and our hot chocolates to the boot room and pulled on our coats and snow boots as fast as we could, all while I tried to act totally normal.

Opening the door to the chalet, Josh exclaimed, 'Wow, it's freezing out here. Are you going to be OK?'

'For the Northern Lights, I'll be fine,' I answered, and followed him through the door.

The world outside was silent, sleeping. The snow was untouched, the top layer freshly frozen over, the imprints from party returners having softened over the past couple of hours. The trees were still and steady. My PJs and my dad's thick jacket were no real match for the deep cold, but nevertheless we stepped further into the clearing and craned our necks, searching between the trees for more swirling colours.

The only sounds were our breath, and the soft crunch of the snow under our feet as we moved in circles, exploring the stars.

'There!' I whispered, suddenly seeing the green glow move behind the very tips of one of the pines, off to one side.

It would have been wonderful to be up on one of the fells, or out in the middle of one of the frozen lakes, somewhere I could see a huge panorama of the sky instead of this small-lensed view from within the clearing of the trees, but even without the conditions being perfect, it felt perfect. I'd been here six weeks and this was the first time I'd been lucky enough to catch the aurora borealis.

Maybe I hadn't been looking up enough. Maybe I'd spent too much time looking down, trying to get Christmas out of the way as quick as possible.

The pale swirl of lime green mist, far, far above, moved softly as if it were in time with our breathing, as if it were another world opening up before us, and I barely noticed I was shaking.

'Are you OK?' Josh whispered into the silent night; his voice close.

'I'm great,' I replied, and realised then that my lips were numbing. I sniffed, inhaling the cold more.

'We should go in; we shouldn't get too cold.'

'Just a couple more minutes, just in case we don't see them again.'

'All right. Then . . . could I put my arms around you? I'm not trying anything; I just don't want you to freeze.'

I glanced at him and managed to move my lips into a smile.

He laughed. 'It's not a line. But it's fine if it's a no.'

'Come here,' I said, and I let him step closer.

Josh tucked me in under his arms, and we stood side by side but leaning into each other. Despite the cold, I felt warm against him. I liked my arms around his waist. I liked the feel of his breath on the top of my head.

I felt him looking down at me, his breathing shallow like he didn't want to make any sudden moves and break the spell. But by the time I looked up at him, he was back gazing up at the night sky.

Under the guise of searching for the Northern Lights, I gave myself permission to unashamedly study his stubbled jaw, his eyelashes, from beneath.

Twenty-four hours ago, if you'd told me I would be standing in the snow in the middle of the night with Josh's arms wrapped around me, wondering if I was moments away from kissing him, I wouldn't have believed you. Well, I would have blushed, denied it, told you he was way too annoying and then secretly wondered what his aftershave smelled like for a while.

Josh turned his head and looked into my eyes, the space dividing our lips no bigger than a whisper. His mouth curved just a tiny bit into a smile, which I returned. This was happening.

'I'm telling you; it's happening!' came an excited voice from the door of the chalet, and we broke apart with surprise as five of our colleagues spilled out into the snow, their faces turned towards the sky. 'Look up between the trees, over there, I saw it from the bathroom.'

Josh kept one arm around me and I glimpsed up to see him biting his lip.

At that point, Angelique spotted us. 'Hey, it's Myla and Josh. Did you guys see the aurora?'

'Yep, just a little bit,' I cleared my throat and called back.

'Was it amazing?' she asked.

'Yeah,' I said, and my hand found Josh's and I slipped my cold fingers inside his, buried between us and within the ends of our coats, something only we knew about.

Angelique pointed. 'Oh look, now I see them, you guys, come over here by Myla, the view is better.'

With that, the five other bodies waddled over the snow in their PJs and coats, giggling and whispering about Christmas miracles.

The spell was broken, but the magic was glowing both above and around us. With a final squeeze of Josh's hand, I broke away and, with a smile, said, 'I think I'd better go in before I turn into a snowwoman.'

Josh followed me back into the chalet, and I was wondering if we'd be able to steal any more alone time in the sleeping house, when I opened the door and it was like a slumber party from an American high school movie.

In the boot room, to the kitchen, to the living room, the staff were ambling about in PJs, having midnight feasts, pulling on outer layers, crowding around windows. Esteri was in the kitchen singing loudly and making another batch of rice porridge. She looked up when we came in and smiled.

'There you are, roomie!' She then clocked Josh next to me. 'Oh, *there* you are. Good morning, Josh.'

'Hi, Esteri,' he replied. 'Smells good.'

'It'll take a while to make. You know. I'll be in the kitchen for a while.' She winked at me.

Flustered, I just let out a nervous laugh.

'Josh, what was that camera setting you were telling me about that would make night photos come out better?' one of the other elves called across the room.

With a last smile at each other, and a pang in my heart, I whispered to him. 'Goodnight, Josh. See you in the morning.'

'Night, Myla. Thanks for the hot chocolate.'

'Thanks for keeping me warm.'

'Anytime.' Stuffing his hands in his pockets and treating me to a last smile, he made his way towards his friend with the camera, and I turned to Esteri.

'You don't want to use the room?' she asked me, quietly.

'No.' I brushed her away.

She shrugged. 'OK. Rice porridge?'

'Isn't it, like, three in the morning?'

'Is that a no?'

'No, I'll have some,' I said, and got myself a bowl, stealing a glimpse back at Josh, bent over the camera, explaining the settings.

'You all right?' Esteri asked, spooning me some of the warm, creamy porridge.

I nodded. 'Yes. I'm all right. More than all right.' In fact, ever-so-slowly, like the moving parts of a mechanical clock, things were starting to work themselves into a place pretty close to perfect.

Chapter 29

On Christmas morning, at a more respectable hour, I returned to the room from the shower to find Esteri FaceTiming with my dad.

'Here she is,' Esteri said with a smile, angling the phone towards me and my wet, straggly hair.

'Um, good morning!' I said, a burst of love popping through at seeing my lovely dad's face, smiling, from within my phone.

'Merry Christmas,' he called back, but Esteri was back facing my phone towards her.

'All right, so I'll let you speak to your daughter in a minute, Mr Everwood. Where was I? Ah yes, so he's an elf which means he has to *be* an elf all the time so it doesn't ruin the Christmas illusion. But she definitely *likes him* likes him, you can tell, you know?'

'Whoa whoa whoa,' I said, snatching for my phone. 'What are you doing?'

'Just filling your dad in on all the fun you've been having,' Esteri said, all innocent.

'She's been telling us about Josh,' came Shay's voice, and I looked at the screen to see my dad holding the tablet he was using further away.

'Oh great,' I said. 'You're all there.'

'Merry Christmas, sis-in-law!' Tess called out. 'Josh sounds delicious, go get him.'

'Yes,' said my dad. 'Go get him.'

Oh my god.

Esteri picked up her toiletries bag and left the room, chuckling, while I propped my phone on the side and ran my brush through my hair before twisting it up into a braid. I then took a seat by the window and looked at them all properly. 'Anyway, *yuletide greetings* to you all.'

'Merry Christmas, Myla,' they chorused, then Shay added, 'Are we allowed to say that to you?'

'Yes,' I laughed. 'But it's merry for me because it's nearly over.' *Was that still true?*

'What do you mean?' Dad asked. 'You're not home until the end of January, are you?'

'No, I just mean Christmas itself.'

'Doesn't all the Santa stuff in Lapland carry on after Christmas?' asked Tess.

'Well, yeah, and that's fine, that's what I signed up for, don't panic, Shay. But *I* know Christmas is over. Anyway,' I changed the subject, aware I was teetering on buzz-kill territory, 'how's your Christmas morning going?'

Dad checked his watch. 'Well, it's not yet eight here, so it's not been going long so far.'

'Speak for yourself,' Tess interrupted. 'Shay had a craving

for rice pudding at three in the morning so I was here in the kitchen digging in the back of the fridge for a Müller Rice in the middle of the night. Merry Christmas, me.'

'I had rice pudding, or porridge, in the middle of the night, too!' I cried. 'It's a traditional Christmas brekkie in Finland and Esteri makes a delicious batch. The whole house was awake and eating it because the aurora borealis were out last night.'

'Oh that's right, that's where I got the idea,' Shay said, absent-mindedly stroking her stomach. 'I'd been reading about Finnish Christmas customs yesterday to see what you might be up to.'

'What were the Northern Lights like?' asked Dad.

'And did you watch them with Josh?' added Tess.

'Yes, Josh was there but so was practically the whole house,' I white-lied to my sister-in-law. 'But anyway, the lights were incredible. We're living right in the middle of the forest so the view wasn't great, but I'm going to try and see them again while I'm here. Hopefully I'll get lucky and run a Northern Lights safari trip and see them then. Fingers crossed.'

'I'm keeping all my fingers crossed for you, honey,' Dad said.

'Thanks, Dad.'

I was glad he was spending Christmas with my sister, as he usually did. He'd lived alone since I'd left for university at eighteen, and although he insisted he was fine, I knew he enjoyed the holidays and I was glad Shay was able to be there for him.

As if he could read my mind, he asked, 'Are you going to call your mum today?'

'Yeah, at some point,' I replied.

'Shay wants to ring her a bit later because of the time difference in Malta.'

I nodded. I loved my mum, of course, but we weren't close any more. She had a whole new life and family, and she was happy, which was great, but it didn't undo the fact she left us. 'Are you turkey-ing today?' I asked them, pushing thoughts of Mum aside for the time being.

'Yes, we got one that feeds ten,' Shay said with pride.

'For three of you?'

'Four, excuse me.' She pointed at her stomach and licked her lips. 'What will you do today?'

'I'm on snowmobiles, I think.'

'Good luck!' they chorused.

'Oh, before you go,' Shay said, and I saw her reach for her phone and start tapping. 'I got you something.'

'What? But we don't do presents,' I said. Several years ago, when I'd stopped spending Christmas with my family, I'd told them not to worry about buying me gifts and that chatting to them on the day was enough. I know, who gives up presents, right? But it was just something I was able to control at the time. So over the years, although Shay and Dad exchanged gifts, I kept myself out of it.

'I know,' Shay said, 'but it's from all of us.'

'I told Shay that her getting you that job in Lapland was present enough,' Tess said, bluntly, and I smiled. I'd always liked Tess.

'Done,' Shay said, and my phone tinkled with an incoming email. 'I didn't want to send it over until today, but there you go.'

'What is it?'

'It's a ticket to go to an ice bar. You know, one of those experiences where you get shut in for half an hour and drink vodka through ice sculptures or some such thing.'

I gasped. 'No way! Wasn't that expensive?'

'Well, I just thought it would be fun for you to be a tourist one evening. There's a restaurant and bar made of snow and ice not that far from you, it's built every year and looks amazing. Besides, I'm using it as another bribe to stop you quitting early. You've made it this far.'

'When is it for?'

'Whenever you like – you have until the end of January, obvs, but you'll need to check availability on the day.'

'Shay ...' I said, touched, looking at my sister's face, all those miles away.

'Well, shush, I'm allowed to treat my baby sister from time to time and it looked nice.' She waved me away. 'Enjoy, and take photos.'

'I will. Thank you.'

'You're welcome.'

When I'd hung up the phone, I smiled to myself for a moment, reading the email confirmation Shay had forwarded to me. That was so nice of her. I wish I'd got them a Christmas present, now. And then I remembered ... I had. The *kuksa* that I'd bought at the Siida museum. And the reindeer for my dad. I'd bought them all Christmas presents without even realising ...

222

OK. I had to go to work now.

I put a little make-up on my face, including a red lipstick, because it probably was the right thing to do in Lapland on Christmas Day, not because I was feeling festive or anything like that, and certainly not because I wanted to draw attention to my lips in case I ran into Josh because all I could think about was the longing to kiss him. *Totally* not for those reasons.

Leaving the room, I made my way downstairs to where the kitchen was a mess but the members of staff who weren't on first shifts were cleaning up with a spring in their step.

I joined them, and was dumping cold rice porridge remnants in the bin when Angelique walked into the kitchen carrying some more empties and said, 'You know who I feel for today? The elves.'

I turned. 'What do you mean?'

'I mean, their job is amazing, and I bet they love being elves here on Christmas Day, the atmosphere is probably so fun, but after we were all awake for ages in the night, I would not have wanted to be out of the house by nine, greeting guests.'

Of course. Josh wouldn't be around all day. 'Yeah,' I agreed.

'Nice lipstick,' she said, smiling at me. 'What are you working today?'

'Snowmobile Safari.' I grimaced, unable to keep the trepidation from my voice.

'You don't like those? They're one of my favourites.'

'It's more that the snowmobiles don't like me. I've yet to take a trip out on them that's gone one hundred per cent smoothly.'

Angelique looked at her watch. 'Oops, better run, I'm on reindeer. Hey, maybe your Christmas gift this year will be that perfect, smooth, run.'

Chapter 30

Although Christmastime would go on here in our corner of Lapland for several more weeks, I was still feeling that change in myself when I stepped out of the house that morning for work. Like I wasn't so worried any more. And like I could appreciate the beauty around me.

'Morning, hello!' I greeted people I passed as I made my way first to the activities' lodge and then around to the snowmobile park.

Despite being Christmas Day, I was sure today wouldn't feel quite as busy as it had been recently. Not so many day-trippers, and the overnight tourists appreciated having a later start and a chance to open gifts with their families in their hotels before hitting the snowy hills for activities.

I hoped I didn't get us all lost in the woods and ruin everyone's Christmas or anything . . . No! That wasn't going to happen. It might be a little premature but I was going to believe we were *out* of the woods now.

I was taking a family out today for one of the longer Seeking Santa Claus snowmobile safaris, where we'd stop to spend time with the reindeer, huskies, Santa's cabin and I'd take them to some viewpoints. When I met them that morning, they seemed friendly and relaxed, here on holiday from Italy, and ready for a day of adventure. After showing the young teenage boy how he could transfer from his wheelchair to the snowmobile, his parents helped him on and off we went.

'Did you see the Northern Lights last night?' I asked the family when we stopped on the first fell for everyone to take some photos and have a snack. After the clear night, the sky was lit up with pinks and blues today, the sun still sleeping below the horizon but casting Happy Christmas colours up into our world.

'I did!' said the boy, whose English, like his parents', was brilliant. 'I woke up in the night and my bed is right by the window, so I said, *Mamma*, *Papa*, wake up.'

'It was incredible,' the mother agreed. 'My favourite thing about the trip so far.'

It had been pretty incredible. And with that, my mind flitted back to a memory of Josh watching them with me at three a.m. I was bursting to tell this family about how I'd watched them and with whom, but they probably wouldn't care so I should just focus on the job.

And what a job this was. For the first time on one of these snowmobile adventures, I found the wind stretching my face into a genuine smile as we zoomed and sliced our way through the snow to our different stopping points.

Everything was going well, much to my relief, and finally I could see why the other guides loved being on them so much. It was freeing, not scary, not if you let yourself be in the moment.

After I bid farewell to my family at the end, and was packing up my stuff in the activities' lodge ready to head home, Daan came up to me.

'Myla, great job today!'

'Really?' I said, pleased because . . . I thought so too.

'That family you took out just came up to me and wanted to sing your praises. They said you were a kind, friendly guide who made their Christmas incredibly special.'

'I made their Christmas special?' I repeated, the words catching in my throat. But I was the buzz-kill, had been for years. Making Christmas special was a talent that was beyond me, I thought.

'That's what they said. And I was watching when you came back in. You're confident on the snowmobiles now, aren't you?'

'I wouldn't say *confident*.'

'That's how it looked. Well done. You've come a long way.'

I beamed. 'Thank you.'

'Merry Christmas.'

I took a pause and a breath. I'd really made their Christmas special? I could do that, despite everything? And then out popped the words that I'd long felt like an imposter saying, only this time, it felt different. I meant them. 'Yeah. Merry Christmas.'

Chapter 31

It wasn't until I got in from work that I looked at my phone again. By this time, a sleepy Christmas spirit had swept over the chalet, the proverbial chestnuts roasting on an open fire. Candles burned, the fireplace was lit, workers were strewn around the living areas quietly chatting on phones or reading, old-fashioned Christmas music played from an Echo in the corner. It seemed we were all feeling the after-effects of the late night last night, followed by the three a.m. outdoor fun, and then a full day of manual work.

Trudging my weary limbs up the stairs, I opened the door to my room to see Esteri's towel and slippers gone, so she must be soothing it all out in the sauna. I would join her, but I had a call to return.

'Hi, Mum.' I smiled into the camera when FaceTime connected, hoping my face was still able to convey a modicum of festive spirit.

'Hi, sweetheart! Merry Christmas,' my mum said from all

the way over in Malta. Her hair, dark like mine, was swept up in a clip, with loose bits hanging down that probably hadn't been there at the start of her day. She wore a gold T-shirt and gold, sparkling earrings, together with her classic understated make-up. When she was my mum, at home, she was never the glamorous mum. She was just 'Mum'. She wore jeans and cosy sweatshirts. Now she lived some-where she probably rarely needed sweaters. She was now a restaurateur, so she'd evolved into dressing smarter, looking smarter. I don't remember her ever being down about the way she looked, but I guess people just change when their circumstances change.

My stepbrother stepped into frame behind Mum and waved. 'Hope you had a good day, Byron.'

'How was your day, honey?' Mum said, carrying the phone onto her porch, the sun dipping low behind her as she settled into a wooden chair overlooking the ocean. 'Did you cope all right with all the Christmas stuff?'

'Yeah, it was fine.' Mum knows I don't participate in Christmas, of course, but I've never actually listed all the reasons to her why. I know she's always felt guilty for leaving and there's no benefit to me piling that on. 'I went snowmo-biling today, and we had a big party yesterday evening which was actually a lot of fun.'

'Oh right, with the new boyfriend, Josh.' Mum nodded.

'What? No, he's not a boyfriend, nothing happened. I take it you've already spoken to Shay, then?'

'It was actually your dad that let it spill.'

Oh Dad. I loved him and his interfering ways, usually,

229

but the fact they even knew about Josh at this stage was a smidge mortifying. 'Anyway,' I changed the subject. 'What about you? What have you all done today?'

Mum went off telling me about the family present-opening, the family trip to church, the family meal and the family movie night they were about to sit down to, and even though it felt like a lifetime since she left, I couldn't help this nagging little stab that wanted to twist through me and remind me, *you're not part of her family any more* ...

I put my hand on my stomach to try and calm the angry little voice inside (that's where I imagine she hides and grumbles at me from), and as if sensing a shift, Mum changed tack. 'Myla, sweetheart, enough about boring old me. Please tell me everything about Lapland. Are you enjoying yourself?'

I hadn't meant that memory to bubble to the surface. Not now. With one more deep breath, I pushed it back down and released my hand. 'I am. It's been a lot of work, but I think I'm going to really like January.'

'Will it be quieter?'

'Not for a while, but I think I just feel a bit more settled now. A bit more like I actually live here, you know, so I can appreciate it more.'

'I do know.' She nodded, and I knew she was thinking of when she first moved over to Malta, once I'd started university. Before that, although Shay and I had both insisted on continuing to live in Yarmouth with dad, we'd gone to stay with Mum every other weekend, and we'd visited her in Malta a couple of times. It *was* beautiful.

'Is it hard to feel festive at the beach?' I asked, thinking already about where I should spend next Christmas.

She thought about it. 'No.'

Oh, maybe not then. Not that I would have definitely gone to *her* beach, but just some beach. Perhaps further afield.

When she didn't elaborate further on the 'no' (she didn't have to, I predicted she was thinking something along the lines of *it's always festive where family is*), I thought it might be time to ring off.

'Well, Mum, I don't want to keep you from your Christmas movie night. What are you all watching?'

'*Die Hard*, apparently.'

'You like *Die Hard* now?'

'No, but Byron wanted to watch it and I made us all sit down to *The Nutcracker* yesterday, so . . . '

I smiled at my mum. 'Still *The Nutcracker*?'

'Always *The Nutcracker*.'

'All right. Well, Merry Christmas to you all.'

'And to you, Myla. Call me again soon, OK? I want a video tour of your winter wonderland.'

I promised I would, and we ended the call.

So that was it. I'd made it not only *to* Christmas, but now to the end of the day itself as well. I yawned, visions of sugarplum fairies beginning to dance in my head.

Chapter 32

Over the following week, while December took its last stretch prior to New Year's Eve, I had a spring in my step as if the snow was giving way to the flowers. It wasn't, of course, it was thicker than ever. But with Christmas now officially back in its box for another year, I felt free, like I did every January.

It was like coming out of an anxiety episode, but one that always lasted a couple of months every year. Finally, I could see clearly again, and stop obsessing over the past, or, more accurately, stop trying to run away from the past. At least for another year.

Today I had the perfect day lined up. A morning at the reindeer farm – no specific tours, just being around to help and chat to visitors about the animals, which was always nice, followed by an evening on a snowmobile safari where we were going to be travelling for a while and then setting up a campfire and hoping to catch the Northern Lights.

Why was I excited about a snowmobile safari for a change? Well, two reasons . . .

1. Daan had recommended me to be included on this trip, following my Christmas Day family leaving the loveliest review on TripAdvisor. I'd been out on them once again since and I really felt like I'd settled into a confidence that I'd been missing before.
2. After my taster in the early hours of Christmas Day, I was beyond excited at the prospect of seeing the Northern Lights in all their glory.

It was a big group going out on the aurora safari today, so a few of us staff would be going. I didn't know if Esteri would be one of them, but I hoped so. She might sleep talk, and tell my family awkward things, and shove her boobs in my face on the daily, but she had fast become my favourite person in Finland.

The elves, and I'm really talking about Josh here, if I'm honest, were still just as hard at work as the rest of us, and that wouldn't let up just because the Big Day had now come and gone. Holidaymakers would still be arriving in Lapland in droves, certainly all through the remainder of the school holidays around the world, and then after for the great opportunities in Lapland for winter wonderland fun.

So what I'm saying is, I hadn't seen Josh again since Christmas early in the morning. But perhaps I'd give him a knock when I got back tonight.

The reindeer were, as ever, wonderful. And it was a nice

change to not spend my time there nervously watching the clock because of the impending snowmobiling. Instead, later on, when the clocks turned to late afternoon, and the light dipped from the deep inky blue of astronomical twilight into the star-sprinkled black of night-time, I looked up and felt a shiver, both from the chill, and the excitement. I made my way back to the activities' lodge to get ready for the tour, packing my bag with food and a big flask of hot berry juice, and hoped for the sake of the group that we saw the lights tonight. The forecast and that clear sky were looking good.

Josh had looked good, in close-up, under the Northern Lights . . .

And just as I was thinking about him, as if I'd manifested him, there he was. Crunching over the snow in the dark was Josh, kitted out in his padded suit and a helmet under his arm.

'Hi,' I spluttered, hoping my face didn't betray what I'd been thinking. 'Are you taking a tour out?'

'Actually, I'm on your tour,' he replied.

'You're coming to see the Northern Lights?'

'I hope so.'

'As an elf?'

'It's my day off, so I spoke to Daan and asked if I could tag along, as a volunteer. I checked, and all the guests tonight arrived today and leave tomorrow morning, so they won't have seen me as an elf. Nor will they.'

I tilted my head at him. 'Did Daan ask you to come in case I needed help again?'

'No,' he laughed. 'Daan thinks you're great, this is all me.'

I brushed some snow off a fence for no reason other than I needed my hands to do something. 'Well, thank you, it's always nice to have extra company.'

'You don't mind me coming?'

'Of course not.'

Josh turned to fiddle with something on the snowmobile and I allowed myself to glance back towards him, wondering, hoping, feeling my heart open up for the first time in a long time.

Angelique appeared then, together with another guide and a group of guests. 'All right, let's get going! Who's ready to see some Northern Lights?'

The guests let out collective cheers, and we climbed on our snowmobiles.

We drove in convoy, taking it slow because the dark made it much harder to see, though the moonlight and the lights of our skidoos provided some illumination. Beside me, phantom trees whooshed past, and the slice of the machine through the thick snow sounded oddly comforting.

The snowmobile moved through the wilderness. Again, it felt like the first time I was noticing the curves of the hills, the cold on my cheeks, the brightness of the Milky Way above our indigo surroundings.

Lapland – its colours, its snowbanks, its wildlife – was utterly breathtaking.

Eventually we entered a large clearing, driving the snowmobiles onto the flat of a frozen lake, glowing a baby blue in the dark.

'There you are,' I whispered up to the magnificent sky.

If I'd thought the aurora the other night was spectacular, this was a whole other level. With uninterrupted views of the skies for miles, the black above was painted with water-colour brushstrokes of luminous green that breathed and moved. It was kind of ethereal. Whoa, mamma.

I pulled my snowmobile to a stop along with the other guides, and signalled for the guests to do the same.

There was a collective gasp that filled the silence that wrapped around us once the engines were turned off. 'Oh my gosh, look at that!' I heard somebody cry from a few vehicles back.

'We got lucky this evening,' I told the guests nearest me, as I stepped from my snowmobile. Seeing their hesitation, I added, 'It's OK, it's safe to get off here. The ice is so thick you won't fall through. Typically the lights might not last longer than half an hour, so please make the most of it while they're here.'

They climbed out and all the guests started meandering about on the ice, wobbling as their feet sank into snowy banks while they stared up at the sky with awe and an infectious excitement and phones and cameras held high. Josh was wandering between them giving them photography tips, and I held back, just taking it all in myself.

I could see why Esteri kept coming back here year after year. Lapland was completely beautiful. And if you could tolerate Christmas too it was kind of the perfect place to work over winter.

Did I *actually* just think that?

I knew my next duty was to get a campfire going, so while

the other adventure guides led the guests a little further onto the lake, I stayed near the snowmobiles and pulled out logs, kindling and matches from the bag, and carried them off the edge of the lake.

Some clever people can build campfires *on* frozen lakes. I think we all know how that would likely go if I were to try it. So I would stick to the gently sloped shoreline, thanks.

I sat down in front of my makeshift campfire while it got going, and closed my eyes, breathing in my surroundings along with the scents of the woodsmoke. And when I opened my eyes again to the unmistakable sound of boots treading over knee-deep snow, Josh was approaching.

'Hey,' he said, his American accent as warm as the campfire flames.

'Hi.'

'Do you need a hand?'

'Not really, but some company would be nice, if nobody needs you?'

We couldn't just start snogging here ... *could we*? No, that would be totally inappropriate. Besides, he might just have come over for a toasted marshmallow.

'Pretty amazing, huh?' Josh took a seat beside me, resting his elbows on his knees, as the embers began to ignite.

'It's incredible,' I agreed. Even through all the winter clothing, I felt the proximity of his arm like we were back at the party. It caused my mind to go blank, and I struggled to think of conversation. Instead, I poked at the fire, which crackled under my touch. 'Have you ever seen them before?'

'While in Lapland? No, only when we were, you know ...'

'Outside on Christmas morning?'

'Yeah.'

We both laughed, shyly.

'That was a good night.' He held my gaze, his eyes soft and his voice low.

'It was.' I nodded. 'Plus, I realised you're not *always* annoying.'

He chuckled at that. 'Thank you.'

We were quiet again for a bit, until Josh leaned back in the snow, propping himself on his elbows and watching the sky above. The only sound was the distant chatter of our group being watched over by the other guides, and the crackling and hissing of the fire. The lights were soundless, just breathing, much like us.

'Do you feel better now?' Josh asked all of a sudden, his voice quiet. 'Now that Christmas is over?'

'I do,' I murmured. 'It takes the pressure off my mind a little. Not that Christmas is ever really *over* here, I suppose.'

'That's true. Can I . . . ' He paused and I waited, leaning back next to him. 'Can I ask what it is about Christmas? Like, there's no rule that says you have to like Christmas, I just wondered though if there was a reason you weren't so into it.'

I kept my eyes on the sky, but I didn't mind that he was asking. 'Yeah, there's a reason. A few, in fact. It's just that over the years I've built up a bit of a wall between myself and the holiday season. It just happens that the worst things in my life always seem to happen at this time of year, so it's kind of painful.'

'Because it brings back bad memories?'

'Yeah. And I don't really want to add to them, you know? So I tend to hide away over Christmas and pretend it's not happening. It sounds a bit weird now I say it out loud, because you can't really hide from Christmas.'

Josh shook his head. 'No, I think I get it. Might I say, you picked an excellent place to hide out this year.' I laughed, and he continued, meeting my eye and smiling. 'Were you going for a "keep your enemies close" kinda theme this season?'

'Something like that.' I smiled, looking away from him and back up at the green hues above.

'I'm sorry, though,' he said, softer.

'What for?'

'I'm sorry you've been through some stuff. I'm sorry you feel this way.'

'Oh, it's fine,' I said. 'I'm actually kind of embarrassed to talk about it because I don't have it bad at all. Some people have really horrible Christmases and my experiences seem so . . . petty. It's just that . . . '

'Those are *your* experiences. I'm sure whatever they were meant something to you and you can't feel bad about feeling the way you do.'

As if to prove him wrong, I turned to him and countered with, 'Well, would you give up Christmas because you once went to a school dance and the guy you thought you were in love with was kissing your friend?'

At the word kissing, I saw his eyes do that thing where they flicked down to my lips. He hesitated for a moment, before his mouth curved into a smile. 'Wait, is that what you were remembering at the party, on the edge of the dance floor, when "Bleeding Love" was playing?'

'Busted,' I laughed and covered my face with my hands, wetting it with the snow on my mittens. Oops.

Josh looked thoughtful for a moment. 'Maybe it's not about trying to forget the past, but about finding a way to . . . I don't know . . . make peace with it? Sometimes it can help to try and reframe things, I guess?'

I nodded, but it didn't feel that easy. How could I make peace with all those things to the point they didn't cause a black cloud to follow me around at this time every year? Where was the sunshine? 'Maybe,' I said, eventually.

'So do you wish you were still with this guy now?' he asked, and the thought struck me as funny.

'No. We're barely even in touch any more. Thinking about it, it was the best thing for me at the time, because I followed *my* future, whereas back then, knowing how I felt, knowing who I was, I very possibly would have tried to tag along with his. So, I had to move on somehow, I guess. No, I don't wish things had turned out differently, not at all . . . Anyway, that was just one example, really. There are others, some a little harder to swallow.'

'Do you want to tell me about them?'

'Yeah, maybe I do,' I said, surprising myself. I was so used to only discussing all this with my family, or Willow and Max, and if I mentioned it to anyone else, I would always joke over the details. It would be nice to open up to someone new, and there was something about Josh, perhaps his own openness, that made me want it to be him.

At that point though, three of the group walked over to warm their hands around the fire, so we sat up and I started fiddling about with kindling.

One of the group – a girl in her late teens who I think was a little besotted with Josh (weren't we all) – came over to him and asked, 'Excuse me, Josh, could you show me again the ISO setting on my mum's camera to get the best shots if I want to try a time-lapse?'

'Sure,' Josh said, leaping up, always on hand to help out.

He walked off and I made small talk with the guests warming their hands while I cooked a batch of sausages over the fire. I liked that he was good at photography. It was a little link we shared.

When Josh returned, along with the other guests, the only space for him to sit was opposite, so while I tried to keep my eyes on the fire I was stoking, I couldn't help but keep meeting his across the flames.

Why was I so drawn to him? We had very little in common. We lived in different countries. We didn't even know each other that well. But although I hadn't realised it at the time, ever since we'd met on the plane we'd forged this tiny connection and I couldn't help but wonder if, somehow, he was going to change my life.

Chapter 33

I love New Year's Eve. For me, this is the anti-Christmas, and my night to shine. I know it's a cliché to be all 'new year, new you' but I don't mean that I change a lot about myself come January the first, it's more that, for me, the end of the year is a fresh start. I like to wear sparkles, drink fizz, dance all night, whirl sparklers in the air, kiss people at midnight, the whole shebang. Basically, take all the fun other people have had at their Christmas parties throughout December and channel it into this one night.

So when I heard that, unlike at Christmas, the staff of Love Adventuring Lapland wouldn't be working beyond mid-evening and that Daan and the management were letting us have a celebration at the staff lodge, I was excited. I was *sparkling*.

'What are some New Year's traditions in Finland?' I asked Esteri when we were back in our room after sharing our last glass of sparkling wine with guests and now were ready to be left to our own devices. And open more sparkling wine.

Esteri was adjusting her boobs inside her sequin-covered sweatshirt, frowning down at them like they were doing something wrong. 'Do they look like two disco balls in this top?' she asked, ignoring my question.

'No,' I laughed. 'They're wonderful, you look amazing.'

'Oh. I was hoping for disco balls, haha! Um, Finnish New Year's traditions, let me see . . . Well, first of all you need to say *"Hyvää uutta vuotta!"* when the clock hits midnight – that's Happy New Year.'

It took a few tries of me attempting to twist my tongue around the words before Esteri rolled her eyes and said, 'Good enough. Now, what else. We used to melt tin and then put it in cold water and see what shape it solidifies into, and use that to tell our future.'

I blinked. 'Are you just messing with me?'

She laughed. 'I'm really not. Though tin is now banned so we won't do it this year. Let me think if there are any more and come back to you.'

I slid my delicate, dangly earrings into my lobes, watching as the gems danced against the low lighting. Since we were staying around the lodge tonight, being both inside and out as we'd be lighting a campfire, I was dressing in warm layers as opposed to my usual I'm-going-to-get-my-sweat-on-dancing NYE outfit. I was wearing a blue velvet top with a heavy, fluffy, soft grey cardigan draped over the top and some jeans. I'd crumpled my hair into waves and was feeling excited, not just from the fizz. Kind of from the fizz.

'You know what's cool?' Esteri said, coming beside me to look in the mirror. 'I sent a message to my Lapland family and they came straight back to ask me if I wanted to come and stay with them after we've finished working here at the end of January.'

'That is cool,' I replied, and Esteri looked pleased.

'You look lovely,' she said, admiring me in the mirror. 'Very cute. I'm sure Josh would agree.'

'Shut up,' I laughed. 'You look lovely too. Disco ball boobs especially. I'm sure the husky men would agree.'

'Thank you,' she said, giving them a wriggle.

All dolled up, we went downstairs, where the New Year's celebrations were already flowing. It was a couple of hours until midnight, so Esteri and I grabbed a glass of bubbles, courtesy of Love Adventuring Lapland, and spent a while mingling, dancing a little in the living room and making merry.

'Shall we light the campfire?' someone called, just as I'd finally spotted Josh, chatting with Angelique on the other side of the room.

Esteri took my hand and raised it in the air. 'This girl makes a mean campfire,' she declared, louder than usual with a little alcohol in her system.

'No, I don't,' I protested, pulling my arm down.

'Yes, you do, Josh told me,' she said, which threw me for a moment, like she probably anticipated. Nevertheless, she dragged me outside and started bundling my arms with kindling, causing little damp patches on my rather thin velvet top. Thank God for this thick cardigan.

'All right, I'll do it, but only because it's freezing out here.'

While I was assembling the fire, acutely aware that people were relying on me and watching me, and I hoped I wouldn't be about to ruin New Year's, the party started to move outside. Someone brought me out my dad's coat, someone else gave me a drink top-up. Then a speaker was brought out and hooked up to a phone so the music could fill the cold air. My co-workers were filtering out and taking seats on the logs around the firepit, bringing with them cushions and blankets from inside.

Josh came out of the chalet, with Angelique. He came towards me and because I hadn't spoken to him all night, and I'd had a couple, *ahem*, of glasses by this point, I wasn't really thinking and greeted him by throwing my arms around him. 'Hi, happy new year!' I enthused, and as I pulled away, he left his hands on my back for a moment, grinning down at me.

'Happy new year to you too,' he laughed, unused to me being so openly affectionate, I guess.

There weren't many seats left by this point, so he moved to the other side of the campfire from where I stood.

'You know, Myla,' Esteri said, her voice calling across the chatter.

I looked up to see her standing behind Josh.

'There's a New Year's tradition here in Finland that I forgot to tell you about earlier. If someone lights a fire in the first try on New Year's Eve, they will be lucky in love.' She stood beaming, her hands on her hips, not-subtly angling her eyes down towards Josh.

'Is that so?' I said, unsure if she was pulling my leg, and hoping my blush didn't show in the dark.

'Happy New Year to Josh,' called one of his elf friends, who then descended into happy-tipsy giggles.

'Shut up, man,' Josh said, sounding embarrassed through his laugh and when I glanced over, I spotted him glancing away from looking at me.

My heart thumped and I felt chills tickle the side of my cheeks, willing me to smile. Did that mean ... did that mean Josh's friends thought he liked me? Did that mean he did like me? I was already ninety-nine per cent sure he did – I can't have totally imagined those near-kisses, but was this the confirmation I was searching for?

Well, I did light the fire first time, but I'm sure that was just because I'm an excellent fire-starter as opposed to anything mystical. Nevertheless, it took everything in me to not look over at you-know-who when the flames stroked over the kindling and took hold.

For a while, a deep, satisfied quiet descended on the group, with the exception of the low playlist in the background and the crackling of the campfire.

'Did anyone make any resolutions for the new year?' Daan asked the group, breaking through the lull.

With chatter starting up again, some left the campfire to restock drinks or head back inside to warm up a bit. I was staring into the flames, wondering whether or not my resolution counted if it wasn't something I could enact until the following December. Then through my eyelashes I saw Josh get up and move over towards the empty seat next to me, on my right.

'Hey,' he said.

'Hi,' I answered. 'Do you want to sit?' I shuffled over on the log I was perched on.

'Sure, thanks. Are you cold?' He held out a blanket to drape over the two of us.

'No more so than I've been for the past month and a half.'

'You get kind of used to it, right?'

I nodded, and accepted the blanket, pulling it over my lap, and with the fire not needing any more prodding for a while, tucked my hands underneath as well.

'Do you have any resolutions?' I asked him, my voice coming out totally confidently and smoothly. Not really. It came out as a weird squeak, but I don't think he noticed.

'I can never think of any. Do you?'

'I do have one,' I confessed, then swept my gaze around at the group. 'But I shouldn't say it out loud.'

'Whisper it to me.'

OK, I would. I edged closer to Josh and leaned over, placing my right hand on his left shoulder for balance, and bringing my face close to his. Under the blanket, he reached his right arm over to hold me close and I felt him squeeze me softly. Nobody but me could tell, this was just for us.

Up close, Josh smelled of pine and sandalwood. I whispered into his ear, 'My resolution is to enjoy Christmas next year.'

'Is there any part of you,' he replied quietly, so nobody but me could hear, 'that enjoyed it this year?'

Under the blanket, he still held softly onto my forearm.

Taking a breath and a leap of faith, I rolled my arm, turning it upwards, and, sliding it backwards a few inches, took his hand in mine.

To the outside world, nothing had changed, but in that secret world under the blanket, it had for him and me.

As midnight approached, I could feel nerves kick in. Although Josh and I hadn't held hands the whole time, he remained next to me, our legs pressed together under the blanket, even when we chatted to the people to the other sides of us. I couldn't keep my mind straight, thinking of whether or not we'd kiss at midnight.

I liked a midnight New Year's Eve kiss. Did I mention that already? I usually didn't mind who I kissed, and if Josh and I were still nothing more than colleagues, friends even, I'd plant one on him, and Esteri, and anyone else willing. But could I do it in front of everyone? What if kissing at midnight wasn't the vibe here?

I picked up my glass full of sparkling wine from where I'd jammed it into the snow and took a swig, snorting into the bubbles remembering last New Year when Jamilia and I had held a house party with all her cool friends, and at midnight I held my arms wide and shouted, 'Jammy, come here and give me a kiss!' and she'd said, in her deadpan way, 'No thanks, babe, you smell like garlic bread.'

Oh God, what if I smelled like garlic bread now?

No, I hadn't had any garlic bread, we were OK.

'Sparkler? Sparkler?' Daan was walking around the campfire, handing out short little unlit sparklers to everyone as the clock counted down the last minutes of the year.

Josh and I turned back to each other and I breathed in the smoky air, keeping my eyes on him.

'Shall we light these?' he asked me.

Around the fire, people were sticking their sparklers into the flames and oohing and ahhing as they ignited with a fizz.

'Sixty seconds!' somebody called into the night air, but my eyes were still on Josh.

'Let's light these bad boys,' I replied, immediately feeling awkward at my choice of words, then immediately not caring because who cares, right? It's New Year, and I don't need a 'new me', I just need the old me back.

Whoa, hey there, feelings.

As the thirty-second countdown began, my co-workers calling numbers up towards the tops of the trees, we stuck our sparklers into the fire and watched them burst to light.

The seconds moved slowly, like falling snow on a gentle breeze, the wait for the moment that was on the edge of my lips feeling like for ever away. The glitter from my sparkler edged downwards, illuminating the dark.

'Ten, nine, eight . . .' we chanted as a group, and because it was New Year's and I couldn't help myself, I stood up, holding my sparkler high in the air like I thought I was Harry Potter or something.

Over the next few seconds, there was a scrabble of shoved blankets and knocked drinks as the others followed suit, and we collectively whooped a, 'Three, two, one, HAPPY NEW YEAR!' into the night air.

The sparkler in my hand faded to black, as did Josh's beside me, as did most people's, and in the amber-flame-hued darkness I reached my free hand up towards Josh's neck, and he turned to me, pulling me to him, just as I was doing to him, and he caught my kiss. Pressing his lips to mine, tasting of sparkling wine and woodsmoke, it was over in a second but the feeling imprinted on me.

We slipped apart, our eyes meeting, before we were both distracted by other people reaching in for hugs, cheek-kisses, high-fives and choruses of 'Happy New Year!'

I was so lost in my own giddy mind that I didn't notice Esteri standing in front of me until her lips were on my mouth, giving me my second kiss of the night. 'Happy New Year to the best room-mate I have ever had,' she said, raising a bottle in the air.

I laughed, chuffed and happy and kissed and blissed.

It was tempting to stay up for hours, to try and get some more alone time with Josh in case he wanted to revisit that tiny moment in our lives. But after a long day, most people drifted off towards their rooms not long after midnight, ready for work again the next day.

Back inside the chalet, I was wearing a headband I'd found that said 'HNY, bitch' and helping carry bottles into the kitchen. Josh was wandering about blowing out candles and collecting glasses alongside several others, and anytime we passed we'd meet each other's eyes and smile, but I didn't know what to say when all my lips could think about forming was another kiss, and there were too many other people around to be thinking about things like that.

Eventually, with a yawn and a lean of my head on Esteri's shoulder, I was ready to hit the sack.

'Sleepy?' she asked, letting out a big yawn herself.

'Yeah.'

'Done for the night?'

I snuck a look at Josh, engaged in a conversation with Daan and looking pretty sleepy himself, and said, 'Yeah.'

We climbed the stairs. I kissed Josh. It had been a good night, a really good night, and now it was January. Told you New Year's was brilliant.

Chapter 34

'I would love to have eyes like him,' I said to Esteri, staring into the most beautiful set of peepers I'd ever seen. One eye was iceberg-blue, the other log cabin-brown, and it gave the husky puppy the most interestingly appealing face in the world.

Esteri was too busy smooching her own puppy to answer, so I buried my nose back into mine. His name was Juno and he was ten weeks old. His fur was a marble of snow-white and charcoal-black, his nose splotchy pink and black, and his ears little concaves.

Esteri and I were both, separately, leading groups on husky tours today, so had arrived early to the farm because who would ever give up a chance to sneak in some snuggles with the pups?

'Oof, Juno is heavy,' I commented, shifting my weight and hoping not to topple back in the snow. With his long legs dangling down from my arms, he kept trying to wriggle in order to lick my face, which meant my skin kept being tickled by gloriously lustrous and soft puppy fur, so thick to keep them warm, even at this age. Around me, husky dogs spread out into the distance, howling and yapping and eager to stretch their legs on a lovely long run.

'OK, our groups will be arriving soon, come along,' said Esteri, putting her own puppy down and looking over at one of the husky men. 'We will come back under the cover of darkness for more kisses.'

With one last stolen peck on the top of Juno's head, and in turn one last lick of my nose for him, I put him back in his enclosure and followed Esteri to where the husky team were setting up the dogs that we'd be taking out today.

Rows of excited huskies stood in the snow, looped together with a long harness. Happy howls continued to ring out loudly as they all bellowed at each other and demanded to get going. They loved to run so much, and it was nice knowing that when visitors took the husky sleigh rides, the dogs really were having a great time.

Some of the more mellow dogs were chilling in the snow, occasionally dipping their noses in to graze a little. Others were standing with their heads tilted right back, seeming to go off on some kind of monologue they were forcing the others to listen to from start to finish. Some wandered out of formation and spaghettied themselves in amongst the harness.

I went down the line for the sled I'd be part of, saying hi to all the dogs and giving them all equal attention and ear-strokes. If this were a longer excursion, the husky guides would take the guests out, but for shorter loop trails we took them ourselves.

When my guests arrived, a middle-aged couple from Brazil named Davi and Lucas, both men were so entranced by the line of dogs they had to have photos with every single one and I promised they could meet the puppies on our return.

'Shall we get going?' I said, coaxing the men onto the sled, sensing the dogs were getting restless.

'Yes, yes, absolutely,' said Davi, and then quickly took another ten photos.

'Come on, Dav,' said Lucas, rolling his eyes at me with good humour, and pulling his boyfriend by the hand where they took their places, seated on the sled.

Lucas turned back to look up at me. 'Do we say "mush"?' he asked.

'Well, who wants to start?' I asked.

'You?' Lucas suggested. 'I think we'd quite like to just sit back and let you do the work.'

I laughed, and made my way to stand at the back of the sled. 'OK, no problem. I'll get us started. It can feel a bit funny to begin with so we'll have you enjoy the ride and the scenery and get a feel of it all first and then I'll teach you some commands and if you want you have a go in a while, if that's all right?'

'Definitely,' said Davi, snuggling back against Lucas and pulling the thick blanket over them both.

I stood on the back of the sled, held on tight, and instructed the dogs to get going. On my command, all eight dogs started trotting forward, happy as Larry, and Davi let out a happy cry.

As we began to slide along the trail, the sled

bump-bumping over the snow, the fresh, cold air whipping at my cheeks, a smile spread across my face. Back here, nobody could see me as the smile turned into a grin.

The trees rushed past, the dogs brushed their noses in the powdery snowy drifts either side of the trail for on-the-go slushie drinks, their tails whooshing, bottoms wiggling, the wooden sled creaked against the packed snow trail in the most satisfying way, the sky overhead was muted pinks and mauves, and my lips were freezing.

I loved this. I *truly* loved this. This was the best part of my job, and I never would have known how much I loved working outside in somewhere like this if I hadn't quit my latest office job.

Come to think of it, if I'd still been in my 'dream job', I also would have never known how much I could enjoy something like this.

Like an icicle drip, the thought dropped into my mind that maybe, just maybe, I'd been wrong about my dream job being the be-all and end-all.

After a little while, we stopped to give the dogs a rest and a chance to have a snack and eat some snow, and I went through some of the techniques with Davi and Lucas, so that they could have a go themselves.

I took a seat behind Davi, while Lucas tried to begin with. It always felt a little odd snuggling up to someone else's partner at this juncture, but usually everyone involved was just pleased to keep the body heat sharing going.

'All right, Lucas, so say "Mush" and the dogs will start to pull forward. Remember to hold on tight and lean your weight in the direction you want to turn. Say "Whoa" to stop. And remember to have fun!'

As we set off, I was pleased at how quickly he'd got the hang of it. The dogs were off on their fast trot again, relaxed and happy, and Davi kept holding his camera in the air to take photos of Lucas, standing up at the back.

It was all going so well. Until . . .

Boof. Something under the snow hit the sled, hard, and I, distracted by keeping an eye on both Davi, Lucas, and the dogs, wasn't holding on tight enough.

With an embarrassing yelp I tumbled off the side of the sled, face-planting the snow, one arm protecting my head, the other crushed under me at an odd angle.

I heard Davi shout 'Whoa!' in a panicked voice.

Lifting my head, I saw the huskies pull to a stop and Davi scrambling to get up. 'I'm OK, sorry, guys, that was completely my fault.'

Lucas reached me while Davi hesitated beside the sled, one hand on it. 'Should I come over or stay to make sure they don't run away?' he called out.

'You stay, I'm fine,' I said.

The two dogs at the front, Whisky and Bourbon, pulled themselves around, nudging me with their noses and licking at my face, and then Whisky started howling his head off as if calling for help. Or maybe he was just going off on one of his monologues again.

Lucas pulled his gloves off. 'I am a first aider back home, let me take a look at you. Did you hit your head?'

'No, just my pride. I think there was a rock under the

path, buried under the snow right at the edge so we happened to miss it before now. I guess enough snow had shifted that we felt it that time.'

'But you aren't hurt?'

'Well . . .' I didn't know what to admit here, because part of me felt like I should just put on a brave face because these were paying guests and I had to show them a good time no matter what, but part of me was like, *has my arm actually been broken or am I just dying*?

Before I could answer, Lucas asked, 'Is it your head?'

'No, no, just my arm, it's nothing.'

'Can I decide that, please?'

As best he could, considering we both had a lot of padding on, he assessed my arm's mobility while I winced and the dogs got restless. 'It hurts, right?'

'Yeah,' I admitted.

'OK, I think it's just a sprain, but I know they can be painful. It's not broken, but it would be best if you didn't use this arm for a little while.'

'But I have to, for work,' I protested.

'Maybe it would be worth a doctor taking a look at it, to make sure.'

I nodded and got to my feet, giving Whisky and Bourbon a thank you head stroke as I passed. 'I'm so sorry, you two,' I said to my guests. 'I hope this hasn't taken anything away from your trip?'

'Not at all,' cried Davi. 'We're just glad you got up.'

'I know, right, otherwise the huskies might have eaten me.' Seeing their faces, I quickly added, 'Just kidding, they don't do that. Um, where were we? Lucas, how did you find driving the sled?'

'Amazing, hard work but incredible.'

'That's great. Davi, you want a go now?'

'Actually, I'm pretty happy as a passenger, if that's all right?' he asked.

I nodded, trying to inconspicuously twitch my fingers and not let the pain register on my face. 'Of course that's all right. We're doing a loop and we've gone a little past halfway, so there's about another twenty minutes to go. Are you both warm enough?'

'Yes,' they both chorused, their eyelashes partially frozen.

I began to walk to the back of the sled, wondering exactly how not-recommended driving a husky sled with one arm was.

'Where are you going?' called Davi.

'Oh, I was going to drive again. Unless you want to carry on for a little bit, Lucas?' I sounded super nonchalant . . .

Before Lucas could answer me, Davi shook his head. 'No, you cannot use that arm. Will you let Lucas do the rest of the driving?'

I mean, I shouldn't really, since they'd specifically requested that I do the bulk of the leading, but as my arm throbbed and I considered the amount of pull and control I was supposed to have to drive the husky sled, I felt myself relenting. I looked at Lucas. 'Would you mind? I know you wanted to mainly be passengers, so I'll be sure to arrange a refund—'

'Are you kidding?' Lucas replied, practically running back

around to the back of the sled. 'I would actually love to. When will I ever get the chance to do this again?'

Davi helped me onto the sled with him, being careful with my arm, and added, 'Instead of a refund, maybe we could just get an extra ten minutes with the puppies back at the farm?'

'You can stay around and help with feeding time, if you want,' I said, full of gratitude (and still a little embarrassed at my fall and my loud yelp).

Once again, I settled back behind Davi and watched twelve furry husky bottoms lead the way around the curve of the path, their tails high in the air, their legs scampering along. The small bumps slightly twinged at my shoulder, but it was OK.

But what did it mean for my job?

Chapter 35

Back at the husky farm, while the activities' lodge doctor looked over my arm and Davi and Lucas got an extra-long playtime with the puppies, I explained to Daan what had happened. Or, more accurately, I was trying to convince him I was to blame.

'But you didn't know about the rock,' he said.

'I should have been holding on properly,' I insisted. We were going around in circles, and eventually he just laughed and, on doctor's orders, sent me back to the chalet for the rest of the day to take some painkillers and rest my arm.

When I arrived back, I spent a long time in the boot room trying to manoeuvre my way out of my snow boots only using one arm. The chalet was pretty quiet save for a few other workers on funny shifts or with their days off, and I admit, I kind of hoped to find Josh there. But he was nowhere to be found so he must have been out elfing.

Up in my room, I wriggled out of my ten million layers and considered heading down for a sauna but decided first to have a bit of scroll about social media. Being only a few days into January, much of the content consisted of work Christmas parties and family gatherings, and, well, I managed to 'like' seven pictures before I'd had my fill and instead navigated to Love Adventuring Lapland's page to see the latest posts and tags.

'Oh it's me!' I cried out loud to see that the second most recent picture that had tagged Love Adventuring Lapland was a selfie of Davi, with me behind him on the sled, and Lucas driving at the back, the snow bright white and a second photo of scampering husky bottoms. The third and final photo was a portrait of both of them holding puppies and grinning so widely it looked like a toothpaste advert. The caption was written in Portuguese, but thanks to the translate option on Instagram, I could see it said, *Amazing husky ride – thank you Adventure Guide Myla of Love Adventuring Lapland! You are full of smiles and made sure our holiday memory would be filled with smiles too.*

Ahh, that was nice. And sweet of them not to have mentioned my little accident! Scrolling through the other tagged photos on the company's Instagram, I paused at one showing three of the elves captured in the middle of what looked like a dance-off outside Santa's cabin. Josh was one of them, and I zoomed in on his face, which was beaming away. He was such a goof. *So* annoying, really. But, I realised, catching a glimpse of myself in the mirror, with a smile so infectious . . .

I navigated next to WhatsApp to send my sister a message about my latest misadventure.

This morning I took the huskies out on a trip and guess what? I typed.

What? She came back almost immediately.

Dum-dum here fell off the sled and sprained my arm, so now I can't do my job. Typical! But something stopped me from pressing 'send'. Because sure, that unfortunate thing had happened, but that didn't mean it had to be the part I focused on.

I deleted the text, took a breath, and typed instead, It was such a gorgeous day with some lovely guests. And I had lots of husky puppy snuggles. And you know what? When the sun doesn't come much above the horizon, it's like the sky is a new painting every day.

Send.

Shay typed back, Is this Esteri?

No, it's Myla!

No way, my sister doesn't like to admit she's having fun.

Up yours! I laughed.

She sent back a smiley face and wrote, I'm really happy to hear you're enjoying yourself.

I am. Now Christmas is out of the way, anyway.

Yeah, yeah . . .

I was about to sign off when I asked, No baby yet, right?

Nothing yet. Just a big stomach and a need to pee 85 trillion times a day. Speaking of . . .

I sent her an emoji of a waving hand and a toilet, and then went off for that sauna.

*

262

That night, just as Esteri and I were about to head upstairs with some hot chocolate to have a gossip, I ran into Josh.

'Oh, hi,' I said to him, managing, just, to avoid both knocking my arm and spilling my scalding drink down him.

'Hi, whoops, haha,' he answered, and we did that awkward thing of shuffling from foot to foot to try and pass each other while making small talk.

'Oh, um, how was work today, still lots of Santa love going down?' I asked, like a total dork.

'Some,' he said. 'And how was your day? You were with the huskies, right?'

'Yes, they're so lovely.'

'They're the best. I just want to take them all home.'

'Me too!' I cried. 'Especially the puppies. I sound like Cruella de Vil but I honestly would just love them all. Not make coats out of them or anything. Hahahaaaaaa.'

Josh chuckled and cleared his throat.

'I fell off the sled!' I yelped suddenly, babbling to fill the silence.

'What? Are you OK?'

'Yeah, totally fine. Well, no, my arm is sprained but it's nothing.'

'Your arm?' He reached over and touched it gently, lifting it. It was a sweet gesture, almost reflexive, but his touch, even through my jumper, tingled.

'Yeah. That one.'

'Oh, no.'

'What?'

'I think it needs surgery.'

I laughed. 'It does not.'

'I think I would know.' He shrugged. He smiled, and lowered my arm, breaking our connection. 'Can you still work?'

'Daan has me on reindeer duty tomorrow, just at the farm. I'll be on low-impact work for a few days, I guess, but then I'm sure it'll be back to normal.'

'That's good.' We hesitated in front of each other for a moment.

Standing beside us, watching, blowing on her drink, was Esteri. 'Hello, Josh,' she said all of a sudden, alerting him to her presence.

He snapped to attention and smiled at her. 'Esteri, hi, how are you?'

'I am just fine, thank you, Josh, and you?'

'Yes, good, great. I mean, not great, is that rubbing it in considering you just told me you're hurt?' he asked me.

I shook my head, grinning, and Esteri raised her eyebrows at me.

'All right, well, see you later,' I said to Josh, and followed my room-mate up to our room.

Inside, we climbed into our bunks, and I put my hot chocolate on the small shelf above my bed and propped myself on my good elbow, staring out of the open curtains to the darkness beyond. A lining of snow coated the window frame, and I could see flakes still fluttering down in front of the lights at the bottom of the pine trees below.

I took a sip of my drink, holding the sweet, warm liquid in my mouth for a moment, right as Esteri said, 'Are you and Josh having sex?'

Spluttering and dribbling a little hot chocolate onto my chin and pillow, I exclaimed, 'No! What? Why would you . . . ?'

From the bunk below, cool as a cucumber she continued, 'I knew there had always been something between you two, it was so obvious, but something's altered.'

'What do you even mean, there's not been anything between us, he's like, the most annoying guy I've ever met.' All right, that might be overkill.

'No he's not, he's cute, if you like that kind of thing.'

Not sure what *that* meant.

She continued, 'Did something happen at the Christmas party? Or New Year's?'

'No, nothing's happened.'

'Yet?'

I hesitated a moment too long because she made an *ah-ha!* sound and leapt up, moving to one of the chairs so she could sit and look up at me.

'We had a bit of a moment at the Christmas party, that was all, he was taking a break, and so was I, and there was no one around.'

'The magic of Christmas,' Esteri sighed and I tried not to roll my eyes.

'But the moment was broken when the band stopped playing and, I don't know, we've had a couple of times since then that I've felt like we're on the brink, but nothing yet, apart from a tiny kiss at midnight on New Year's. Just before you kissed me.'

'What are you waiting for?'

'I don't know,' I admitted. 'I guess I don't want to mess up our friendship. And I *don't* want to get hurt.'

Esteri made a derisive snort. 'Come on, you have like, one month left together here. Then he will go back to America, and you will go back to your sad little life in England, and you might never see each other again. So live a little.'

'My life in England isn't sad!' I protested.

'Hey, I'm just paraphrasing you, Miss No-Job, No-Home.'

I lay back on the bed and stared at the ceiling. Of course I wanted to be with Josh. I couldn't stop thinking about him. If I was honest with myself, the spark had been sparkling long before the Christmas party. But was there any point? Like Esteri said, in a matter of weeks he'd be gone.

'What are you thinking?' she asked me.

'Just wondering what to do.'

'Do you want my advice?'

'Do I have any choice?'

'No,' she laughed. 'I bet you're thinking, oh, maybe it would be better if I didn't rock the boat, if I didn't have any fun so then I can't be sad at the end. Well, that is crap. You like him. He clearly likes you. Don't waste an opportunity just because you're worried about hypothetical outcomes.'

Hmm. She sounded like my sister, when Shay was trying to convince me that coming to Lapland was a good idea.

And she was right, wasn't she?

Hmm.

'Come on, you stupid Brit, get up and go and kiss your man, and I'll go and have an extra-long sauna so you have the room to yourself.'

I laughed. 'No, not now, I don't want to do anything right this minute.'

Esteri shrugged and took a drink. 'OK, suit yourself. But don't leave it too late, OK? Don't wait for someone else to solve your happiness problems.'

'Yes, ma'am.'

'Now, I need your help.'

I propped myself back on my good elbow again, glad to be moving the topic away from me. 'What's up?'

'I know we talked about this before, but ... What do you think about me moving to Lapland?'

'Permanently?'

'Yes. I'd need to go back south to tidy a few things up when we're done on this job, but then I'd come back up ready for summer.'

'Would you live near your family?'

'I don't know ... I don't think I want to uproot everything to move right next door to them, but being a little closer would be nice. They were nice, right?'

'Really nice.' I was flattered she was asking my advice about such a big decision. 'Would you consider moving around here and continuing to work for Love Adventuring Lapland?'

'Perhaps,' she answered. 'If they'd have me.'

'I think you should speak to Daan, tell him what you're thinking and scope out his thoughts. You don't have to agree to anything, but at least it would give you some time to think about it all if you had the information already.' I watched her mull this over, swirling her drink as snow lightly tippy-tapped on the window pane. 'Sooner rather than later, and all that.'

She narrowed her eyes at me and smirked. 'Are you using my own advice against me?'

'Maybe a little.'

Esteri sighed. 'It would just be a big change, you know? My family all lived in Turku so I've always gone back there. But I love it up here.'

'And you still can go back there. You wouldn't be leaving for ever; you could still visit. It wouldn't be like you were trying to push the memories away, just accepting them and moving forward.'

'So you think I should do it?'

'I think so, if it would make you happy.'

'Would you visit?'

Would I come back out to Lapland again, to the land of Christmas? 'Yes, of course.'

Chapter 36

The following day the snow was falling in fat flakes from a cloud-filled sky, and I was standing in it, hanging out with the reindeer, doing odd-jobs that didn't involve too much bicep work, helping out Kirste and Johánná with anything they needed, and mulling over what Esteri had said. A sparkle of excitement kept fizzing through me every time I thought of Josh, because I'd decided: I was going to take matters into my own hands.

Everything felt better now. Even with the overcast sky, the colours were vibrant, the air was fresh, and I wanted to show Josh what he'd come to mean to me over the weeks. Even when I hadn't really known it myself, he was always one of the first people I looked for when I entered a room, one of the only ones I was drawn to across the snow.

The snow had fallen throughout the night, and today it continued kissing the ground in layers, softening every path and coating every fence. The visitors were loving their winter wonderland, even with the low lighting that the arctic circle brought at this time in the late morning.

I was brushing a reindeer called Phil and chatting away to him while all around me other guides were helping their guests get ready for sleigh rides.

'So, Phil, in conclusion, I think he might just be lovely.'

'Excuse me,' said a lady, approaching. 'Is this reindeer friendly? My daughter wants to meet one of them but she's a bit scared.'

'Oh yes, he's very friendly.' I looked around the lady to see a teenage girl, her eyes downcast, layered up but looking like she wanted to be anywhere but here. 'What's your name?' I asked her.

The girl looked up but wouldn't meet my eye, and mumbled, 'Nadia.'

'She's shy,' said Nadia's mum. 'She had a bad experience with a horse once and hasn't wanted to go near them since, so she's a bit worried about this.'

'All right.' I stepped over to Nadia and said, 'This reindeer is called Phil, if it helps.'

A small laugh escaped and Nadia said, incredulously, 'Phil?'

'Yep. He thinks he's a heart-throb but he's actually just a typical, farty guy. I've made him sound really appealing.'

'Yeah.' Nadia smiled, looking back at the ground.

With a little more coaxing, and a little more explanation about Phil, and a lot of Nadia watching him and how he interacted with me, eventually Nadia was gently running her hand over Phil's pelt. I stepped back a touch to give her and her mum a little bit of space, but to be on hand in case anything went awry.

Then, out of the corner of my eye, I saw Josh approaching. He was in his elf outfit, rosy cheeks and all, and striding straight towards me.

Was this it? Had his heart taken over to the extent he was marching over to kiss me, right here, right now? My breath caught with the possibility, and when I smiled at him, he returned the smile, only, something was different . . .

'Hello, Elf Josh,' I said, playing along as I knew he'd have to remain in character with all these guests and children around.

'Hey, Adventure Guide Myla,' he replied, stopping before me and clearing his throat, searching my eyes for a moment.

'Everything all right?' I felt hyper-aware of Nadia and her mum right there next to us, and I couldn't leave my post in case they needed me.

'Everything's great!' he said, though it sounded anything but. 'I just needed to come and tell you that I have to take a trip.'

'To where?'

'The United States of America.' He gestured playfully. His eyes betrayed him.

I tried to play along. 'Wowzers, Elf Josh, that's a long way. When are you going?'

'I have to go now,' he said through a sad smile.

'Now?' I breathed out the icy word, feeling my heart drop.

'My elf grandfather lives all the way over there and he's had to go to elf hospital because he's kinda poorly, so my elf mom needs my help. I'm just going to pack some things and join one of those sleigh rides that fly over the seas.'

Despite the gung-ho voice, it wasn't hard to translate that he was saying his grandfather must be really sick and his mum couldn't cope and needed him home ASAP.

'Is he OK?' I asked quietly.

With a glance around he nodded and sighed, 'At the moment.'

'I'm sorry,' I whispered.

I didn't want to disturb the experience for any of the visitors, so in a normal voice I asked, 'Um, will you be coming back to Lapland during January?'

'I don't know,' he said, smiling.

'OK.'

His eyes looked deep into mine and I tried to tell him silently how I hoped he was OK, how I hoped everything would be OK. How much I would miss him.

How I would miss the us we wouldn't get the chance to be.

He was leaving. *Now*. Maybe for good. And neither of us could say a proper goodbye and I felt my poor, protected heart begin to crack. In an attempt to hold it together – and because it was one of the only actions we could take that wouldn't look out of place – I reached out and wrapped my arms around Josh and squeezed him. I didn't care about the pain in my arm, I didn't care about the people watching. I felt his arms wrap around me too, holding me tight, and I pressed my face into his shoulder.

We probably held the hug for less than five seconds, but I savoured every single one of them, weaving a memory just for us out of all of the particles of hope that had never had a chance to form.

'Bye, Myla,' he whispered, his voice so quiet it was barely more than a snowflake drifting past my ear.

I couldn't manage a reply because I thought it might cause the crack in my heart to deepen, so instead we broke apart and I watched the best thing about this Christmas walk away.

'Does Phil get on with the other reindeer?' Nadia asked, pulling me back to my guests.

I took a deep breath and pasted on a smile. 'Yes, he's a big hit, who couldn't love Phil? He has such a kind personality.'

Nadia and her mum continued to ask questions and pet Phil, who basked under their adoration, all while I spoke and moved on autopilot.

When they walked away happy, I finally managed to exhale and whisper, 'Bye, Josh.'

Chapter 37

Twenty minutes later, Esteri rounded the corner, having just returned from an early reindeer ride. She led her reindeer around to the paddock, where I helped her unharness and brush him.

'The clouds make today feel dark, don't you think?' she said.

'Yeah,' I agreed. Nearby, guests pottered around taking photos of our furry friends.

Shaking out her blonde hair, Esteri studied me for a moment. 'What's up with you?' she asked, keeping her voice low.

'Josh is going home,' I replied, staring forward at the reindeer, stroking his neck mechanically.

'Home to the chalet?'

'No, *home* home. His grandfather is in the hospital and I think his mum needs him or isn't coping or something. So he has to leave. I mean, he wants to leave. Of course.'

Esteri let out a soft sigh. 'That is sad. When's he leaving?'

'Now.'

'Today?'

'Like, *now*. I guess he had a call this morning, must have cleared it with Daan, and then was stopping here to tell me before heading back to the chalet to get out of his costume and pack up his things. He must be planning to catch the shuttle bus taking guests back to the airport in Rovaniemi.'

Esteri turned to me, her brows furrowed. 'But he's coming back, isn't he?'

'He doesn't know. I guess it depends what happens.'

She looked around. 'So you might not see him again?'

I couldn't find any words so just shrugged.

'Go.'

'What?'

'Go and say goodbye, properly, without all of us around.' She gestured towards the guests, the staff, the reindeer. 'Without him dressed as a damn elf.'

'I can't, I'm working, and he's probably gone already.'

'I will cover for you. I have your back, Myla, believe me. Just go. You'll regret it if you don't.'

I hesitated, though the pull of the chalet was already tugging at me. 'I don't want to make this about me, he's got other things on his mind.'

'So don't make it about you, or the two of you. But if nothing else, you're his friend, right, so go and say goodbye to him properly.'

'Isn't it a bit selfish?'

'Isn't making the decision for the two of you without his input selfish?'

275

I nodded, and backed away, blowing a kiss to Esteri before taking off through the snow.

It wasn't far to get from the reindeer farm back to the chalet, and I ran all the way, hoping to catch Josh, all the time wondering if I was doing the right thing.

At one point I skidded to a halt, right in the middle of the trees, with the snow falling around me, and took a breath. It didn't matter if nothing happened. I know I wanted it to. But if I could just tell him goodbye and that I hoped everything would be OK, and that I was glad to have known him for the winter, that would be enough. It would have to be enough.

When I emerged from the trees, I saw him coming out of the chalet, his backpack beside him as he closed the door, his coat done up, his eyes downcast until he glanced up and they met mine.

I crossed the clearing towards the chalet, and leaving his backpack on the ground where snowflakes began to settle upon it instantly, he walked towards me too.

'What are you doing here?' he asked as we drew close.

'I don't know,' I admitted. 'I just wanted to be able to say goodbye properly. I'm not trying to ... I just wanted to let you know ...'

That's when I shut up. Josh took a step closer to me, his dark eyes searching mine, his eyelashes low and catching snowflakes. His breath was warm on my face and I blinked as snowflakes kissed my face.

Josh reached his fingers to my hair, which was damp, the edges stiff in the cold, and pushed it back from my face, leaving his hands on my neck. I moved my hands to his waist. And just for a moment, we stayed like that, memorising each other, memorising this moment, which I knew would for ever be a winter memory I would do anything to keep instead of push away.

I tilted forward then, touching us together with a kiss, feeling his warm lips and cold nose press against me, his chilly fingers causing shivers on the back of my neck, the feel of his inhale and exhale underneath his jacket.

As we kissed under the falling snow, I forgot all about the freezing cold, because my heart was warm.

After too short a moment, he let me go and brought his face away from me, his eyes still swallowing mine, his mouth curving into that smile. I smiled back, and he pulled me into his arms for a final hug, resting his chin for a second on the top of my head while I breathed in the exposed skin of his neck.

With a gulp, I pulled back, and before he could say a word, I whispered, 'You have to go.'

Josh nodded. 'Yeah.'

'I hope everything is OK at home,' I said. 'And I hope you know you'll be missed.'

'So will you.'

I was not going to cry. I was in no position to ask *him* to comfort *me* right now. So instead, I widened my smile and untangled myself from within his arms, though it might have been the hardest thing my heart had ever had to do, being pulled away from its source of warmth. 'Bye, Josh,' I said, keeping my voice steady.

'Bye, Myla. Thank you.'

I shook my head. 'Thank *you*. Take care.'

Josh nodded. 'You too. And be happy. You do deserve it, you know.'

I couldn't speak any more, so with one last look at his face, I turned and walked away.

After Josh had left, I took myself into the forest, not far from the chalet, and sat down upon a tree stump, while the snow fell around me.

What if I just let it cover me? What if I wrapped myself in the snow like it were a duvet, and I hibernated for the rest of my time here, then when it thawed I would go home and forget the whole thing.

Because I had to forget it, didn't I? He wasn't likely to come back here before I would leave anyway.

My face and my hands were getting colder.

It was fine. This would just be another memory of how Christmas brought nothing but failed memories into my life.

I pressed my lips together, and remembered him kissing me, and that memory fought with my own mind. It didn't want to be boxed up, forgotten, pushed aside. It wanted to be heard, and loved.

With an inhale that chilled my lungs but woke me from my daze, I stood up and made my way back into the house, where I methodically changed into some dryer clothes, redid the braid in my hair, made myself a cup of tea, took some deep breaths and was about to head out the door again and back to the reindeer farm when I noticed something. It was a flannel shirt hanging on a hook by the door, one of Josh's that he'd left to dry and forgotten to take. I knew it was Josh's, without a doubt, I recognised the emerald green because I remember thinking how nice it looked on him. Should I try and run after him?

Then I noticed something I hadn't spotted before. A small rectangle trimmed off the hem of the left panel, barely noticeable, but with a gasp I realised it matched the bracelet on my wrist.

'It was from Josh,' I whispered. *He* was my Secret Santa, not Esteri.

No, I wouldn't run after him, I'd hang onto his shirt. This stupid lumberjack shirt that belongs to my goofy elf. Maybe one day I could give it back to him. In the meantime, I could smell his aftershave on the collar, and so I'd keep it with me.

Chapter 38

'Hey, wake up. *Hey.*'

I was awoken the next morning by Esteri poking me while I lay huddled under my duvet.

'What?' I croaked. 'Is it really time to go to work? It *is* dark in the mornings now, isn't it.'

'No, we have a while before work, but I'm borrowing Daan's car and taking you somewhere.'

'What?' I sat up and bumped my head on the ceiling, cursing these bloody bunk-beds, and actually, *all* the bunk beds in all the world.

'I am sorry Josh has gone, I really am, and I feel for your heart. But he wasn't everything about Lapland. *I* am here. *That* is here.' She gestured towards the window. 'So before you bury yourself in the snow and hibernate I am taking you on an adventure to wake you up.'

'I just wanted a little time to feel blue, I wasn't— *Hey*— I'm coming!' Esteri was dragging me down from the bed by my leg.

She regarded me in my PJs while I scowled. 'You will probably want a swimsuit.'

'Where are we going?'

'It's a surprise.'

'But we're not going too far?'

'No, maybe half an hour away. You're going to love it.'

Feeling sceptical, I changed into my swimsuit and layered clothing over the top. I considered pretending my arm hurt more than it did and begging to crawl back into bed, but got the feeling Esteri would have absolutely none of it.

It was just after six in the morning. Josh was probably still trying to make his way back to America at the moment. Even if he 'only' had to change in Helsinki, London and New York, like on the way over, it was still a trek, but combined with the fact he'd had to go last-minute and take whatever was on offer ...

'Hey!' Esteri snapped my fingers in my face, pulling me back to the present. 'Let's go.'

We slid out of the chalet and crunched our way silently through the snow to the other side of the activities' lodge, where Daan kept his car. It had stopped snowing, I noticed, and the stars twinkled overhead like it was still midnight. No sign of the aurora, though.

Driving out, we left Luosto behind us and followed the same road that had taken us towards Esteri's family back in December, though we evidently weren't going that far today. The roads were clear and dark, and Esteri put on the radio to some soft music I didn't know, and I was grateful that she wasn't trying to get me to talk about my feelings and whatnot.

After we'd been driving for a short time, we turned off towards a lake, and pulled to a stop beside a wooden cabin, where Esteri entered our details via a tablet and a gate opened. We slid the car silently to a stop beyond the gate, and then Esteri led us towards a changing room.

'You can relax, we're just going to sauna,' she said, as I started to undress without knowing why.

'Oh, a sauna! I thought it was going to be something far more painful. Why have we driven all the way out here when we have one at the chalet?'

'For a change of scenery, and to be tourists ourselves for a moment. Besides, this is where I come every year when I get that day when I think, *ugh, I'm done here.*'

'You get that in this job?'

'Everyone gets that in every job sometimes, it's human nature. You've never had that in other jobs?'

I thought back to my numerous temp jobs over the past year. Yes, yes I had. And usually I quit at that stage.

'Do you feel like that now? Is that why you're cashing in your trip to this sauna?'

'No, I just thought you could do with it. Now let's go in.'

Leaving the changing room, we stepped across the heated pathway through the snow, and opened the door of a fairy-light-decorated wooden chalet. Inside, the steam was already misting the air, scented with sage and frankincense. It was like being hugged the minute you entered a wonderfully welcoming spa.

The sauna back at the staff chalet was blissful, but this was a whole other level. Wide, long benches lined the walls so both of us had plenty of room to stretch out. Water dripped carefully and precisely from a feature above, ensuring you never had to get up to manually wet the hot stones to create the steam. Tiny spotlights with warm gold bulbs scattered the ceiling like stars, and one side of the sauna was entirely glass, looking out over the pre-dawn frozen lake and forest.

'Esteri, this is ... *wow*,' I breathed, feeling my crumpled, tense body relax as I climbed onto one of the higher benches while she did the same. I lay down on the warm wood, silky smooth.

Esteri, as usual, was naked and I in my bathing suit. She let out a big, deep sigh from her end of the sauna. 'It's pretty nice, isn't it?'

'How long do we have?'

'In the sauna? We should limit to fifteen minutes. So relax, shut up and enjoy.'

I'd been told, and I closed my eyes with a chuckle.

The skin on my legs and arms began to warm and tingle. A rivulet of sweat trickled its way from my forehead and down my temple. My breathing became long and deep. And as the scent of frankincense entered my nose, a memory of that party, Callie's party, back when I was twenty-five and nervous and pulled down the Christmas tree, entered my mind.

As quickly as it came, I forced the memory away again. That wasn't what I wanted to think about now. If I went down that road, I'd be punishing myself all day. So after some calming breaths, I began to settle on happier things.

My thoughts drifted to Josh, to our kiss and to all our near-kisses. To the time we met on the plane. But they also danced past memories of the first time I managed to drive the snowmobile, plus, of course, the problems I'd had getting it back. But, I had got it back, hadn't I? Not really what I'd class as a disaster. I thought about my reindeer and husky friends. The trip to visit Esteri's family. The Christmas party.

This sauna was lovely.

At least it was . . . until Esteri suddenly sat up and shouted happily, 'Time's up!'

I opened my eyes, wiping the sweat from around my neck, having let myself be thoroughly baked. 'Already? We have to go home already?'

'Not quite,' she said in a voice that was both mysterious and a little dark. 'Follow me.'

With a heave-ho I hauled myself from the bench, sweat beads shimmying their way down the backs of my legs, and followed her to the door, allowing myself one last inhale of the aromatic steam.

With her hand on the door, Esteri said to me, 'You're feeling pretty hot, right?'

'Very,' I replied.

'OK. Just remember that.'

'Why?'

'You'll see.' Esteri flung open the door to the sauna and took my hand, and began running across the snow.

'What in the actual—'

'Trust me!' she shouted.

I barely had time to register the chill of the packed snow beneath my feet, nor the flicker of fire from inside ice lanterns that lined the path we were following, nor the millions of stars overhead, because all of a sudden I was faced with a drop. A jacuzzi-sized rectangle of inky black water carved out of the sea of snow. In the dawn light I could make out slivers of ice clunking about atop of it.

And then Esteri released my hand from her vice-like grip and jumped in.

I started to back away. 'No, no, no, that's not a nice warm jacuzzi, I see ice in there.'

'Yes, it's ice swimming, come in, it's amazing.'

'You liar. I'm going back to the sauna.'

'This is the best thing you can do for yourself in Scandinavia,' she protested, while I stood on the sidelines getting chillier by the second. 'We do it all the time, it gets your blood circulating, your endorphins pumping. Get in.'

'Wait, I wanted to ask you something.' I stalled, and held out my wrist. 'This bracelet, I thought it was from you, but was Josh my Secret Santa?'

'It's not a secret if I tell you, now get in,' she replied.

'But I need to know. And did you ask to swap with him or did he want to swap with you?'

She regarded me and then gave in. 'He wanted to swap. He asked around everyone until he knew who had you. He said he had a great idea, something that might make you laugh. The way he was talking, like it was some hilarious inside joke, I assumed you'd have figured it out by now.'

I smiled down at my bracelet. It was funny. He knew I thought he dressed like a permanent Gap Christmas advert, and now, he'd sneakily got me to do the same.

'Come on, I told you, so it's time to get in the pool,' Esteri demanded. I shook my head and she stood up, her hands on her hips and growled, 'Get. In.'

'OK, OK.'

I dipped a toe into the water and then to Esteri's screeches of, 'Just do it! Jump! Jump!' I hurled myself into the ice pool.

And died. *Goodbye, cruel world.*

Actually, it was all right ... Cold – awfully, awfully cold – but kind of a rush. I exhaled into the darkness and shrieked, 'Oh my *god*!' through a wide, laughing, alive, smile.

Also, it did feel nice after the head-faintingly hot heat of the sauna. Still, though.

'You do this every year?' I asked Esteri through chattering teeth.

'I do it whenever I can. Back at the chalet I sometimes come out of the sauna and have a little lie-down in the snow. You should try it.'

'I think this has boosted my endorphins enough for this year, thanks. Can we get out now?'

'Only when you admit it's done you good.'

'How will I know if it's done me good?'

'Have you created a nice memory?' she asked.

I thought for a minute, looking back at the luxurious sauna and then into this hilarious icy water surrounded by snow. 'Yes,' I laughed.

'Then it's done you good.'

When we arrived back at the staff chalet, the kitchen and boot room was in full swing with staff members getting ready for their shifts. The smells of cooking breakfast filled the rooms and there were the usual cries of, 'Where did I put my ski socks down, I *just* had them?', 'Anyone want more toast?' and 'Myla, how do you feel about being an elf?'

Wait, what?

I turned, my hair straggly and unbrushed, my swimming costume damp in my hands, to see Daan holding a clipboard and smiling down at me.

'What? Pardon?' I said.

'I don't know if you know, but one of our elves, Josh, had to go home yesterday for a family emergency.'

Behind Daan, Esteri made a kissing face at me and high-tailed up to our room. Ignoring her, I said quietly, 'Yeah, I heard. He told me.'

'Oh right, you two were pretty close.'

'I mean—'

'Actually, that's probably even better because maybe you picked up some tips along the way.'

'Tips for what?'

'Being one of Santa's elves. With Josh gone, we're one elf short, and have a big school group visiting for a few days so need the full house. Since you're a little out of action because of your arm, how would you feel about being an elf?'

No, no, no, don't make me be an elf.

I wondered how to tell him I was the last person suited for this role, without telling him anything like that. 'My arm feels a lot better,' I said.

'That's good, but you still need to partially rest it until at

287

least the end of the week, doctor's orders. As an elf, I can make sure you don't have to put any pressure on it at all.'

'But, um ... ' I scanned the room, what for I don't know. 'Don't elves have to do lots of dancing around and throwing snowballs and stuff? That sounds like it could be pretty hazardous.'

'It's fine.' Daan waved my concerns away. 'I can have you meeting and greeting, there may be some singing but we can avoid you having to be physical.'

'I, um ... ' Shiiiiiit, what to say, what to say?

'I know, it's daunting to try a new job, but I'm sure you've thought how much fun Josh was having and how you'd like to join in. Now's your chance! You are going to make a wonderful, happy, festive elf.'

I dragged myself back upstairs and told Esteri the news, who promptly burst out laughing. '*You*? An elf?'

'What's so funny?' I asked. Macabre was more the mood, not funny.

'Oh nothing, nothing.' She wiped her tears. 'I'm going for a shower. See you at the end of the day. Feel free to use my pink lipstick to give yourself those rosy cheeks you need, you look a little pale right now.'

Guffawing to herself, Esteri left the room.

This was getting ridiculous. First, I fall for an elf. *Me*. Then I have to become one?

Chapter 39

The other elves made me feel very welcome. We were standing in the forest near Santa's cabin being given a pep talk and some info about the school group, and while my new colleagues were already buzzing and ready, I was conserving my smiles for a day of being holly and jolly and Christmassy in what might be the performance of a lifetime.

To try to channel some festive spirit from the guy who did it better than anyone (well, except Father Christmas), I was sneakily wearing Josh's shirt under my elf costume.

I know that's a bit weird, but it made me feel a little less alone, so I was going with it. And I liked that I could smell him again.

'So, please welcome Myla into the group, she's going to be getting into the festive spirit with us for a few days,' said Daan, and I smiled at everyone despite deflating inside.

As I listened to instructions on how to be our best elves

and who should do what – and where – during this big school trip they had coming in, that familiar fear set in of, *I don't think I can do this.* I'd been feeling that a lot over the past year, and usually I took the easy way out. I didn't used to be like that. Perhaps I'm just afraid of getting too attached again, so I leave as soon as things don't go my way.

I'd been kidding myself by pretending Christmas was all over once December the twenty-fifth hit, I thought, miserably. Of course it wasn't. If anything, for me, it was now more festive than ever, and I couldn't seem to stop all the painful memories from creeping their way back in, like they were taking advantage of the window I'd opened for Josh.

Nearly a week later and I was still being utilised as an elf, and was at my wits' end. Every time one of my co-elves sang or danced or put on a show-stopper of an improvised comedy performance for the guests, I knew I was as much help as one of the logs in the wall of the cabins. I just couldn't keep this up, all this Christmas spirit, especially when I was feeling a bit heartbroken, and especially when I thought I'd put all this, for the most part, behind me for another year. I was truly enjoying Lapland, and now I felt like I was back to square one.

'Bye, goodbye, have a happy holidays!' I waved to the last family of the day over at Santa's cabin. Once they were out of sight, sledding away on the back of a train of huskies, I stepped back inside and took off my hat, letting my smile drop and rubbing my aching cheeks. I could feel tears behind my eyes, which was so ridiculous it hurt even more.

'You all right, Myla?' asked Jens, one of the other elves and a good friend of Josh's.

'This is exhausting, how have you done it for two months straight?' I said, covering my shaking voice with a laugh.

He chuckled back. 'The benefits outweigh any negatives. I think it's such a fun job.'

'Oh, me too,' I said, quickly, hoping I hadn't sounded insulting. 'It's just not what I'm used to.'

Before I began joining in with the end-of-day tidy, I pulled my phone from my pocket and checked to see if Josh had returned my message asking after his grandfather. He hadn't.

I frowned, not because Josh owed me anything, I just hoped that he and his family were OK. The last I'd heard from him was that he'd made it back to the US and was on his way to his mum's house.

Thinking of Josh reminded me that he'd dressed as an elf in his hospital once. He was a nice guy. A little thought inched closer, wanting me to remember the Christmas that I was in hospital, but I didn't have the energy to go down that road now.

I put my phone away and leaned on the window pane of Santa's cabin. It *was* magical out here, I couldn't deny it, and it *was* nice experiencing first-hand what the elves saw the whole season – the wonder on guests' faces at meeting their real Father Christmas.

'Hello, Elf Myla,' said a kindly old voice, coming around the corner, and pulling me back to the cabin.

Even a grump like me couldn't not smile at Santa's

friendly face and belly full of jelly. 'Hey, just getting cleaned up here. Did you have a good day?'

'I always have a good day,' he laughed with a ho-ho-ho and I wondered if he ever let the jolly act drop or if he was just, well, *him*. 'Did you?'

'The best,' I said.

He tilted his head at me.

I looked around for Jens and spotted him through the cabin window, straightening out some things outside.

'I'm just missing home, I think.'

'And a certain other elf?'

'Not you too, Santa,' I joked. 'But yes, we'd become friends and I'm sad he had to go so quickly, but more than anything I hope everything's OK at home.'

Santa patted my shoulder and waved goodbye, and I finished packing up for the night. This place was made for the Joshes of the world.

Not me.

Chapter 40

I traipsed back to the chalet, the sky overhead covered in thick cloud, and icy snow plopped down upon the top of my head and stung my face. I kept trying to tell myself that nothing was really wrong, that yes, a guy I'd started to have feelings for had gone, and yes, I was being made to be an elf. Big deal. The problems were in my mind, my fight or flight mode activated and itching for me to take the 'flight' option. I just wanted to go home now and close that door.

With Esteri still out at work, I had the room to myself so I climbed up on my bunk, stuck in my earphones, and called Dad – he always offered comfort. Plus, what I really hoped was for him to say, 'Hey, you've put in your time, you can come home now. Shay won't care.'

'Hello, love!'

'Hi, Dad,' I said, making my voice sound chirpier than I felt. 'What's going on with you?'

'Well, I'm actually back up at Shay's. She's just started her maternity leave and I said I'd come and help her out with a few things.'

'She's on mat leave already?' I checked the date on my watch. The tenth of January. She wasn't due for another three weeks or so. Perhaps that was normal, what did I know? 'Is she all right?'

'Yes, she's fine, just wants her old dad around to do everything for her, I think,' he chuckled. 'So what's new with you? How's Josh?'

I hadn't told any of them. What was there to tell? It didn't amount to anything. In the end, it was nothing.

Then why did nothing feel like everything?

'Actually, Josh had to leave Lapland early because of a family emergency.'

'Oh no. He's gone?'

'He's gone.'

'Are his family OK?'

'I hope so, I've not heard from him since he arrived back.' Dad paused. 'Sorry, love.'

'It's fine.' I picked at a loose thread on the duvet cover. 'Actually, I'm a bit gutted. And I know that sounds really selfish because I don't wish he was here with me instead of there, where he needs to be, it's just sad losing someone, isn't it? Even if they were just a friend.'

'It is,' Dad agreed, his voice soft.

Memories of Mum leaving drifted past my mind again like falling snow and though I didn't want to, I found myself trying to catch them.

'Dad?'

'Yep?'

'Are you still sad about Mum leaving?'

I heard him take in a big breath. 'Yes . . . and no.'

'All right then . . .'

'Yes, because it was a sad thing that happened and I can't change that because it's in the past. It's out of my hands. But no because, well, your mum is happier now – actually we both are – than when we were together. Your mum loved you girls to the moon, but in the end her life wasn't meant to be in our house with us, and I don't begrudge her finding happiness.'

'Why?' I asked.

'Because what good would that do me? Apart from stop me moving forward and being happy myself?'

'You are happy . . . right?' I asked with trepidation.

But my dad surprised me, and without hesitation let out a laugh. 'Bloody right I am. I have two daughters I'm intensely proud of – one who's working in Lapland which is pretty amazing, the other who's about to have my first grandchild. I have a house that's all mine now you two have skedaddled, and sometimes I spend whole weekends watching crime dramas with endless popcorn.'

'Dad, that can't be good for you—'

'Hush. I'm healthy . . . *ish*. I've still got a fair amount of hair. I'm doing well. I'm happy.'

That was nice to hear, and for now, I let those thoughts melt away.

'Good.' Changing the subject, I added, 'My other development, which I'm sure Shay will find hilarious, is that

Love Adventuring Lapland have me working as an elf since Josh left.'

'Oh dear, I can't imagine you like that much,' Dad chortled.

'I don't,' I sighed. 'Dad . . . can I come home?'

'Why do you want to come home?'

'I'm just feeling . . . over it. This was never a good fit for me and I don't think I can take it any more.'

'I thought you were enjoying it though, love? Surely there are more pros to cons?'

'There are, but it's been two months now and I'm tired of pretending to be Holly-Jolly-Christmas every second of the day. I want to come home.'

A movement caught my eye. I turned my head. And there was Esteri standing in the doorway, looking furious.

Esteri stepped in the room and closed the door, and I said a goodbye to Dad for now.

'Hi,' I said to her, dragging myself to the ladder and stumbling down from the top bunk, wondering what she'd heard.

She stared at me, her arms crossed, and I didn't think I had to wonder any more.

'Look,' I started, 'I was just letting off steam after a difficult day—'

'Do you want to quit?' she interrupted me.

'No. Well . . . maybe.' My heart thudded. Esteri and I were close, but she'd been with Love Adventuring Lapland for four years. Was she going to tell on me to Daan, and would my sister get in trouble?

'You would give up this experience because a guy left?'

'No, it's really not that. It's Christmas, I just don't . . . I'm not . . . Christmas isn't . . .'

'I know, I know, you don't like Christmas.'

'Of course I— Wait, pardon?'

'I said, I know you don't like Christmas.'

We locked eyes for a moment. She knew? 'You knew?'

Esteri waved her hand in the air, her eyebrows still furrowed together. 'I could tell right from the start, but you know why it didn't bother me? Because you were trying. You were making the most of the opportunity. I may not have understood what exactly brought you here, but I could tell the longer you stayed the more comfortable you were becoming. Now, you don't seem to be trying any more. You're giving up, because a boy you liked has left? What happened to all that progress?'

I stepped back. 'I can't believe you knew. And you still made me do all those Christmassy things with you.'

'Oh, for God's sake, they were your job. They still are. Unless you're planning to quit and run away?'

'You don't understand,' I said. 'Christmas is a really hard time for me and coming here has been tough. It's hard to let go of bad memories.'

'You don't think I know that? You think you're the only one who's done hard things?'

'No, I'm not saying that.'

'Well guess what? You're not the only one. And I know everyone is different, but I choose not to define myself by the things in my past. They have happened, they are a part of me, but so are a million other things.' She shook her head and went to sit on her bunk. 'I don't know what you've been through, but you can talk to me about it if you want to. Or I guess you can just leave. Since you're so tired of pretending.'

Esteri lay back and rolled over, facing away from me, and I stood in the centre of the room feeling pretty crap about myself. I'd never meant her to think I didn't like being around her. It wasn't her, it wasn't Lapland, it wasn't even the holidays, it was *me*.

I'm the problem.

Chapter 41

I'd really messed everything up. Not only had I come to winter wonderland when I had a huge Christmas aversion, but thanks to my shoddy husky-sledding skills I now couldn't do my job, even though I was just getting the hang of it, just starting to actually let myself like it.

And now I'd let myself open up to heartbreak.

I was filling in as an elf and I just knew I was doing the worst job in the world, my best friend here was pissed off at me, and Shay was going to be so mad when I told her I was leaving early.

Well. If I was going to piss off my sister by leaving early, I'd better not waste her Christmas present to me too.

With Esteri not talking to me, and a long, dark evening until bedtime, I needed to get out of there. Grabbing my coat, my wallet and my phone, and before I could think too much about my decision, I left the staff chalet and marched to the activities' lodge, where I called for a taxi to come from Luosto to pick me up. Within the hour I was standing outside the ice bar, which rose from the thick compacted snow as if it were carved straight out of the scenery. Soft glacier-blue lighting guided me to the doorway where I stood in a warm zone with other patrons awaiting their timeslot. I blended in as a tourist and after being kitted out with some extra layers was told I, and the other visitors during this time slot, had thirty minutes in the frozen bar to enjoy an array of icy alcoholic drinks.

Perfect. Thirty minutes was all I needed.

It doesn't take much to get me tipsy. So when I entered the minus five degrees bar, which felt like stepping into a giant, crystal blue ice cube complete with ice sculptures lit from below with vibrant pink and purple bulbs, I went straight for an ice-cold vodka shot. Served in an ice shot glass. And I sat on a stool made of ice while I knocked it back.

As the cold liquid slithered down my throat, burning and scratching as it went, in seeped the first memory I'd been trying to hold back . . .

CHRISTMAS 1999 ~ AGED EIGHT

I glared at Shay from the other side of the living room. We were like two wrestlers in our corners, panting, red-faced, lips curled into snarls. Outside, rain beat against the windows. Inside, Home Alone 2: Lost in New York *played on the TV, though neither of us were paying attention.*

Tinsel framed the picture frames. Cards from friends and family lined the mantelpiece. A solitary bauble dropped from the tree, falling with a tinkle on the floor, like a bell ringing for the next round to start.

Shay picked up a cushion from the sofa and gave it an intimidating punch, so I let out a guttural screech and, wielding the tube of wrapping paper, advanced towards her ready to strike.

Thwack, scratch, bite, pull, rip.

'What is going on in here?' My mum's horrified voice cut through our anger, and I turned, leaving my guard down just as Shay whipped a length of tinsel across my cheeks.

She scratched my cornea with that tinsel, and my, how I wailed. Especially after falling back and bumping my head. And so that year I spent Christmas in hospital.

My mum was still furious, even while I sat up in the hospital bed happily munching on fistfuls of grapes, wearing an eye patch. 'What on earth were you arguing about?'

'Father Christmas,' I replied, spitting grape juice down my chin.

'What about him?' Mum side-eyed Shay.

'Shay said he wasn't real.' Shay looked close to tears, and I added, 'She didn't mean to be horrible, it doesn't matter, Shay, it is what it is.'

'It is what it is' was a phrase I'd heard Dad say a few months back and now I used it all the time, though I didn't really get what it meant.

'I shouldn't have said anything,' Shay said, shame etched all over her little face.

'You shouldn't have got into a fight,' Mum scolded both of us.

'Sorry, Mum,' we chorused.

I wasn't angry at Shay for telling me about Santa, I'd had suspicions anyway and she clearly felt terrible. I was more upset about spending Christmas Eve in hospital, and when I was told I'd need to stay through until Boxing Day, that's when I started *crying again. Big, gulping sobs at not being allowed to be at home for Christmas.*

Dad stayed in the hospital with me that night, and Mum and Shay returned first thing in the morning along with a pile of presents for me and some for them all to open too.

Late on Christmas Day, when Mum and Shay had gone home again, Dad took my hand and helped me out of the hospital bed, and we went on a little walk around the ward. He thought it would be nice for me to say Merry Christmas to some of the other children, and perhaps make some friends. Some of those children hadn't been home in a long time and I was pretty quiet when Dad and I were alone together again.

'Are you OK, love?' he asked me.

I nodded. 'Do you think the other children had a nice Christmas?' I asked, afraid of the answer.

But Dad smiled and said, 'I think they did. I heard a lot of laughing as we were going around. I think the doctors and nurses have made this a very nice place to spend the holidays. But, I'm sure they and their families would prefer to be at home, like you would. So maybe we should remember that.'

'And visit them next year if they're still here?'

Dad squeezed my eight-year-old hand, and kissed my forehead, staying there with his prickly beard in my good eye for longer than he usually did.

With my eyes squeezed shut, I pushed the memory away and asked the bartender for a second vodka shot, drinking it quickly, as if I could outrun what was coming next . . .

They'd been bickering all day, it was nothing new. And nothing serious. In fact, I'd spent the first day of the school Christmas holidays watching the music video for Girls Aloud's 'Love Machine' in slow motion, trying to learn the dance routine in case it ever came on at a party and then I could wow everyone. So I'd tuned out what they were saying hours ago.

Shay, at sixteen, found me excruciating and hilarious, but that hadn't stopped her setting up camp in the corner of the living room to wrap gifts and sing along to the choon.

'Nearly got it,' I said to her after a semi-successful run-through, pausing the video, just in time to hear a thump-thump-thump down the stairs.

I opened the living room door to see Mum standing with two suitcases, Dad sat on the stairs.

'What's going on?' asked Shay, appearing behind me. Her voice had a hard edge, the kind of one she used with me sometimes, like when I'd see her at school holding hands with someone and I'd yell, 'Wooooooooooooo, that's my sister!'

I looked at the suitcases – where could we possibly be going on holiday this close to Christmas? And then I gasped, and screamed, or maybe the other way around. 'Are we going to DISNEYLAND?'

I was dying to visit Disneyland Paris at Christmastime. One of my best friends, Rick, went last year and all he talked about was how good Space Mountain was, and how festive it was, and how big the Christmas tree was. I'd been banging on about it to Mum and Dad all year, and now we were going.

Girls Aloud would have to wait.

What was I going to pack? What book would I take? Would we take presents with us to open there or have them when we got back? What hotel would we stay in?

My thoughts came to a screeching halt when Dad got up and put his arm around me and said, 'Not this year, sweetheart.'

Oh. 'Then where are we going?'

Mum took a big inhale and I noticed, for the first time, that both she and Dad had pink eyes. She came over and wrapped an arm around me and an arm around Shay. I returned her hug, holding her waist tightly, but Shay was stiff and I didn't know why.

Mum took another deep breath. 'Myla, Shay, I'm going to go and stay at Auntie Alexa's for a little while.'

'For Christmas?' I asked. 'Why doesn't she come here?'

'Not just for Christmas,' Mum said, her voice slow, a tremble sneaking through. She shook her head. 'I'll be gone for a little while, but I'll come and see you and you can come and see me.'

At this point, Shay broke away and ran upstairs, shoving past Dad as she went.

'Why are you going?' I asked. Though I think I'd realised by then what was happening, I just didn't want to believe it.

'I think everyone will have a happier Christmas this way,' Mum said.

'Love, why don't you just—' Dad started, with a sigh, but Mum held up her hands.

'Let's just . . . ' She smiled at him, whispered an 'I'm sorry' and then squeezed me so tightly I cricked my neck.

Mum broke away and pulled her suitcases towards the door. 'I'll stop back over in a couple of days, try and talk to Shay then.'

And then she left the house. She left our family Christmas. She left everything.

I pressed the ice shot glass to my forehead, forcing myself to feel the cold because if I felt the pain of that on my skin, maybe, just maybe, I could keep myself present. Isn't that what everyone's always telling me I should do? 'Stay present'? I don't need, I don't *want*, to be dancing with ghosts of Christmas past . . .

CHRISTMAS 2011 ~ AGED TWENTY

I got off the bus and walked the last five minutes along the lane to Dad's house with a smile on my face. It was icy on the dark ground, I was shattered from the long journey back from university, I was even more exhausted from my course, which, in my second year, was sucking the life out of me. My suitcase had a broken wheel so it made a thunk-scrape-thunk-scrape sound as I walked it along. I'd left my book on the ferry. It was Christmastime; not my favourite.

But I was actually excited. Four whole days with Dad and Shay was just the break I needed. Yes, I'd be forced to watch Home Alone 2 *again because it was Shay's favourite, yes, I'd be force-fed mince pies until it was all I could taste in every burp, but I was determined to enjoy myself.*

I hadn't seen Shay in what felt like so long. She'd finished with uni the year before and seemed to be living the high life in London with some fancy recruitment firm, and she was always busy. I couldn't wait to catch up with her, and found myself quickening my step to get home quicker.

But when I reached the front door, something was wrong. The outdoor lights Dad insisted on putting around the front door every year weren't switched on. The woodsmoke smell from the open fire in Dad's living room wasn't creating the homely aroma in the air around the house. I opened the door, expecting to hear Shay and Dad chattering, or special Christmas TV episodes playing, or the clank of dishes over the soundtrack of carols.

'Dad?' I called into the still house.

At the end of the corridor, my dad walked past an open doorway, listening into the landline phone receiver. He looked up and waved at me, then put his hand back on his forehead and walked out of sight.

I froze on the spot, unable to move with the weight of worry that fell on me. Where's Shay?

Hearing Dad say in an unusual, croaky voice to the person on the other end of the phone, 'All right, thank you for letting us know. My other daughter's just arrived so, um, I'll call back in a while to get the latest. Thank you. Thank you. Goodbye.'

'Dad?' I whispered.

A moment later he reappeared in the door and walked straight over to me, wrapping me in a tight squeeze.

'Dad, what's happening? Is something wrong with Shay?'

'She's OK, she's OK,' he said, kissing my forehead.

'Then what is it?'

He took my suitcase from my hand and led me to the living room and sat me on the sofa. My heart thudded the whole time, and as he took a deep breath, I readied myself for bad news.

Dad cleared his throat. 'Your sister isn't going to be coming home for Christmas this year,' he started.

'Why? You said she was OK.'

'She is. Well, in a way. She's—' Dad choked on a sob and in a second I was there, throwing my arms around him, because I rarely saw my dad cry, and the last time was the Christmas Mum left. He cleared his throat again, trying to compose himself quickly. 'Shay's unwell, My, she's realised she's got a problem with alcohol.'

'No, she doesn't,' I said, confused.

'Apparently she does.' Dad shrugged. 'I didn't know either. But that was her friend from uni on the phone, Helena, do you remember her?'

I nodded. 'I think so.'

'She said that she worked with Shay at that recruitment firm, but since she was let go, Helena's been worried about her for a while.'

'Wait, Shay was let go? When?' But Shay was always talking about this amazing, flashy job and all the fancy dinners and parties she went to.

'Back in the summer, Helena said.' Dad rubbed at his forehead in the same way he'd done when on the phone. 'And last night, when Helena got home from a night out, she found Shay on her doorstep, passed out. Alcohol poisoning.'

Oh, Shay. The thought of my headstrong, confident sister lying unconscious and helpless on the concrete was heartbreaking. 'But a night of binge drinking doesn't mean she has a problem with alcohol,' I tried to justify.

'According to Helena, Shay's been trying to hide it from everyone, but Helena hasn't seen her without a drink in her hand or on her breath in months.'

'But Shay's OK?'

'She's OK. She's in hospital in London, Helena's with her. And when she woke up, Shay told Helena the reason she'd come to her house last night was because she was scared and wanted help. So ... Shay's going to be checking herself into a rehab facility later tonight.'

'But tomorrow's Christmas Eve, she wouldn't want to miss this,' I said, my voice small. Of course she should be going to rehab instead of being with us, but I couldn't understand how all this had happened in her life and I didn't know any of it. What kind of a sister was I?

I hated letting my sister down. I really hated it. And now I was going to do it again. I glanced at the clock on the wall, and took another shot.

CHRISTMAS 2016 ~ AGED TWENTY-FIVE

I'd never knowingly smelled frankincense before tonight, but Callie loved an essential oil so had rolled out the big dogs for her Christmas-slash-engagement party.

To try and make it through the party with a genuine smile on my face, I'd tried everything beforehand to calm my nervous energy: meditation, dancing in my bedroom, breathing exercises. I really wanted to be jolly-Myla tonight. I was so happy for Callie and her fiancé and I wanted to support them.

'Myla, what are you doing?' Willow whispered at me as I leant over the diffuser, wafting the mist at my face.

'Smelling the gold, frankincense and myrrh,' I replied with a stifled laugh, and Willow gave me a kick. She could tell I wasn't quite myself; that my nervous energy was manifesting itself as some kind of extrovert party animal.

Standing up straight, I tried to calm down and centre on Callie and her partner, standing at the head of their pristine living room, where they'd been giving a little thank you speech to their guests that had evolved into the engagement story. I shuffled from foot to foot, focusing my eyes, trying not to look like I never usually went to anything with the words 'party' and 'Christmas' in the same sentence. Trying to look natural. For good measure, I even let out a loud laugh at an opportune moment, as proof I was listening hard.

Callie shot me a look. That was the moment it became my night's obsession to get back on her good side and make her other friends and family like me.

I trailed her around, slinging my arm around her back and telling anyone she was chatting with that she was just the best person ever. Sometimes I pulled her into me and kissed her cheek. One time I slapped her bum and she pushed me away. Then I decided everyone knew I was funny about Christmas so I might as well make a joke out of it. Add some entertainment to the night.

I painfully remember trying to get everyone to look at me while I mercilessly roasted myself for being how I was at Christmas, all with a thumping heart and a too-wide grin and a never-ending thought stream telling me to stop being such a twat and just shut up. It was as if all my self-shame and loathing were being turned into a comedy routine, and I was doing it to myself. But also, I was doing it to Callie. I made fun of her matching decorations. I tried to pull a little beaded string from the tree as a prop, and the whole thing crashed over, tiny gold baubles scattering and rolling across the hardwood floor.

Callie asked me to leave.

I did, and I was never invited back.

I lay awake in the depths of that night, the room spinning, and vowed not to be the reason anyone else's Christmas fun got wrecked. Callie and I would never be the same again, because her memory of that big night would always be tainted by my behaviour. And it was that, more so than the one prosecco cocktail, that had me throwing up for the remainder of the long night.

'I can't change the past,' I whispered to myself, or more accurately, down at my drink. I wished I could believe that, wished it could turn off the tap that was now flowing. At least I knew I'd never make that mistake again. Perhaps being the worst friend had turned me into a better friend. Perhaps I'd better have another drink before I got kicked out of here. Maybe this next drink would make me happy again ...

LAST CHRISTMAS ~ AGED TWENTY-SEVEN

'It's the Most Wonderful Time of the Year' was playing out of someone's computer and I didn't even mind this year. I mean, I didn't love it, but it was mid-December, and for the first time in years I was planning to attend the office Christmas party.

It had been a good year; things were going well. I'd started in the art department of the advertising company, YOLO Number 1, in January and it was the dream job I'd always hoped to land. I got to be creative, I got to be artistic, and I got to work with lovely people in a nice, friendly building.

Phoebe, my co-artworker at YOLO Number 1, slung a length of tinsel around my neck as she passed. 'Is someone actually getting in the Christmas spirit?' she asked with a laugh, seeing my small sway to the music.

'For one night only,' I countered. 'From tomorrow I'm heading back into my hut of denial.'

She winked at me and slipped me a small gift as she perched on my desk.

'What's this?' I asked.

'Secret Santa.'

'But I didn't join in with Secret Santa.' I picked up the box, wrapped in red and silver paper, and gave it a little shake. 'Also, this isn't very secret.'

'I know, but I wanted you to have it. 'Cause I love ya.'

I grinned and ripped open the parcel, a small box inside which, when I lifted the lid, revealed a palm tree brooch, a couple of inches in length, with green painted leaves.

Phoebe took the brooch out and fixed it to my black velvet top which was the extent of my Christmas party outfit. She pressed a button on the back and stood back admiringly as flashing lights danced up and down the palm fronds. 'There. Now you have a festive, flashing tree brooch but with a Myla twist. Merry Totally-Not-Christmas.'

'I love it!' I cried, looking down as red, green and blue twinkles flashed. 'Thanks, Phoebe, that's so sweet of you.'

I had trousers on too, by the way. I wasn't just in a velvet top. Just to clarify.

'My pleasure,' she said. 'Ooo, better go. Don't leave for the party without me, OK?' She hopped off my desk just as my manager, Rose, appeared.

'Myla, could you come with me, please?' she said.

A frown crossed my face. The tone of her voice wasn't laced with Christmas spirit, like all the other employees at YOLO Number 1 today. I followed Rose across to her office, where she shut the door, and the festive music was silenced.

'Is everything all right?' I asked her, taking a seat. I bet this was about that infographic I'd messed up last month. Or maybe it wasn't even a bad thing, maybe she was going to give me a Christmas present?

But as she opened her mouth and started speaking about how she was sorry to do this today, but cuts had to be made in each department, and it wasn't any reflection on me, her words were drowned out and all I heard was the faint sound of my own breathing. I looked down, watching as red, green and blue lights from my brooch made patterns on the grey plastic tabletop.

'I'm sorry,' said Rose, and I looked up at her to see genuine regret in her eyes.

'That's OK,' I lied. 'These things happen. When do I have to go?'

'If you like, it might be easiest if you don't come back after Christmas.'

I nodded and stood up, heading to the door, letting her words settle over me like snow over a fallen branch. With one hand on the door handle, I said, 'But, this is my dream job.'

'I know. But you'll find another one really soon, I have no doubt. And I'd be very happy to write you a letter of recommendation if you ever need it.'

'Thank you,' I whispered. Outside the door the music hit me like a blast. My co-workers were happily lost in their world of sharing make-up, pouring wine into mugs, adjusting each other's outfits. And with a scribbled note for Phoebe, I walked away.

It was time to leave, the bartender said so, and I slid off my block-of-ice bar stool and swayed towards the exit. The colours beneath the ice sculptures blurred, and I tilted my head to try and figure out what the one in front of me was supposed to be. A dragon, perhaps? Or a dog? I licked it to see if my tongue would stick.

'OK, ma'am, time to leave,' the bartender said, appearing behind me and ushering me to the exit, where I grumpily swapped the special ice-bar coat back to my own and then stepped out into the cold night air. It was always so cold here, so *Frosty the Snowman*. Uggghhhh. So glittery and beautiful and perfect all the time and I was annoyed that Lapland had won me over and that actually I would be so sad to leave, and why did I always have to leave, and why did Josh leave, and Mum, and why did I have to lie to Esteri, and why was that bloodyyyyyyyy Santa Claus ice sculpture just *staring at me*?

I sauntered up to the sculpture, four-foot high atop the low, wide gatepost at the entrance to the bar's gritted car park. I didn't even care that the other bar-goers were all still milling about outside too, everyone waiting for their rides back to their homes or hotels.

I sighed at Santa, at Christmas itself, and muttered, 'What are you looking at?' Then I gave him a nudge. A tap! I swear, officer, he nudged me first!

Icy Santa wobbled. Or maybe I wobbled. Either way, a moment after I turned away, I heard a sound like shattering glass.

The car park became very silent, and I turned, suddenly very sober, to see Santa. Dead.

I had killed Santa Claus.

The bar's ice sculpture version, at least.

The bar staff came running out and with everybody watching I stumbled and tripped over apologies in both English and what little Finnish I knew. 'I'm so sorry, I'm so sorry, I didn't mean to, I'll pay for it, *olen pahoillani*.' I waved my credit card in the air, my heart beating fast.

You stupid idiot, Myla! You selfish, stupid, idiot!

The sculpture surrounded my feet like diamonds on the ground around me, twinkling in the moonlight, reminding me of every fault I owned.

'Please, let me pay.' I couldn't get away with ruining Christmas for anyone else, not any more.

The bar manager hesitated, and then nodded, taking my card and charging me probably not as much as he should have, but enough to make me realise just how much time and effort it must have taken someone to make that sculpture.

When my taxi came, I climbed inside, the vodka a distant memory, unlike the others that had visited me tonight.

'I'm sorry,' I whispered again, my breath misting against the glass of the taxi window.

Chapter 42

Esteri was asleep when I got back that night, and she left for work before I was even up in the morning.

My memories were weighing on me heavy, and every direction I turned something else was reminding me of them. I had the day off, and a hangover, and a heart full of sorrow, so I waited until early afternoon, with the sun at a whopping one degree above the horizon, and then I headed out.

Though the temperature outside was noticeably sub-zero today, and the snow so thick it reached the top of my boots and then some, I made my way to the activities' lodge and borrowed a snowmobile. I needed to clear my head, and what better way to do that than by rushing as fast as I could through the open air. Besides, while the sun was poking up, I wanted to see Lapland in all its glory again, before I quit and went home and left all this behind. Just one last time.

Taking it outside and manoeuvring it away from the lodge

and towards the path that led into the forest, I paused, and took a breath. Everything was silent. Still. I let the pale blues and glittering whites and streaks of yellow and pink envelop me. My hands gripped the handles of the snowmobile, and I felt the dull remnants of ache along my arm where the sprain hadn't fully healed.

I flexed my fingers. It was *pretty much* fine now, though. Really, they should just let me go back to being a guide for the last two weeks here. Things were better back then, even though I found them hard at the time, I ... I was enjoying myself.

Why was I doing this? Was it really about seeing the views again, or was I trying to prove something to myself?

I climbed on the seat and started the motor. The machine hummed to life below me, and I took off, driving carefully and slowly, but confidently, the headlamp helping to guide me through the dense trees. In this world I was isolated, and when I reached the top of the fell I stopped for a while, breathing in the unspoilt scene in front of me, trying to breathe out the memories, and the feeling of how I knew I shouldn't have come to Lapland. I knew it would all go wrong again.

But, actually, I have enjoyed Christmas this year, a small voice in me piped up. I told her to hush but she persisted. *And that's thanks to Lapland.*

I cut the engine, hearing nothing but silence, and my thoughts stopped whirring and instead drifted, settling down into one simple fact: *I love it here.*

Shaking my head, I decided to push further, run further.

I wanted to keep feeling the snow spray onto my legs, smelling the pines, tasting the icy air, hearing the carving of the skidoo. Maybe I wanted to stay in this moment, just for a little longer.

Onwards I went, faster, the rushing scenery causing my eyes to stream, or perhaps it was my heart.

Esteri was right, even though she hadn't said it directly. I held those memories, those experiences, so close that year after year I let them define me. And now I looked for bad things to happen, just so I could say, 'See, I was right.'

But I couldn't change how I felt, I couldn't force myself to not care.

I drove upwards, climbing a long, gently sloping fell I hadn't travelled before, reaching for where the stars soon would be, wishing on every one of them to fix me.

Reaching the top, I jolted to a halt and switched off the motor, and my breath was taken away. Before me were miles upon miles of the most serene landscape, a glowing white vista bathed in the sunset pinks and purples, undisturbed other than by twinkling pockets of lights from villages afar. Soon, the sky, large and colourful and domed above me, would drift through the last of its slow-motion sunset into twilight above the distant fells. Whispers of clouds hung silently, that might be replaced by aurora borealis come nightfall.

I hugged my arms around myself, imagining they were Josh's.

After I don't know how long, the purples began to turn mauve and the pinks seeped into the shades of blue known here in the Arctic as the famous 'blue moment', when the twilight causes everything from the sky to the snow to glow a glorious sapphire.

I sat for a long while, my back against the snowmobile, my knees up to my chest, just watching the sky and letting emotions and thoughts wash over me, too tired to keep running from myself and my story.

Eventually, since I was beginning to feel like the cold was seeping through my clothing, I called my sister; something I wanted to do before I headed back to the chalet to start making arrangements to come home.

'Hey, everything OK?' Shay said, down the phone, picking up on the first ring.

'Hi, Shay . . .'

'Hi. What?' she asked. She sounded kind of annoyed, like she was in the middle of something.

'I just wanted to call and tell you that, um, Shay, I want to come home.'

'Nope. No, you don't.'

'I do. I can't do this any more. It sucks.'

'It does not suck, get over yourself. Don't forget I know a thing or two about these jobs and what you're doing is both fun and a privilege.'

Wow, OK. 'But—'

But Shay was going off on one now. 'Dad filled me in on what you spoke about yesterday, and it's crap, so don't call me and tell me you're giving up because you need to escape from the job I gave you specifically *because* you wanted to escape.'

'But how could I ever really escape, here, or anywhere? I can't escape my own head.'

Shay took a steadying breath. 'Look. I know that you don't like Christmas, but you were having a good time there, I know that's true. You were enjoying yourself. Don't forget that. Don't create this story for yourself that is all about the setbacks so that's all you remember.'

'I'm trying, Shay, I am, but I don't know how to just forget about the things that I see in my mind every time Christmas comes around. Every year, year after year.'

'Nobody's asking you to change the emotion you felt at the time, or forget how you feel in favour of a silver lining. I just think you need to . . .'

'Reframe?' I rolled my eyes, thinking back to Josh's words.

'Well, yes, actually. Let me help you.'

'No, not right now.'

'Then when? What are you doing right now?'

'Freezing my bottom off on top of a hill, waiting for the Northern Lights.'

Shay stuttered and then said, 'Oh, right, OK, yeah I can see why it's so bloody awful there.'

'No, it's not awful, it's incredible.'

'Come on, then, why don't you hit me with one of these big bad memories and let's see what we can do about it.'

I didn't want to do this, not now. *Then when?* Shay's words echoed back at me.

I swallowed. Should I open this door? A tear came to my eye and I swept it away. I'd never delved into the details about all this with Shay before, not fully at least, but maybe it was time, after all.

'Spit it out.' Shay interrupted my thoughts.

'Well, there was the time you, you know, were in hospital.'

'The Christmas I went to rehab?' she said, and then she hissed to someone in the background, '*No, I'll be there in a minute.*'

'I should let you go—'

'No. Myla, is that one of your worst Christmas memories?'

'Of course it is,' I said, quietly.

She went silent. Shit. I hadn't meant to bring this up. I felt my heart quickening, worrying, jumping to the worst conclusions. She was sad, or angry, or . . .

'You stupid idiot,' she said, but softly, kindly. 'You think of that as one of the worst Christmases?'

'Of course. You were at rock bottom. You were poorly. You were alone and in rehab.'

Shay let out a small laugh. 'Well, I consider that the best Christmas I ever had.'

'You what?'

'You heard. I know the specifics were horrible, but that was when I got sober, I got my life back. For me, for my own personal journey through this life, that was my Christmas miracle.'

How could two people have such different takes on the same event?

'Ow, crap,' Shay suddenly said and then growled to whoever she was with, 'Yes, all right, I'm coming.'

'Shay, are you OK?'

But then my dad's voice came on the other end of the phone. 'She's only bloody standing here yapping with her waters broken all around her.'

'WHAT?' I shouted. 'Is she ... but she ... wait!'

In the surprise, the phone slipped from my hand, and as it dropped deep into the powdery snow I heard the voice of my dad saying, 'She's OK, she just—'

Then everything was silent, only my breathing audible in the night forest, my phone a dark shape peeping out of the muted white snow.

'Dad, hang on a mo,' I called out, dropping to the ground, causing sprinkles of flakes to fill the narrow slice created by my mobile. I pulled off my outer glove and stuck my hand in, trying to move the snow aside without disturbing it too much, feeling a bitter sense of déjà vu at coming full circle from my first Lapland excursion – when I'd taken the snow-shoe couple out and he'd dropped the engagement ring – to now, what might well be my last Lapland excursion if I did, indeed, go home.

Gripping the casing, I pulled my phone free and tried to use my sleeve to wipe the screen, only smearing it with more wetness. 'Dad?' I said, holding it to my ear, but nothing. I looked down at my phone, now just a dark rectangle. I pressed the home button ... nothing. My phone was dead.

Chapter 43

'Arghhhh!' I yelled into the night sky.

It was fine. It would be fine. Wasn't this one of those situations where you could fix your phone by chucking it in a bowl of rice, or surrounding it with packets of silica gel or something? *Well, no problem then, Myla, let's just empty all this uncooked rice out of my pockets . . .*

Jumping back on the snowmobile I started the motor, ready to race back to the staff chalet so I could fix my phone and call back to make sure everything was OK. It had to be OK.

All right, pause, breathe. I was clearly doing something wrong because the snowmobile wasn't starting. But no matter how many pauses or breaths I took, it still wouldn't start.

I reached for my phone to call Zoë or Daan for help again, and then smacked my forehead with my wet glove, remembering it was dead.

Fine. This was fine. Using the maintenance kit, I fiddled

about with the fuel lines, since that worked last time. But still nothing. I didn't know how to make this right. I wasn't strong enough. I was cold.

Pulling the blanket off the back of the snowmobile, I snuggled myself under it and sat on the seat.

Sitting there, with no phone and no escape, I had nothing to do but think, and that's when the floodgates opened.

Esteri was right to call me out. As was Shay. I was defining myself by these things that had happened in the past, to the point I was now looking for the bad in every situation over the winter. And this happened year on year.

There was so much to enjoy here in Lapland, and I *had* enjoyed myself. From the friends I'd made to the boy I'd kissed, from the adventures and saunas and experiences, from the views and the skies my eyes had taken in. How could I lie to myself and cling on to anything 'bad' as if it was the only thing that mattered?

I didn't want to be like that any more.

I couldn't forget the past, and maybe I didn't want to – it was still part of me after all. I didn't need to knock back shots of vodka or escape on a snowmobile or even lock myself in my home or take a plane to a tropical island. But perhaps I could reframe the memories, just to make them easier on myself. Even though thinking of them was hard. Though as I sat there in minus temperatures, keeping myself safe wrapped in these arms that I had to accept were mine, not Josh's, I felt like maybe I could do hard things.

It certainly wasn't easy, and it didn't come naturally. It's possible it wouldn't, unless maybe I sought some help from a doctor. But I concentrated, my whole mind and body focused on finding the light patches in my dark thoughts.

If I hadn't spent my eighth Christmas in hospital, I wouldn't have developed an understanding and appreciation for what other kids were going through at this time of year.

If my mum hadn't left during the holidays when I was thirteen, she wouldn't have gone on to have the happy life she was missing.

If, at sixteen, Rick had kissed me at the school Christmas dance, instead of Ashley, we would have broken each other's hearts at some point, because I knew I didn't want to be with him now.

If, at twenty, my sister hadn't gone to rehab instead of spending Christmas with us, she wouldn't have got her life back on track as soon as she did.

If I hadn't made a huge mistake at twenty-five and ruined the engagement party, I might have carried on being a sucky friend, and bringing other people down, rather than trying to be better.

If, at twenty-seven, I'd not been let go from my dream job, I would never have been here.

And if I'd never been here, I'd never have lived through one of the most amazing winters of my life.

I knew none of these reasonings made up for the things I'd done wrong, or negated the things I'd been through, but it was time to at least try and let go, at least try and change how I react when things go wrong. I owed it to myself to look back on these experiences with fondness and care rather than push them away. Because sixteen-year-old me could use a confidante. Because twenty-five-year-old me still feels crappy about what she did. And because eight-year-old me had loved Christmas, and she'd be pretty mad if she knew I'd let a handful of problems change who I was. I wanted to change again, so it was time to accept.

I don't know how long it had been that I'd been sitting there, lost in my mind, but it struck me like a flame on a match that I *was* strong enough, after all. Because I could light a fire. I was good at fires. I could keep myself warm, and once I'd warmed up, I'd move onto the next step, and perhaps, step by step, I'd make it back.

So that's what I did. Using the supplies in the emergency kit under the seat of the snowmobile, I lit a small campfire, and warmed my hands in front of the flames until it felt like they had blood pumping through them again.

I watched the fire having a good flicker, twinkling the glittering snow on the ground around it. I briefly closed my eyes again, focusing on the smoky scent that enveloped me, the tingle in my fingertips, the crackle of the wood burning and the cold of the night air. Then I opened them and smiled.

Who would have thought that in Lapland, the Christmas capital of the world, I could stop seeing winters-past every time I closed my eyes and start seeing the present again?

Then, using the tiny torch, and a lot of guesswork, I started prodding at bits of the snowmobile.

The fire crackled and hissed as I stepped around it, flicking it with snow, and it took me a minute to realise the extra light on the snowmobile wasn't coming from the flames.

And suddenly the silence and dark were cut through with

that familiar, wonderful sound of snowmobiles vrooming through snow.

I turned, shielding my eyes from the brightness, protecting my fire from the incoming blades of the snowmobile.

'Ah, here you are, you silly Brit,' came Esteri's voice from inside a helmet.

'Esteri!' I cried. 'You came to save me!'

'It looks like you were saving yourself,' she commented, removing the helmet and pointing at my fire and dismantled snowmobile.

'Well, I was getting there. How did you know where I was?'

'The snowmobiles have GPS,' she said, like it was the most obvious thing in the world.

I let out a relieved laugh. 'Yay! Could I use your phone quickly? I think my sister's gone into labour but my phone died and I want to check she's OK.'

'She's fine.'

'How do you know?' I asked, perplexed.

'Your dad called the head office to ask to get a message to you that she was all right, in case you were worrying. She's doing great. But she did say something about not letting you meet the baby if you came home early.'

I shook my head, smiling. Thank God. 'I'm sorry to have dragged you out in the middle of the night to rescue me. And for . . .'

'It's like, seven p.m., calm down,' she laughed.

Oh. It had felt like I'd been out longer than that.

'Besides,' Esteri moved aside, 'somebody couldn't wait any longer.'

Behind her, another person dismounted the other snowmobile and removed their helmet, but my breath had stopped the second I saw the flannel shirt sticking out from the top of the coat.

'Oh my god,' I said, stepping right on the campfire. 'Shit!' I stamped my boot out in the snow and looked back up.

Josh was here. Smiling at me. Putting his helmet down. Walking over. Putting his hands up to my face. Pulling me close. Kissing me.

I savoured him, touching his hair and his neck, hoping this wasn't just some delusional dream from being out in the cold for too long.

'Are you a mirage?' I whispered when he removed his lips from mine.

'No, I'm not Nicki Minaj,' he whispered back, and I laughed.

'What are you doing back here? How's your grandad? And your mum?'

'He's fine, they're both fine. It was looking worrying for a minute but he pulled through better than before, and when he came out of the hospital and I was telling him about you he told me I'd better come back here or I was an idiot.'

'So he didn't realise you were an idiot anyway?'

Josh grinned, his eyes twinkling into mine. I couldn't believe he was back. He came back. That can't have just been for a final two weeks of work, it had to mean more than that.

I *knew* we meant something.

Esteri cleared her throat. 'Can we put this fire out of its

misery and head back now? As much as I love to watch the two of you making out and all . . .'

'Yes, of course.' I dropped my hands from around Josh, but he still held onto one of them. 'But what should I do about this?' I pointed at my broken snowmobile.

'We'll tell Daan and he can send someone to pick it up when it's light. Light*er*.'

'OK. Esteri, I've been doing some thinking – I'm sorry about everything.'

'I'm not. It's in the past. And it helped us get to know each other better. OK?'

She was a good friend. The best. 'OK.'

Esteri climbed on her snowmobile and Josh on the other and I said to him, 'You drove this?'

'Yep!'

'Want me to drive back?'

'That's OK. You can be my passenger this time.'

I climbed on the back of Josh's snowmobile, and gave myself permission to enjoy the ride, enjoy the moment, every spray of snow on my legs, every scent of pine, every taste of icy air, every sound of my heartbeat.

Chapter 44

We arrived back at the staff chalet a short while later, and after Josh had said a few hellos to his fellow elves, he took me by the hand.

'You want to take a walk?'

'Back outside?' I asked. I was just warming up.

'Just over to the activities' lodge.'

'Isn't it closed now? *Oh*.' I got it.

We ducked out of the chalet and walked over to the quiet lodge. I still couldn't believe he was back, and I kept sneaking looks at him, and more than once caught him sneaking looks at me, too.

Unlocking the door, Josh held it open for me, and I stepped into the darkened reception area.

From there, he led me into the hall and then disappeared, returning a minute later with an armful of fleece blankets from the storeroom. We took a seat together in the centre of the hall, facing the large glass windows that overlooked the winter wonderland outside. Those wonderful, heavy, snow-blanketed forests that had become my second home.

'I just figured, since I'm still off the clock for another ...' he checked his watch, 'nine hours, maybe we could spend some time together before I go back to being annoying again?'

'Sounds good to me,' I laughed. 'You will be annoying by tomorrow, for sure.'

'Oh, for sure,' he agreed. 'I hear you've been after my job, anyway.'

'Yeah, I was really good at it.'

'I bet. You must have loved being an elf.'

'It was actually OK,' I said, surprising even myself. But you know what, maybe I needed to change the story I was telling myself. After all, things were working out pretty well since I got off my ass and lit that fire.

'I'm sorry I didn't keep in touch more, while I was home,' Josh said, sincerely, but I shook my head.

'I didn't expect you to. You were dealing with a lot.'

'Yeah, my head was all over the place. But I still thought about you a lot.'

'And your grandad's definitely OK?'

He nodded, and told me all about his journeys and his visit, and how the hospital had been taking care of his grandfather brilliantly. I then opened up to him about what had been going around in my mind over the past week, and it felt good. Really good.

Our conversation faded, but in the best possible way.

Josh propped himself up on his hand. 'I didn't think I would see you again.'

'Same. I surprised myself with how grumpy I got after you left. You must have some effect on me, Josh Roberts; I never usually let a guy get under my skin.'

'Except Santa Claus.'

'Yeah, that guy ...' I shook my head. 'I'm glad you came back.'

'Me too.' He kept my eyes in his, his eyelashes flickering, as he leant in close and kissed me again. He kept holding my gaze as we lay back. As he pulled the blanket over us. As we slowly, so slowly, peeled off our winter layers.

I caught sight of a grin spread across his face out of the corner of my eye. 'What?' I laughed.

'Is that my shirt?' he asked.

'No.' I shook my head, smiling.

'No?'

'No, it's *my* flannel shirt. I love it.'

I didn't go home. I stayed right where I was and made the most of every single second of my time in beautiful Lapland. Sometimes memories from Christmas past floated in to say hello, and sometimes I felt sad, but I didn't stress about feeling that way. And in the times I felt OK I sometimes made myself think of them, so I could practise reframing them. It would be a long road still, but I was pretty confident I was strong enough to save myself eventually.

I was back to being an adventure guide, and I treated every day like it was one more amazing memory to add to my collection.

And Shay and Tess, proud mums to baby Lila, whom I

already loved to bits even from afar, were doing well, everyone happy and healthy. Dad was enjoying being a grandpa, and I was looking forward to meeting my new niece when it was the right time for me to come home.

On the last day of January, after everybody had spent the night before staying up late, squeezing every drop of friendship out of each other, the staff chalet was a hubbub of backpacks, lost items, goodbyes and tears, and I was among them.

'Did you decide if you're going to move here yet?' I asked Esteri, as we hauled our bags from our room. She'd been dilly-dallying for the last few days, having been given a job offer from Daan but not being sure whether or not to take it.

But now she beamed at me, confident and sure. 'Yes, I'm doing it. I'm going to go home for a bit to sort out my things, then I'll be back for the spring.'

I hugged my friend. 'That's amazing, I'm so happy for you!'

'It won't be the same here without you though,' she said into the hood of my dad's coat. 'Would you like to live here too?'

Would I ever do that, what Esteri was doing? Giving up everything I knew to follow my dream?

What exactly would I be giving up, though? What exactly *was* my dream? It was clear to me now that I'd changed over time, and that if my 'dream job' had really been all that perfect for me still, wouldn't I have tried harder to get back into it after I was let go?

When I came to Lapland, I thought I was so out of place, like everyone would see how I didn't fit in with anyone else.

I hadn't even noticed that the job was fitting in with me. That being outdoors, that working alongside happy holiday-makers every day, actually made me happier than I could ever have known, and brought out more creativity than I'd felt in a long time.

Check me out, reframing the heck out of my latest Christmas.

To answer Esteri, I said, 'I don't know. I think I need to figure out some new plans for myself.'

'In Lapland?'

I shrugged. 'Let's just say my answer isn't what it would have been three months ago.'

When we reached downstairs, I saw Josh waiting for me by the door to the boot room, leaning against the pane, flannel shirt on (of course, Mr Gap Christmas advert), all dark eyelashes and big smile and folded arms.

Esteri, who before heading back to Turku was making her way north to her family again, pulled me into a final hug.

'I will miss you, you silly Brit,' she said to me.

'I'll miss you too,' I told her. 'Thank you for everything. *Everything.*'

'Back at you. We'll see each other again soon, OK?' She stepped back, pulling herself together and wiping away a sneaky tear that had spilled over. 'In the saunas, naked.'

I laughed. 'I'll be there.'

With that, Esteri waved, and I blew her a final kiss. I'd never expected to make such a great friend out here. But though it felt awful to watch her leave, I was so beyond grateful to have had the chance to have her be a part of my life.

Turning to Josh, I said, 'I can't believe this is it.'

He moved away from the door frame, and walked over to me, and held me against his chest. 'You don't want to go home now? You want to celebrate Christmas all year around?'

I let out a snuffly, snotty chuckle. 'Yeah, maybe I do.'

I couldn't let myself think about leaving Josh. I tried to push it down and pretend it wasn't happening, but though we were travelling to the airport together, that would be it for us. We were heading off to our different parts of the world, taking different flights this time, and I was so envious of whoever was the lucky person who got to sit next to his funny, annoying self on their journey.

Josh carried both our bags towards the bus outside the activities' lodge, and as I walked, I focused on every crunch of snow, every tall tree, and knew I would miss all of it. Lapland was magical, for a lot of reasons.

On the shuttle bus we were quiet, and I leaned into Josh, his arm around me, and occasionally he would turn his face from the window and kiss my forehead, his stubble tickling my chin.

At Rovaniemi airport, once we'd bid goodbye to the others, the two of us stood outside for a moment, letting the last snowflakes kiss our skin before we left.

Josh's eyes were on mine, his smile sad. 'I don't want this to end,' he said quietly, and my heart leapt a little.

'Neither do I,' I sighed. 'Does it have to?'

'I don't think it should.'

'Does that mean we could be long-distance?' I asked. 'Would that even work?'

'I think it's worth a try. What's a plane ride away, anyway?'

'It's nothing. A few hours.'

His smile widened. 'So we're going to give this a go?'

I nodded. 'I don't want this to be just one memory.'

As we said goodbye for as long as we could, I knew I wouldn't change a thing about my winter in wonderland. And if they'd have me, I'd treat myself to a trip here every Christmas. Because it had certainly changed me, in the best possible way.

Chapter 45

Summer

It was beautiful. The detail in this tiny ornament, glittering under the spotlights of London Heathrow's boutique Harrods store. I picked up the bauble, made of clear glass, where inside a tiny Big Ben was surrounded by shakeable white dust, snow-globe style.

It was the perfect gift to give someone in the middle of summer. Especially someone like Josh.

I paid for the ornament, stuffing my change into my shorts pocket and retying the flannel shirt wrapped around my waist, and went back to hang around the concourse for my flight.

My phone bleeped and I looked down to see a message from Shay. Don't you dare quit this one, will you?

I replied straight away. I promise I won't. You don't need to worry about me any more.

You're one to talk xxx

Smiling, I looked up at the board, to see my gate finally announced.

Although I hadn't figured out my new career path yet, I was beginning to think it involved being outdoors. After some arm-twisting, Shay had been convinced to put me forward for a role working for an adventure tourism company in a national park in Washington State in the USA for the summer. I was going to be a ranger, and I think I was going to like it.

I didn't need somewhere this time that provided accommodation. I had somewhere to stay.

I was still working on myself, but now I had the help of somebody professional, who was teaching me all about cognitive reframing and restructuring, and I was learning, slowly, to live with – and love? – my story.

'Ladies and gentlemen, welcome to flight BA49, we will soon begin boarding for your journey to Seattle, Washington.'

I smiled. It was time to bring on the new memories.

Acknowledgements

And then everybody died . . .

Just kidding! Imagine if that was the ending to this book!

We climbed through a lot of snow but have all made it to the end together, so thanks for sticking with us.

I just want to throw out a few more snowballs of thanks before I go . . . .

Thank you to my Editor, Bec, for all your enthusiasm and help. You're a star, and I hope one day you get covered by beagles. I mean that in a nice way. Thanks for shaping this novel with me and hope we can share some more lunchtime cocktails soon.

Thank you to the whole team at Little, Brown and beyond: Thalia (for your patience and kindness, you deserve a stonking great medal), Liz, Frankie, Lucie, Bekki and Robyn. You're all invaluable: thank you thank you thank you.

Thank you to my agent Hannah and the Hardman & Swainson team. Hannah, you're a total legend, and thanks for never hanging up on me when I call you with another ten random book ideas. Can't wait to see you again soon.

Thank you, Phil (Husband Phil, not farty reindeer Phil), for putting up with my endless waffley worries while I'm writing, dropping everything to read a draft, and not minding too much when the dog gets more of the bed than you. And Kodi, thanks for not minding too much when Phil gets more of the bed than you. You're both everything.

Thank you, Mum and Dad, as always, for being such good cheerleaders. Lots and lots of love and happiness and dog fur being thrown in your direction.

Thank you to Paul, Laura, Beth and Rosie for sharing your memories with me, and let's hope we can start making some more together soon.

A hundred thank yous to Hanna, my lovely reader and friend, who kindly answered all my questions about Finland, laced them with extra wonderful detail, and patiently helped with all of the Finnish language bits.

So much thanks to the various kind tourism offices over in Lapland for answering my questions, and to Lapland itself, for being one of the most serenely beautiful places that I hope one day to visit in person.

Thank you to Mary, David, Robin, Jude, Eleanor and Peter – love you all. Thank you SJ, Sarah, Emma, Ellie and Alison for always helping with last minute questions like 'why would a kid be in hospital?' and 'what's a word for peen?'. Thank you, Reuben, Ziggy, Nicki and Tom, for your helpful help. Thank you, Holly and Belinda, for always being ace.

And finally, thank YOU all for reading my book, and from me, Myla, Esteri, Josh and the whole gang: we wish you a wonderful wintertime xx

Escape to the mountains and fall in love this Christmas ...

Alice Bright has a great life. She has a job she adores, a devoted family and friends she'd lay down her life for. But when tragedy strikes, she finds her whole world turned upside down.

Enter, Bear, a fluffy, lovable – and rapidly growing! – puppy searching for a home. Bear may be exactly what Alice needs to rekindle her spark, but a London flat is no place for a mountain dog, and soon Alice and Bear find themselves on a journey to the snow-topped mountains of Switzerland in search of a new beginning.

Amidst the warming log fires, cosy cafes and stunning views, Alice finds her heart slowly beginning to heal. But will new friends and a charming next door neighbour be enough to help Alice fall in love with life once more?

Would you marry a stranger to live the life of your dreams?

August Anderson needs somewhere to live. Dumped by her boyfriend who would rather be alone than move in with her, she has almost given up on happiness. Until she notices that the beautiful Georgian townhouse she's long admired is seeking a new tenant, and suddenly things begin to look up . . .

There's just one catch – the traditional, buttoned-up landlord is only willing to rent to a stable, married couple and August, quite frankly, is neither. Competition for the house is fierce and August knows she'll have to come up with a plan or risk losing her last shot at her happy ending.

Enter Flynn, the handsome, charming and somewhat unsuspecting gentleman who August accidentally spills her coffee over. Flynn is new to the area and is looking for somewhere to live, and August thinks she knows just the place, but only if he's willing to tell a little white lie . . .

'Sunday afternoon bliss!' FABULOUS magazine

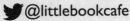